SCARLET KING AND NADINE O'KEEFFE

Broken Vows

For Sas
Happy Reading!

Nadine O'Keeffe

Scarlet King

First edition

ISBN: 978-1-7399387-6-5

Cover art by Samantha Wildeboer of Sunset.Bibliophile Graphics

This book was professionally typeset on Reedsy.
Find out more at reedsy.com

To our meds, for keeping us alive and sane enough to finish this book. Truly couldn't have done it without you.

Contents

Author's Note

Broken Vows is an ADULT, DARK sapphic (FF) mafia romance. This book is written in British English. It is a stand-alone, and the first in a connected series of stand-alones.

This book contains explicit sexual content, including kink and is NOT, in any way, representative of safe sex or kink practices. This is a work of fiction and not in any way meant to represent realistic BDSM activities, nor should it be taken as such.

It contains content that may trigger some readers, and we heavily advise you to read the following list before continuing.

Trigger Warnings:

- Blood
- Death
- Death in childbirth (past mentions)
- Torture
- Violence - including gang violence, gun and knife violence
- Mentions of substance abuse
- Explicit sex
- Sexualisation of religion
- Parental death
- Kidnapping

Mentions of childhood abuse

Mentions of sexual assault (past assault and threats, no graphic on page SA)

Persistent verbal abuse from a parent

Anxiety

Depression

Homelessness

Mentions of past abandonment

The following is a list of kinks included in this book, some of which may be triggering for some readers: praise, degradation, knife play, blood play, sexualisation of religion

Prologue

Siobhán
Two Weeks Ago

"You're twenty-five now, Siobhán, it's time to pull your fucking weight in this family."

I force myself to sit still, hands under my thighs so I'm not tempted to fidget and annoy him. The room is cold and dark, the curtains pulled shut, keeping me from the outside world. The only light emanates from the lamp on his desk, casting a yellow glow over his face.

My father isn't even looking at me as he speaks. Instead, his icy blue eyes flick between the paperwork in front of him and the line of men at my back.

I do my best to suppress the shudder working its way down my spine as I feel the weight of their glares boring into the back of my head. I blink quickly, desperate to hide the tears stinging my eyes before looking at my father once more. I feel myself shrinking as his brow furrows and a sharp frown pulls wrinkles from his clean shaven face. His salt and pepper hair is neatly trimmed and sits perfectly in place. A tailored black suit clings to his arms as he rhythmically taps the table with the gold signet ring emblazoned with our family crest on his pinky finger.

I swallow thickly as I ready myself for the dance I'm about

to do. The practised steps I'll have to take to defend myself. I open my mouth and hope like hell that he'll let me get a word in edgeways during this sham of a meeting.

"But I-"

"But nothing," he snaps and I try to hide the way I flinch. Someone coughs behind me, a poor attempt to cover their laughing, and I know my fear is clear to everyone in this damn room. "I'm sick of you sitting on your arse, lounging around like a spoiled brat. You're the fucking *heir* and it's time you act like it."

I look down at my lap. I don't care how cowardly it makes me seem. I don't care what any of them think anymore.

I'm well aware of how much I disappoint my father. And given the kind of man he is, I've begun to doubt whether or not I even want to make him proud.

"Tá brón orm," I murmur, silently hating the way my voice cracks on the last word. Silently hating the way that, even after all these years, I'm still not used to the weight of his glare. To the way that his words split me in half, cutting so deep their mark is forever etched into my heart.

I can feel myself crumpling inwards.

"I don't want your apologies, Siobhán," he says gruffly, pushing his chair back from his desk suddenly. The wooden legs screech across the floor and I grit my teeth as the shriek slices through me. "People are starting to doubt our family. To test the weight of the Branigan name. I don't think I need to explain why that's a bad thing." His voice is thick with condescension, and he snaps his fingers at one of the men, whose hand lands heavily on my arm.

I'm dragged out of my seat before I can yank my arm away, glaring at the guy who dared to touch me. Smith. He's the oldest of them all, and unfortunately, he may as well be family at this stage given that he's been around since my childhood. I don't bother to make an effort to learn the names of the rest of my father's men. They're disposable. Nothing but young pups begging at my father's heel for a scrap of attention. Besides, getting attached only spells danger, for me and for them.

The three men surround me, trapping me as we exit the office and head through the familiar corridors. It's late, and the air is thick with a looming storm. Someone's left a window open in the hall, and in the distance, a low rumble of thunder rolls through the city. It hasn't reached us yet, but it will.

Soon.

Pulling my gaze from the windows, I peer over my father's shoulder and I know where we're heading within seconds. Nausea curls in my gut. My footsteps drag with dread, but Smith nudges me forward, delighting in my fear, and I stumble. I grind my teeth as I force myself to keep moving, desperate not to give any of them the reaction I know they're hungry for.

My father idly adjusts his gold cross cufflinks on either wrist as he leads the group down the steps. The wooden stairs creak a little with our combined weight. The house is old and sometimes I swear the stone is alive. It settles around us, soft groans and sighs as if it too laments the things that happen within its walls.

I've never known another home, and yet I'm sure that this isn't what one should feel like.

We keep descending, rounding a corner on the first floor and through the door to the cellar. The damp scent in the air gets worse, the steep steps an unforgiving concrete. They're dented in the middle from years of use, and I'm suddenly mad at myself for not putting my runners on before I leapt to my father's summons. I curse myself silently as I look down at my feet. Thin black slippers cover them, a dainty silk bow resting on top, with smooth soles lightly padding each step I take. I have no grip. I flatten my hand against the wall to try to steady myself. The cold steadily begins to seep into my skin.

Nobody speaks until we're at the bottom of the stairs. Only then does the dim light flicker on.

At first, all I can see is the stained floor. This, I'm used to. The dark spatters are slightly lighter in places where it's been scrubbed with bleach. It's hard as fuck to get day-old blood out of stone, particularly if you're only given a toothbrush to do it with.

But as my gaze rises, my stomach drops.

There's a small wooden chair in the centre of the room directly beneath the naked lightbulb. Weak yellow light spills over the figure hunched over on the chair, his hands tied behind his back, shoulders pulling at their sockets as he slumps forward.

"Up you get, fucker," one of the older men, Tierney, jeers.

I'm frozen, shivering despite the warmth radiating from the bodies pressed against either side of me, as the guy raises his head. I grimace as I take in the sight of him. His nose, recently broken and still bleeding, slants to the left. His greasy hair sticks to his forehead as he lowers his brows. Blood drips into his mouth as he bares his teeth at my father, hatred in his dark eyes.

I have no idea who this man is.

But I know he isn't here for a friendly chat.

"Da-" I whisper, but he holds up his hand in a fist, not even turning to look at me. Dread pools in my stomach.

"You know the punishment for sharing family secrets, don't ya Jackie boy?" my father says scarily slowly.

He's completely calm as he pulls out his gun. I've seen it many times, and yet sweat trickles down the length of my spine as I watch the way he carries it so casually, running his hand over the barrel, one finger resting on the trigger.

"Fuck you," Jackie spits back, eyes fiery as they meet my father's. Da's spine snaps straight, the hand holding the gun rising until the man is staring down the barrel.

I shuffle my feet, desperate to look away, scared that something worse will happen if I do.

Nobody says anything. The whole world seems to still. Jackie doesn't back down, and neither does my father.

"Siobhán," my father snaps, not looking away from his latest victim. Bile stings my throat as my stomach heaves, but I somehow manage to force my slippered feet closer to them.

This close, I can make out the hazel of Jackie's eyes, the chip in his front tooth, and the slight smell of weed on his clothes.

He doesn't look high, but maybe he's a low level rat. That's what my father calls those who work for him. Those not high enough in the ranks to truly be part of the family.

"This *rat* betrayed us. Endangered our family. Tell me, daughter, what's the punishment for such a crime?"

I know.

Of course I know. You don't grow up raised in a literal fucking gang without knowing this shit.

No matter how much I wish I didn't.

"Bás trí fhorghníomhú," I answer, the Irish words falling from my tongue, thick and heavy.

I clamp the inside of my cheek between my teeth hard

enough to taste copper as I force myself to stand perfectly still. I can't show weakness right now, and I'll be as good as dead if my father catches me shaking like a leaf.

Warm metal presses against my hand and I start. I look down to find my father's hand outstretched, the butt of the gun held out to me. I raise my wide eyes to his, finding them narrowed and expectant.

"That's right," he says, ignoring Jackie completely now as he presses the weapon into my palm. I have no choice but to take it. The weight of it in my hand is unwelcome and unnatural. "Death, Siobhán. Execution style."

Realisation makes me stumble back.

I'm no stranger to death. But I've never been the one to bring it before.

I've never wanted to be.

I don't know this man, but he won't walk out of here alive, whether it's me that ends him or one of the others. I'm staring down at a dead man, whose eyes are sad as they meet mine. His mouth is open as if he wants to say something, but no words come.

He doesn't look afraid. Not half as afraid as I feel.

"Give him what he's earned, petal."

The nickname comes out in a harsh hiss and I shudder as I stare down at the gun. I don't want to do this. I can't do this.

"I don't want to," I say out loud, and immediately regret it. My father steps towards me and I stumble, my back hitting the stone wall. I focus on the scrape of it through my thin top, pressing my palm to the rugged surface as I try to ground myself.

"Do not make us look weak," my father hisses as his face comes close to mine. I can smell the whiskey on his breath.

"It's time to grow the fuck up, Siobhán. I have sheltered you for too long and now look at what you've become. Nothing but a fuckin' useless lump of skin living off of my hard earned money. Off my blood, sweat and tears. No more. Get rid of him, petal, before I've half the mind to get rid of you."

I wince. My father is a sure man. He doesn't speak for the sake of hearing his own voice.

Staring at him, I struggle to control the tears streaming down my cheeks.

I open my mouth, desperate to say something, anything, to appease my father. But I can't find my tongue. I think I've swallowed it. Maybe that would explain the lump in my throat.

I think I might be sick.

He steps away and I follow with shaky steps. Tierney and Smith are blocking the only way out and I know I wouldn't make it past them. I've never fought anyone in my life, wouldn't even know where to start. Clearly, nobody here views me as a danger even with a fucking loaded gun in my hand because they all look at me with delight shining in their eyes. Aside from Jackie, of course, who still looks resigned and almost disappointed.

Slowly, I raise my hand, the gun pointing at the man's chest. I know how to shoot it. That, at least, my father taught me. Reluctantly, but still. I may not know basic self-defence, but I know how to use the weapon I fucking despise the most.

It's backwards as fuck.

I don't feel *sheltered* but he's right, in a way. I've never been shown how to save myself without a weapon. I've never had to fight. Never killed.

"Pull the trigger."

My eyes are blurry. My whole body feels fuzzy. The dim light looks like it's flickering but I can't tell if it's me or the bulb that's on the fritz.

My stomach is rioting and I'm shaking hard.

There's no way out of this. No way to escape this nightmare. No way out but through.

"Jesus Christ, pull the fucking trigger, Siobhán!" my father roars.

So I do.

***

"You're nothing but a disappointment," my father tells me, sipping from his pint glass.

I flinch as his words land like a blow to my chest. I killed a man for him tonight and this is all he has to say.

I threw up after, smelling the coppery stain of Jackie's blood on me, unable to stop seeing the spray of red as it arced from his chest. The sound of the man's groan, the soft *thud* of his body on the floor when Smith cut him free of the chair, replays over and over in my mind.

It's been two hours, and I can barely hear my father over the memory.

"I don't understand," I whisper. I had to throw my slippers out, and my feet are cold. Bare. The wood beneath them is unforgiving and dark and I hate it.

I hate this whole office.

This whole house. Fuck, this whole damned *city*.

"You're the fucking *heir!*" he shouts suddenly, slamming his palm down hard on his desk. "And you can't even take out a rat without being sick! You know what makes me sick, Siobhán? You. You, the pathetic fucking excuse for a daughter that your mother stuck me with."

I will not cry.

I will not cry.

I will not-

"Get the fuck out of my sight," he sighs, sitting back and pinching the bridge of his nose like he has a headache. Everything's blurry again. Shame wraps tight around my bones and I can't breathe as it squeezes my ribs.

I nod, standing and stumbling to his door. I run towards my bedroom, swearing to God that I can hear the muffled groans of the man I killed at my back.

But I'm the only ghost that haunts this house. Not even my mother's ghost has the desire to step foot in this place.

I did everything my father asked tonight and it wasn't enough. I don't know why I even bother trying to earn his approval anymore. Why I want to.

After all he's done to me. After what he did to Conor.

I bypass my bed for the attached bathroom and tumble into the shower. I've barely managed to strip before I turn it on, the scalding water mixing with my tears as it clings to my body before watching the blood swirling down the drain.

I sit there for hours, until I find the courage to drag myself out and into bed. My room doesn't have a lock, but I prop a chair under the handle. Nobody's ever dared to break in here, but I can't sleep knowing it's open.

I find my phone tangled in my duvet and briefly click it on to check the time.

11:59

I watch it turn to midnight, and the date change, breathing a sigh of relief when my birthday ends.

Twenty-five may be the year that breaks me.

1

Siobhán

My wedding dress is beautiful. It's a shame it's about to be covered in blood.

I stare into the full length mirror across the room from me, barely recognising myself. Corseted floral lace hugs my waist and flares out at my hips. It's pure white and delicate, crafted with care. A small train *swishes* at the back with each movement I make. I feel the faintest brush of the material against my chest as I take heaving breaths. The low cut neckline exposing the swell of my breasts presses closer against them, holding me captive.

My wavy copper hair is pulled back into a low hanging up-do. The gentle waves slipping over my shoulders, grazing lightly against the thin straps of the dress. My makeup is soft and romantic, pink lips and a neutral brown eyeshadow that compliments my dark eyes. I look pretty, feminine, and if I smile just right, I almost look happy.

Under different circumstances, I'd cherish every bit of this. I'd take a second to appreciate how beautiful I *should* feel. How wonderful this is for my family.

But today is not that day.

I'm alone in the bridal suite, with its large windows and the sickly sweet scent of too many flowers staining the air. I shiver as I think about the crowd gathering in the church just a few streets down. I catch my eyes glazing over as I consider how important today is.

The Branigans and Cavanaughs are waiting for me to arrive. My *fiancé*, I assume, is standing at the altar.

Today, two rival families are coming together as one.

My mind swims with quick flashes of curly black hair, broad shoulders and sharp blue eyes as I force strangled breaths in and out of my lungs. I've barely had a chance to get to know the man I'm about to marry.

Oisín and I grew up in similar situations, or at least I suppose so considering we're both heirs to two very powerful families. Despite that though, we were never allowed to interact. It would be 'treason" for us to be friendly towards one another, or at least it would have been prior to today.

For years I've listened to my father plotting ways to destroy the Cavanaugh gang.

Our families have been on the verge of war for so long I'm shocked we've made it this far without the declaration of destruction. The Cavanaughs are the oldest crime family in Killrover, in the entire south. But my father has risen to his standing with blood and brutality, exploiting even the smallest of weaknesses in the others until he'd taken the east of Killrover for himself. I've been raised the same way as the gang.

And yet, I stand here now, in my wedding dress, preparing for my life to be sold to the enemy.

To the one person I've been warned to never go near, all so

that we can put an end to the brutality that's cursed Killrover city for decades.

Brushing my hands against the skirt of my dress I briefly wonder if Oisín feels the same trepidation I do. If his family has pressured him the way that my da has me. Or if instead, he's delighting in the idea of an unwilling bride joining him in his bed tonight.

Closing my eyes, I try to take slow measured breaths but when someone knocks on the door I jump.

"Come in!" I call, trying to sound enthusiastic. My heels click on the wooden floor as I turn, offering a strained smile at the person who opens the door. It's the event coordinator, a tall woman with bright blue eyes and dark hair and, currently, red lipstick smeared on her teeth. I don't remember her name. I only met her this morning when my father's men were dragging me through the front door of the McBride's Hotel.

She holds out a bouquet of classic pink and white roses and I thank her as I take it. A thorn scratches the soft underside of my thumb and I press my skin harder against it.

"It's time!" she chirps, taking my arm and ushering me out of the room.

The words sound like she's sentencing me to my death.

Still, I manage to steady my breathing as I follow her, allowing her to lead me through the clean, white corridors and down the grand staircase. In truth, it's a lovely hotel that my father's booked, with elegant furnishings and a white and gold colour scheme. The bannister beneath my hand is soft and smooth, forgiving even while I clutch it tightly. The walk down doesn't take nearly enough time and all too soon I'm standing before my father. His blue eyes narrow at me, and I know, *I know,* he's seeing my mother when he looks at me.

"Ready, petal?" he murmurs, taking my hand from the organiser and placing it in the crook of his elbow. His grip on my fingers is too tight and I clench my jaw. He doesn't compliment me, but he doesn't criticise me either, and a soft wave of relief washes through me.

I'm ready.

Just not for what he thinks is about to happen.

We exit the hotel and slide into the back of a white limousine decorated with white and gold bows and ribbons trailing along the front and back of it. The city blurs beyond the window, my eyes unfocused as nerves spike through me. I fight the urge to chew on my bottom lip, knowing it'll ruin the gloss painstakingly painted there by the make up artist my father hired for me.

He's spared no expense for this grand facade and I can't afford to have so much as a hair out of place before all is said and done.

I count the minutes as we take the short drive to The Church of Blessed Hearts. As the old, tall building appears in my line of sight, I forget how to breathe, the pinprick of pain in my thumb the only thing tethering me to my body. I've been here hundreds of times, and each time is a reminder that my father pretends to be a devout, holy man and not one who's forgotten what God's name is supposed to mean.

For as long as I've lived, I've never known him to put the practices he insists he believes in to use.

Thou shalt not kill.

Thou shalt not steal.

Thou shalt love thy neighbour as thyself.

All words my father claims to hold above all else on this

earth, including his family.

Yet, to me, this very church has never been anything but another building my father holds meetings in. The confessional booths the perfect place to orchestrate his deals, to sell supply, the hushed conversations in the pews during prayer aiding in his ever growing presence in the city. A place where he can conduct his business while keeping up the deceptive ruse that he is a kind and loving father. A family man. A man with good morals and a man of honour. It's simply another reminder that my father is nothing but a pretty picture made with swift, brutal strokes.

Despite all that, the building is still breathtakingly beautiful, at least to me. As I exit the vehicle, I tip my neck back to take it in.

Rows upon rows of stone lined with cement climb towards the heavens. Stained glass windows shine in the morning sunlight, the colours refracting into numerous iridescent rainbows.

My neck cricks as I stretch it back further to look at the gleaming bronze bell sitting high above in the steeple.

Lowering my head, I take a steadying breath as my father rounds the back of the limousine and latches on tightly to my arm once more. Without looking at me, he drags me forward toward the large wooden church doors. My heels click on the pavement as I force myself to follow his lead.

Digging my nails into the crook of his arm, I stare at the red carpet lining the floor as we enter the church.

My heart gallops inside my chest and I know that if I dare to look at my father, or the hundreds of people gathered in the pews beyond us, I'll break before I can afford to. With my pulse pounding in my ears, I focus on holding my legs steady as I feel my father straighten his spine. His hand lands firmly on mine, almost as though he can sense I'd rather be anywhere else than here.

Glancing up from beneath my lashes I spot Oisín standing at the altar. He's wearing a fitted black suit, and he looks just as resigned to the situation as I first felt when I'd been asked, no, *ordered,* to wed him just two short weeks ago.

I hold the bouquet in my left hand with a death grip and swallow my nerves as the wedding planner nods once to my father and proceeds to wave a hand at the orchestra set up at the side of the church.

I force my face to remain neutral as the orchestra begins to play the *Wedding March* by Felix Mendelssohn in C Major. Every inch of me recoils at the intense tune, but I push my heel clad feet to take a step forward.

"Lift your head and smile, for fuck's sake," my father admonishes through clenched teeth. I do as he says, praying that by the time this is all over, he won't be able to snap at me, hit me, or order me around ever again.

My eyes fix on the gleaming gold statue of a thorn crowned Jesus hanging from a cross placed in the reredos behind the altar. I soak in the imagery carved into the white marble stone and feel myself gulp. I've never been overly religious, but a part of me wonders if God will ever truly be able to forgive me for the sins I'll be committing inside this church today. If I'll ever be welcomed through the gates of Heaven after the things I've done. The things I'm about to do.

Sweat beads at the nape of my neck, and I beg my mind to focus on anything else. I hope like hell the rest of the congregation gathered can't tell that something is off with me, but given the amount of arranged marriages that have taken place in both families, I wouldn't be surprised if they saw my nerves and simply chose to turn a blind eye to them instead.

As we reach the front of the church, I turn to look at Oisín. His blue eyes rake over me from head to toe and his lips press into a thin line. He's clearly unimpressed with the effort that was made to make me look like a puffed up princess, but truthfully I couldn't give a fuck about what he thinks.

The elderly priest I'd elected to ignore this entire time steps closer to me as he clears his throat. He gingerly lifts his hand before resting it on my shoulder. Every muscle in my body tightens with the unexpected move, but I don't allow myself to show how much I dislike his touch.

I know the things he's done to appease my father. The sins he's committed.

I loosen my grip on the bouquet when I realise that the stems of the flowers are beginning to crumple beneath my hold.

"Don't let me down, petal," my father grunts through clenched teeth as he smiles toward Oisín, and I contort my face into a watery smile once more.

Locking my hand in Oisín's, I ignore the clamminess of my palms and focus on looking at the stained glass window past the reredos before me.

My eyes flit back and forth over each dazzling colour, and I allow myself to zone out while the priest welcomes the guests and runs through the beginning of the mass.

I grit my teeth and keep my pathetic excuse for a smile in place as the show begins in earnest.

"Who gives this bride away?" Father Donnelly asks and I swallow my pride as my father proclaims his,

"I do."

If I have my way, that will be the only *I do* heard within these sacred walls today.

Adjusting my stance, I subtly shuffle my feet further apart and work to steady myself on the stilts for shoes that I've been forced to wear.

I count the minutes down, ignoring everything around me as I wait for my moment. Father Donnelly's voice drones in the background as Oisín loosens his grip on my hand. His fingers recoil from mine as though they want nothing more than to never feel them again.

I don't mind, if anything, it makes what I'm about to do so much easier.

My mind settles as I remind myself of the plan I've concocted in secret.

I don't let myself think about the repercussions.

I don't let myself feel the guilt that's been eating me alive since I made this decision.

Instead I take shallow breaths and pray like hell that I can survive the next few minutes.

I feel my focus snap back as Father Donnelly finally says the words I've been waiting to hear.

"Siobhán Branigan and Oisín Cavanaugh, have you come here to enter into marriage without coercion, freely and wholeheartedly?"

My heart rate climbs in my chest, every muscle preparing for what's to come as I lift my chin and stare the priest in the face.

"No."

The word leaves my mouth just as Oisín prepares to answer with his bullshit, "I have."

Gasps ring out around the church, voices climbing with

shock but I don't let myself care.

Throwing the bouquet in Oisín's direction, I hastily grab the edge of my dress, and run toward the side of the church. My father lurches from his seat, ready to catch me, but I'd expected no less from him.

Slipping a gun I'd holstered in the garter beneath my dress, I point it towards his chest and lock my eyes on his. Hatred simmers there, but I don't let it touch me.

I don't allow myself to give two shits about his feelings.

For twenty five years I've done nothing but try to be the perfect heir. The son he wishes he'd had instead of me.

I've felt the weight of his disappointment for long enough, and I refuse to give him any more of myself.

I thought I could handle it. Thought I could continue to cut myself into strips of nothing until he'd finally see my worth.

But it never happened, and it never will.

No matter how much of myself I destroyed, he simply wanted more and more from me.

And when that still wasn't enough, he tossed me away like I was worthless, and to the fucking Cavanaughs no less.

My father's rats surround me as I continue to stare him down with the barrel of my gun.

My finger rests on the trigger, unyielding as I hold my place and refuse to back down.

From the corner of my eye I catch Smith raising his Glock in my direction. I can't help the smirk that tilts my lips. If he really thinks my father won't kill him for that then he's dumber than he seems.

I might be standing here now with my gun aimed at my father, but no matter what, *nobody* has the right to pull a gun on one of us.

If I can't make it out of here, I'll pay the price for my sins. But it'll pale in comparison to the punishment Smith will face for daring to think he could insult a Branigan so publicly.

My heart gallops in my chest, anger and fear swirling in my veins as I try to control my shortened breaths.

"Put down the gun, petal," my father pleads. The words are soft, hushed, almost as though he believes he can placate me. Like I'm a toddler having a tantrum instead of a grown woman fit to kill him.

"I'm afraid I can't do that Da," I seethe, pissed that even now he's treating me this way.

I'm nothing more than an annoyance to him. I've never been allowed to be more than that.

"Siobhán, you're making a scene. Put down the gun so we can talk. Privately."

Shaking my head slightly I hiss as I feel a single tear track down my face.

I hate that I'm crying. I hate that even now, when I'm finally on the brink of getting what I want, I'm falling apart.

"What the fuck is going on?"

Oisín's voice grabs my attention and as much as I want to keep my eye on him and the rest of the bloody Cavanaughs, I can't.

I keep my gaze fixed on my father as I fortify myself.

"Just a little patricide, nothing for ye to worry about. Figured ye wouldn't mind if I took out dear ol' Da here on my way out."

"I mean, I can't say that I would. But that's not the fuckin point of today now is it, Siobhán?" Thomas Cavanaugh's voice hits my ears, far too close for comfort.

Still, I don't lift my eyes from my father's.

"Truthfully Thomas, I couldn't give a fuck."

Closing my eyes, I tilt my hand to the left just slightly and squeeze the trigger.

Blood sprays from my fathers shoulder as the bullet slices through it. I startle as droplets hit my face and chest. Screams echo through the church as a few people run for cover. More guns are drawn and a few of Thomas' men aim them at me.

I chuckle as I watch them scramble to surround Oisín, but before they can come close enough to cover Thomas, I point the gun in his direction.

"You either let me walk out of here, or I shoot you too. The choice is yours."

Pained groans fill the silence that follows as Thomas drops his gaze to look at my father bleeding all over the red carpet. I marvel at the sight, delighting in knowing that his sins are finally leaving a visible mark in this godforsaken building.

I tilt my head to the side when I realise that my da has the gall to eye his men up like they should move towards me. Sucking my teeth I spin before the rat to my right can so much as shift a toe out of line. The shock of the gun going off vibrates through me for a second time as I hit the rat closest to me in the chest with a bullet. His body lands with a soft *thump* as it falls to the padded floor.

"Jesus, Mary and Joseph, she's lost the fuckin plot!" Thomas roars, a hint of laughter in his words, as he takes a step back from the circle surrounding me. His hands are lifted to show he's unarmed and I smile ruefully.

"Y'know, when you've been told you're a crazy bitch enough times in your life, you start to believe it," I hum.

"Yes, I can certainly see why you might have been told that a time or two," he goads as he pointedly gestures to both of my victims.

I shrug, not caring for his opinion.

My dress swishes as I take a step back and for a split second I want to laugh at the ridiculousness of it all.

My wedding dress is painted red, my hair is tumbling loose from the updo, and I'm standing here talking to Thomas fucking Cavanaugh of all people, while my father is bleeding on the floor.

Sighing deeply, I lift my arm once more and aim it towards him.

I've had enough of this shit show and I want to leave this fucking place.

"If that's all for today gentleman, I think I'll be heading out."

I curtsey like I'm leaving the king of fucking England's presence, disrespect coating each movement I make.

I walk backwards, down the side of the pews, careful with each step I take. The gun stays steady in my hand as every man in the building aims theirs at me in return, unsure of whether to shoot me or not.

When I eventually feel the cold bite of the wooden doors framing my back, I reach behind me and turn the handle.

Before I can open it, I look to Oisín once more. I don't know why, but seeing respect shine in his eyes does more for me than any of this has.

It almost makes going on the run worth it.

Because as soon as I walk out those doors my life will change forever.

I will never be the *Princess* of the Branigan gang again.

I'll only ever be a traitor to them.

Releasing the handle, I push the door out behind me and run.

Shots ring out as all hell breaks loose inside the church. I duck as the sound of the doors bounce off the stone wall ricochets down the street.

But I don't look back.

I beg my legs and the devil below that I never have to see any of them again.

2

Nessa

"She ran."

I frown down at Thomas' name on the phone, sure I must be imagining what he'd just said.

"Ran?" I echo, anger flicking to life in my belly. I stand in front of *Sinners*, watching as the ash tips off the end of my cigarette and falls to the concrete.

"Yes, Nessa, Jesus," he huffs, and I can hear him panting down the line. "The princess caused a fucking *shoot-out*, for fuck's sake."

Confusion clouds my brain. "Why the fuck did she run from her own bloody wedding?"

This marriage was supposed to fix things and now the fucking *bride* has ruined it. Rage burns through me, aimed at a girl I've never met. Thomas has been at that fucking church for hours, supposedly attending his son's wedding.

Or, war declaration.

"Doesn't matter *why*," Thomas spits. It sounds like he's running, and I can hear Oisín yell something in the background. At least our heir's still alive but fuck, I can only hope no other members were lost in the gunfire. "But in the fucking chaos the bitch caused, she escaped. We need our best hound on her trail, Ness."

He only ever calls me *Ness* when he wants something. I swear under my breath, throwing the butt of the cigarette to the concrete and crushing the glowing cherry under the toe of my shoe. My mouth is dry and the cold evening breeze isn't helping.

"I suppose I'm the fucking dog in this situation," I bark back.

I knew I should've gone to this fucking wedding. I'm the best damn enforcer we've got and yet I stayed. I waited fucking hours for a man who didn't turn up. Jackie is four hours late. We'd agreed on this date, this time and this fucking location *three weeks* ago.

And now, this. Some spoiled brat causing a gang war because she wanted to throw a tantrum on her fucking wedding day.

"Find Siobhán Branigan, and bring her back to her fiancé. She's your charge from here on out, Nessa. We can't afford to let her get away again."

"Absolutely fucking not, Cavanaugh!" I snap, my anger boiling over. "I'm not your on-call babysitter. I've enough shit to be dealing with as is."

"You will do as I fucking say. This is bad, do you understand me? Three of our men were *shot* today, Nessa. You're doing this and you're going to fucking keep your trap shut," Thomas barks as he cuts me off. I know then that he hasn't been listening to a single thing I've said. He couldn't give less of a fuck about the mess he's landed me in.

I want to scream. My grip tightens on the phone so hard I worry I'll shatter the damned glass.

"Why can't her fucking *husband* find her?" I ask, running my hand over my holster, feeling for the weapons like a child with a teddy. "She's Oisín's problem, not mine."

I can practically hear Thomas glare at me down the line. I've seen the expression on his face so many times it's ingrained into my brain. He still hasn't learned, even after twelve years, that I don't heel like a bitch when called.

"She fucked off before the vows, and she's not getting near him again. Oisín's going off the grid. He can't be caught hanging around here with those bastards on the loose after this shit show. We can't risk him. Jesus Christ, are you even *fucking listening Nessa?*"

A high pitched ringing starts in my ears and I take a deep breath to ground myself. I move the phone away from my ear as I glare at the sky and remind myself that this is Thomas Cavanaugh I'm speaking to. He's the head of the largest gang in Ireland and I'll be lucky to still be breathing after the way I've spoken to him today.

Gritting my teeth I bring the phone to my ear before shaking my head.

"Yes, Thomas, I hear you loud and bloody clear."

"Good. Now, get a move on. Find her before her dickhead father does," Thomas says, cutting off my retort before ending the call.

I stare at the blank screen for longer than I should, seething. The last thing I want to be doing is chasing down Oisín's wayward bride. I should be tracking Jackie down instead. He's never missed a check-in before and I'm beginning to wonder if I've been played. He's a skeezy fucker, there's no doubt about it, but it makes him the perfect person for going undercover with the Branigans. The fact he's missed our appointment sets off alarm bells in my mind. I want nothing more than to hunt the fucker down and find out if he's turned coat or been made.

Where the hell are you, Jack?

Clenching my fists I sigh heavily as I look up and down the street once more. I grit my teeth, pissed that I've wasted my time. I look back at the neon sign hanging above *Sinners* and contemplate slipping back inside for one more drink but decide against it. I'm about to step into a new kind of hell and I at least need to be sober when I get there. Jim, the bouncer on the door tonight, nods to me as I tip my head in his direction, letting him know I'm heading out. Sliding the phone back into my pocket, I reach for my cigarettes once more and silently curse Thomas Cavanaugh for adding to my already heavy workload. I allow myself two deep breaths before I move, heading in the direction of the Church.

"Sebastian!"

The doors shudder off the walls as I slam them open, the sound reverberating through the abandoned church. The building had been decommissioned years ago, and in place of God, we'd taken it over. Thomas had declared it Cavanaugh territory, and it's my favourite of all our meeting spots. The pews are a little worse for wear, and sure the altar has a little blood spilled across it, but I swear that sometimes, when I sit here in the middle of the night after a job, I can feel something holy in the walls.

"Christ, Nessa, chill the fuck out," Seb calls back, becoming visible at last as he hauls himself up into a sitting position on one of the pews. "What's with the attitude? I thought today was a day of love and celebration." Sarcasm drips from his voice, his signature smirk bright even in the dying light. His deep blue eyes are shaded, something dark hiding behind the fake cheer.

I fight the urge to punch him in the face for the sarcastic comment. He might be my best friend, but that doesn't mean he doesn't deserve a lesson every now and again. It would do him good to remember who the fuck he's talking to.

"What crawled up your ass, Nessie?" he snarks when I do nothing but glare at him.

"Do you have your bike?" I ask, instead of gutting him. *Breathe, Nessa.*

Sebastian stands, sobering, and nods. "Yeah, I came straight here on it when you texted. Abandoned a perfectly good glass of Thomas' whiskey for you and all."

"Good. It's all gone to shit." I pinch the bridge of my nose and exhale roughly, a stress headache already building behind my eyes. For fuck's sake. How can one girl cause so much chaos?

I give him the rundown of the nightmarish phone call, watching horror spread across his face. His blue eyes widen as he shoves his leather jacket over his t-shirt and gun holster.

"Christ on a bike," Sebastian sighs, tipping his head up to the high ceilings. Evidently, they aren't listening, given that he doesn't go up in a ball of flames. The irony of Sebastian calling on the son of God in a church I know for a fact he's killed someone in is not lost on me. "They're not married?"

I shake my head in answer. "If I'm hunting down a runaway princess, so are you," I tell Sebastian, tone brooking no argument. He doesn't even bother scowling at me, instead shoving past me and running to his bike.

His voice is muffled as he pulls his helmet on, but I still catch him call out, "Race you to the wedding!"

3

Siobhán

"Siobhán Branigan and Oisín Cavanaugh, have you come here to enter into marriage without coercion, freely and wholeheartedly?"

"No."

It takes me fifteen fucking minutes to tear the dress off. Whoever the hell designed corseted wedding dresses clearly did not make them to be taken off alone. My shoulders ache from awkward stretching by the time I free myself from the stained fabric. Naked except for my white lacy underwear, I rush for the battered wardrobe hunched in the far corner. The whole thing shakes as I open the door and wrench my duffel bag out, as if the cupboard is as old as the building itself.

I close my eyes and tip my head down as I silently pray, thanking God for willing my cousin Patrick to help me. He'd never agreed with my father's treatment of me, but given that our fathers hated each other, we were kept far apart for most of our lives. Still, when he'd learned about the wedding, I begged him to save me from the future I was facing. I warned him not to turn up at the wedding on our last call, though not why exactly, and I can only pray he listened. My phone stores exactly three numbers: Patrick's, Da's and Conor's. Though the latter is useless now. I have no way of checking if my cousin is okay, because the phone, and the tracking device I suspect is in it, is back at the hotel I got ready in this morning.

Armed with the supplies Patrick stashed here two days ago when he'd booked this room with cash and a fake name for me, I make my way to the adjoining bathroom. I cringe as I switch the light on and notice that the lightbulb's fucked. Squinting, I look up and watch it flicker wildly as it emits a persistent buzzing sound. I hiss a breath at the smell of stale piss in here and take another step forward. I desperately need a shower, but when I try to turn on the water, the shower head only produces a sputter of murky brown sludge.

Sighing, I turn around and settle for the sink. Gunshots still echo in my mind as I scrub off my makeup with a slightly musty smelling towel and cheap hand soap. I reluctantly look up, examining the dark circles under my eyes in the cloudy, toothpaste flecked bathroom mirror. My hair is still curled, but I rip out all the pins and tie it up in a bun on the top of my head. I rinse out the makeup laden towel and frantically rub at the bloody spatters on my skin. My arms, chest and neck are flecked with the stuff, and I refuse to think about whether the blood belongs to a member of my family or not. I try, so fucking hard, to feel no guilt about what I've just done.

God I try, but the sinking feeling in my gut tells me I'm failing.

But this has to be better than being a wife to a man I don't know. Than being under my father's heel for another twenty five years of my life.

Finally, I look less like a runaway bride and more like a normal, albeit exhausted, girl. The towel is beyond saving, and I throw it into the useless shower stall, not caring that it's soaking up the dregs of murky water coating the shower basin.

I'm grateful for my foresight as I tug on my leggings and jumper. I grab a pair of socks and my runners too, internally cheering at the fact I won't have to run in heels any longer. They were pretty, sure, but a bitch to escape in. I'd nearly broken my ankle three times before diving into my waiting taxi.

Shoving the dress in a bin bag, I curse at the giant pile of bloodied lace. Finally winning the wrestling match with the damned thing, I tie the bag closed and push it under the bed. I'm grateful I at least had the foresight to dump the gun out the window of the taxi on my way here. I couldn't stand the sight of it anymore.

By the time I pull myself up from the foul smelling floor, I'm sweating from stress and exertion. I fan my hands in front of my face, hoping to drag air towards my body but the tiny hotel room feels like a bloody desert.

It's a shitty hotel in Abbotsground; a shitty little town I'd never set foot in before, because it appears to consist of nothing but houses and a corner shop. But the hotel is cheap, quiet and remote, which is all I need.

The bed squeaks when I flop down onto it, the springs digging into my thighs. A wave of exhaustion rushes over me, and temptation to lie back and rest follows suit, no matter how fucked this mattress is.

But I can't. I have to keep going, to get far, far away from here and my father and the rest of them.

I want time to figure out who I am, and I can't do that when he's forcing me to be someone I'm not. Someone I hate.

Floorboards creaking outside my door is the only warning I get.

The door shakes on its hinges, once, twice and then it's flying off them, revealing two dark figures in the doorway.

I scream, but no sound comes out. Fear has a choke hold on me as the dim light from the bathroom catches on the barrel of a gun, pointed directly at my chest. I snap my mouth closed so fast my teeth sink into my tongue and blood begins to pool.

I'm up and moving before they reach me, running around the bed so the furniture is between us, my back to the window. Frantically, I reach for the lock, but the fucking thing is painted shut and my nails just scratch up chalky white paint.

For a split second I regret ditching the gun, realising now how useful it might have been.

Panic swallows me whole. I stand there shell shocked, my eyes searching the room for a way out.

All the while, the stranger's gun stares me down.

Only one, I register. The second figure has their arms crossed over their chest as they lean against the doorway, blocking the exit but managing to look completely at ease. My heart is racing so fast I can't hear whatever the man says, and panic is refusing to let me focus on anything except getting the fuck away.

The first person, a woman, I notice vaguely, suddenly darts towards me. She pins me against the wall before I can even think about what the fuck to do. A choked sound leaves my mouth as my breath leaves me, the woman's hand around my throat.

What the actual fuck just happened?

I struggle, but it's useless. Her grip on me tightens as I claw pathetically at her wrists, gasping for air.

"Think she gets the message, Nessie," a man's bored voice says as my vision starts to blur around the edges. I kick out wildly, but my foot barely taps against her thigh.

Just as I think I might pass out, she speaks. "Do not run," she hisses. Her hand leaves my throat and I gulp in air as my vision returns.

I ignore her warning because *fuck this* and run, getting all of two steps before the woman is on me again, tripping my legs out from beneath me and swiftly tackling me to the floor. I land hard on my front, barely managing to slam my hands on the floor to catch myself. Within seconds, she's grabbing my arms and pinning them behind my back, sitting her weight on my thighs so I can't so much as squirm.

I scream into the floorboards, desperation and fear making me sob.

"Scream all you want, Branigan, no one in this shit hole is going to come to your rescue," the woman mocks, tightening her grip for emphasis.

"Who the hell are you?" I pant, trying to bury my fear with the rage I feel pulsing in my veins. But my voice comes out scratchy and wobbly and I can practically hear the smile in the man's voice when he answers.

"The hounds of hell sent to track you down," he says in a sing-song voice, heavy footsteps coming over to us.

Black boots appear in my vision, mud splashed onto the shiny leather. Then he's bending down, kneeling on the old wooden floor next to my face. His blue eyes shine with amusement as he looks at me, his lips curved into a smirk. Everything about him spells trouble, from the messy dark hair to the tattoos climbing his neck.

"Name's Sebastian," he introduces, extending his hand to me before frowning at the woman holding my arms behind my back and shrugging. His arm falls back to his side as I blink up at him, sure I've passed out when the woman was choking me and this is all some sort of dream.

"You know, for the daughter of a fucking gang leader, she's shit at self defence," the woman above me comments dryly, and Sebastian snorts with laughter.

Anger burns in my gut. "Don't talk about me like I'm not here!" I demand. I can't stand it. "Why the fuck are you here?"

"Nessa, let her go, she's harmless," Sebastian says, and Nessa grumbles something about him ruining her fun before standing abruptly, leaving my arms to flop to the floor. Pins and needles seep into my palms as I scramble to sit, rubbing the circulation back into my wrists.

"Why the fuck are you here?" I try again. I know better than to run now. I've had enough of gun wielding gang members today to last a lifetime, and these two have made it more than clear that they can overpower me easily.

No, I need to bide my time and play nice with these maniacs until I can figure a way out of this mess.

Even if every single muscle in my body is begging me to *run.*

"You're coming back with us," Nessa tells me, her voice dark and harsh. She taps her gun against the palm of her hand as she stares me down with narrowed, deep green eyes. Her blonde hair is tied up in a tight braid, though a few wispy strands have escaped around her face. I felt how strong she is just seconds ago, but as I gape at her, I realise just how fucked I am. The muscles in her arms flex as she slides the gun back into its holster, visible through her skin tight black shirt.

I don't have the energy to push myself to my feet yet, but both of them stand over me as I shake on the floor. Sebastian towers over us both, one dark brow raised as his gaze flicks between us.

"Right then, let's get this show on the road," he announces with a clap, the sharp sound ringing through the room. I jump, shaking my head even as he grabs my bag and slings it over his shoulder.

I have no fucking clue where they're taking me.

And I'm all too aware that I have no fucking choice but to go with them.

4

Nessa

It's pitch black out by the time we skid to a stop on the side of the tiny main street of the shit hole town we're in. Furious with myself for not keeping better track of time, I curse into the cold evening air and lower my feet onto the gravel beneath my bike, hands flexing around the handlebars.

My hair whips wildly around my face, strands escaping from my braid as the wind picks up, cutting a path clean through me. I'd had to give my helmet to Siobhán because like fuck did I want to deal with damaging the precious princess.

Glancing at my watch, I curse at the time. We aren't going to make it back to the manor like I'd planned to tonight.

The roads are windy as fuck and full of potholes, the street lights few and far between and we still aren't even halfway home. It's almost impressive how far she's managed to get from the city in such a short amount of time.

Cursing the girl sitting in front of me on my bike, I pry my hands off the handlebars and let my arms fall to my sides. I don't even know what town we're in, but the *vacancies* sign flashing in the window of the pub beside us is good enough for me.

I hear Sebastian park beside me as I slide off my bike and grab Siobhán's wrist, pulling her off with me. She wobbles, her legs unaccustomed to sitting on a bike for so long, but I don't bother to help steady her. Instead I grit my teeth and watch from the corner of my eye as she locks her knees in place and forces herself to stand tall.

"What the fuck is this?" Sebastian asks, a frown marking his face as he stretches his arms above his head. I hear his back crack and grimace. My own body is stiff after the long drive, but I pay it no mind. The ache is welcome.

"You think it's a grand idea to be driving these dodgy roads with no street lights and a runaway bride attached to my Goddamn bike?" I quip back at him, rolling my eyes. I can't help the snark in my tone, I'm pissed off, tired and fucking hungry. We can't even take the easier roads through the city because the entire fucking place is swimming with Branigan men trying to hunt down the girl in my grip.

The girl says nothing, staring up at the pub with wide eyes while Sebastian glares at me, tired of my attitude by now. Glancing in the direction of the pub, I resign myself to the long night ahead.

The place is packed. Drunken shouts from men hardly able to hold their pints spill out of the open front door. The smell of cigarette smoke, beer and sweat makes my nose wrinkle, but the Branigan doesn't take any notice.

Then again, her father owns a string of places just like this.

"So we're getting shit faced with royalty?" Sebastian teases, a terrible attempt at lightening the mood, as he crosses his arms over his chest. His brow lifts with amusement as he watches a drunk as fuck middle aged man fall off the pavement with his limp dick in his hand.

Fantastic.

I sigh heavily, stepping over the drunken eejit as I march up to the front door, shoving Siobhán between Sebastian and me.

I can't fucking wait to get home and put this shit behind me.

"Don't let her move," I growl at Sebastian, leaving him and the girl by the door as I shove my way through the crowd of sweaty bodies to the bar.

A young woman is at the till, arguing with a customer about the price of a pint. I glare at the man, who sneers at me until he takes in the holster straps around my chest. Though the guns are hidden by my jacket, I see the moment he realises that he shouldn't fuck with me.

He huffs, giving the poor server one last dirty look, then stomps away.

"Thanks," the woman says to me, brushing frizzy hair out of her face. Her cheeks are flushed, and she leans against the sticky counter like she's counting down the minutes until she can go home.

I shrug in response. "Do ye still have rooms for the night?"

The woman holds up a finger in a sign for me to hang on, ducking under the counter and reappearing with a battered diary. She narrows her eyes at the open page. "Two singles."

I grit my teeth. There isn't another option but fuck if I don't briefly consider sleeping outside with my bike.

"I'll take them. Thanks." I pay quickly, and she slides two keys across the bar to me. They're heavy with wooden tags, the numbers eight and twelve carved into them.

The crowd is slowly beginning to thin, but I still have to shoulder past more than a few men to reach Sebastian and

Siobhán.

Immediately, he snatches one of the keys from my hand, grinning widely. I barely have time to grab the Branigan brat and hiss at her to follow me before the door to a narrow staircase is closing behind him.

I can hear Sebastian's laughter as I drag her with me in his wake, ignoring the way she huffs and stumbles up the stairs. The staircase opens onto a hallway lined with numbered doors. It smells of old cigarettes and fake florals, as though they'd tried to cover up the first scent with cheap room spray. The carpet is worn thin and an ugly red and brown pattern.

I catch Sebastian just as he reaches room twelve.

"Sebastian, I swear to God-"

He only laughs and winks. "Night, Nessie."

Then he closes the door on my face.

Anger rises, hot and heavy, in me and I kick his door to expel it before I force a breath into my lungs and turn to Siobhán.

"What are you going to do with me now?" she asks. It doesn't escape me that she's attractive, but she looks exhausted, her hair tangled around her face and smudges of lingering eye makeup under her eyes. She stares at me like she's contemplating punching me, though her shoulders are slumped and she eyes the holsters I wear warily. I can't picture this girl swatting a fly, never mind shooting up her own wedding.

"We sleep." I storm off in search of room eight, sick of having to lug the girl after me. I fight with the old lock, wiggling the damned key for what feels like minutes before the door swings open.

I want to scream. Or shoot something.

"What the fuck?" Branigan echoes my own thoughts as she

peers over my shoulder. My fingers are still closed around her wrist, but neither of us moves as we take in the shitty excuse for a room.

"Get in," I snap, not giving her the chance to argue as I step inside and take her with me.

I let her go to lock the door behind us, shoving the key into the inner pocket of my leather jacket.

I can hear her rummaging around behind me, and grit my teeth before I turn and face reality. The room is *tiny*. Barely big enough for the single bed and the wardrobe that are so close together I swear if I roll over in the night I'll headbutt it.

Siobhán hovers over the bed, glancing between it and me with wide eyes. "Uh, there's only one bed."

I snort, rolling my eyes. "No shit, Branigan. Brains to match the brawn, I see."

Her expression shutters and she looks away from me.

"Lie down," I tell her, uninterested in anything else she has to say. She doesn't move. "Lie the fuck down!"

She jolts like I've hit her, her fists clenching at her sides. I narrow my eyes at her, but she's already kicking off her shoes and doing as instructed. She perches on the edge of the bed, her eyes hard as they meet mine, and lies back slowly.

I lift the bag she'd brought with her to the hotel. There's not much in it - a couple items of clothing and some cereal bars. I take the latter and pocket them, then pull out one of her black t-shirts. Pulling my knife from my boot I cut it into strips, careful not to nick myself in the dim light coming from the window.

"Hands above your head," I say, hearing tiredness in my voice. Her big brown eyes grow even larger at my demand, fear skittering over her features. "You can't think I'm going to let you sleep freely?"

She just blinks, swallowing thickly and pressing her lips together. "Why the fuck do you care if I run again? Just let me go."

I raise a brow at her. "People are in the hospital because of you, *princess.* Do you understand? You've started a fucking war. I will never let you go."

She blanches, barely fighting as I tie her to the bed with the thin strands of cotton. When I'm happy she can't escape, I sink to the floor, leaning against the end of the bed with my feet braced against the wall.

It's uncomfortable as fuck but I doubt I'll be sleeping much anyway. The sound of drunkards echoes up from the bar below, and the Branigan girl is silent for so long I think she must've fallen asleep.

"Aren't you going to go sleep with your boyfriend?" she asks suddenly, and I'm so fucking exhausted that it takes me a minute to process what the hell she's on about.

"Sebastian?" I bark out with a snort, momentarily forgetting where I am as the absurdity of her assumption sinks in. "I'm a lesbian. Even if I wasn't, that man makes me want to punch him too often to ever date him."

"Oh," is all she says in response, and then, just as I feel my eyes start to close, "What happens in the morning, Nessa?"

It's the first time she's said my name.

For some reason, the thought stops me short.

"We take you back home to your husband's father."

"Oisín is not my husband."

I sigh, leaning my head back against the bed. "Semantics. Regardless, Thomas isn't going to just let you go now. I hope your five minutes of freedom was worth it, princess."

5

Siobhán

Someone is screaming. Screeching, like they're being torn apart. It's so close that my ears are ringing before my eyes have the chance to open.

The door is still closed, and the fabric holding my arms in place hasn't budged an inch. I twist my head to the right, but I can't see the small window past the damn wardrobe. But there's no breeze or street noise to indicate it's been opened.

I raise my head as best I can while being tied up, muscles straining as I look down the bed to where Nessa had been before I fell asleep.

In the near total darkness, I can make out her shape. She's moving, thrashing, head turning side to side as her limbs kick out wildly. The whole bed shifts as her back hits the frame and I bite the inside of my cheek to kill the urge to scream.

She's fighting, hard. But there's no one in the room but us.

I force myself to breathe slowly, ignoring the pain in my shoulders and neck from the angle I'm holding myself at.

"Nessa?" I call out, softly at first. Fear is still trickling through me, the shock of being woken so suddenly still wreaking havoc on my body. "Nessa?"

She doesn't answer. Another shriek wrenches itself from her throat and her arms drop to her sides. I look wildly for anything to throw at her, or to kick in her direction, something to get her attention, but there's nothing. I'm tied here, in the darkness, while she fights demons I can't see.

Unintelligible but fear stained words fall from her mouth and I realise with utter clarity that she's still asleep.

It's a nightmare.

"Get," she pants, her words clearer now though still muffled with the dream. "Off."

Panic and pity coat my skin. I don't want to feel either for this girl, my *kidnapper*.

"NESSA!" I yell, desperate for her to stop and wake up, but it's useless. The sounds she's making are pained, like a kicked cat, hissing and whining. Adrenaline courses through me in a steady rush as I let my head fall back to the pillow, still chewing at the bloody skin on the inside of my lips to ground myself.

I can't tell if her nightmare ends or I fall asleep first. Only that when I wake again, the sun is streaming through the room and nobody is screaming.

"Please," I plead, beyond caring about how pathetic my begging sounds. "Please don't take me back there."

My arms ache after being held above my head all night, and my body feels awkward and heavy with exhaustion. I'd barely managed a few hours of sleep. I'd spent the night panicking in my forced, uncomfortable position and keenly aware of the enemy that slept at my feet.

Nessa ignores me completely, retying her long, blonde hair into a new, tighter, braid. Frustration threatens to burn a hole straight through me, but I say nothing of the nightmare. What is there to say that wouldn't humiliate us both? *I lay awake and listened to you screaming all night?* I think the fuck not.

Before I can try pleading again, someone's knocking loudly at our door. I freeze, and Nessa exhales sharply, hand on her gun as she yanks the door open. Her face is like thunder as Sebastian grins widely at her.

"I don't know about you guys but I slept *great*!" he declares, kicking the door closed behind him. Even in yesterday's clothes, he looks put together in that annoyingly perfect, rumpled way.

I don't even want to consider what I look like right now. Not that it matters. Not that I care.

I'm about to step into the lion's den without so much as a wooden sword to wield.

All my planning. All those years of biting my tongue and bowing my head and murmuring *yes, Da*.

Just to land myself right back where I started.

"You can't take me back!" I try, aiming my plea at Sebastian this time.

I watch his whole demeanour harden before my eyes. He stands up straight, arms crossed over his chest. The tattoos on his neck strain as he clenches his jaw

"You think so highly of yourself that you'd rather people die than get married?" he asks, voice carefully calm. I still, fear crawling along my spine.

"I think I'd rather die than say those vows," I answer, trying to line my words with steel. I don't want them to shake as badly as I am right now. Sebastian's lip curls back in what I can only assume is disgust and I have to force myself not to fold inward as the weight of it is aimed directly at me.

"That can be arranged," Nessa pipes up, fabric rustling as she finishes readjusting her holsters.

I feel angry tears sting the back of my eyes and hate myself for the way the room blurs before me.

Daughters of gang leaders shouldn't cry in the face of danger. But it's not the threat of death that makes me want to sob, it's the complete and utter devastation of my own failure.

I had one attempt at getting myself out of this.

I don't know if I'll ever get another.

Nessa and Sebastian certainly aren't going to let me go and I don't doubt they won't hesitate to shoot me if I try to run from them.

"Let's go. We've to get Branigan back before anyone else comes looking for her."

My blood turns to ice at the thought. I'm not sure what's worse, being taken to the Cavanaughs or back to my own father.

I fight when Sebastian pulls me upright, my wrists tied together with the damned scraps of my shirt. He doesn't even flinch as he pulls my back to his front, banding his arm around my waist. I kick out, but it's useless. He sighs heavily before lifting me clean off the ground and slinging me over his shoulder.

The dizzying sensation of being carried this way with my arms pinned between us makes my stomach roll. I kick and struggle and shout and he doesn't care.

Instead, he chats happily to Nessa about whether to put me somewhere they call *Church* or at the manor.

I have no idea *who's* manor they're talking about, but none of the potential answers are good. Her's? Cavanaugh's? My father's?

The barmaid gives us an odd look as we charge through the now empty bar, but ignores me completely when Nessa slams a wad of cash down on the bar and gives her a pointed look.

In vain, I shout, "put me down! Please, help! Help me!"

I watch through tangled hair, head tipped back at a painful angle, as the woman turns around and fusses with a row of glasses.

"Shut your fucking mouth or I'll gag you," Nessa hisses, stalking back up to walk beside Sebastian. I can only see their boots and the pavement as we exit and cold air greets me.

I'm about to try screaming for help again, despite the threats, when the world is righted. Sebastian drops me unceremoniously over the seat of his bike, though he leaves my hands tied.

"Hold still," he warns, voice dark, and it's instinct to freeze. I struggle to register the change in him, and why. Clearly, I fell for his charm too fast to see the shadows lurking underneath.

Stupid, naive girl.

The leather seat beneath me is cold and hard, and I wince as Sebastian shoves the helmet over my head. It's too big, and he yanks harshly at the strap under my chin to make it fit better. I bite my tongue and say nothing, not even when he traps me between him and the handlebars.

"You move, you fall. You fall, I'm not scraping you up off the tarmac," I hear Nessa shout over the roar of the engines coming to life. The bike vibrates beneath me and just like last night, my stomach lurches dangerously as we tear away from the B&B.

I resist the urge to launch myself off the fucking bike. Barely, and only because Sebastian drives like a madman. I cringe as I watch the speedometer climb to twice the speed limit. Hitting the road at that speed would surely kill me.

I want out, but I want to live to see my freedom more.

I wonder if that pisses my father off more than anything. My utter determination to *live*. To survive everything he's thrown at me, no matter the cost.

I'm sure he'd rather I'd died with my ma.

I lurch forward as we pull up with a screech outside a massive house. We're in the middle of fucking nowhere, and that surprises me more than the size of the fucking mansion in front of me. I expected to be taken back into the city, not into the fucking wilderness. The mansion is well kept, though it's clearly an old build. The stone is weathered, and ivy is climbing its way up the front wall. I'm gaping at it when Sebastian yanks me off his bike, ridding me of the damn helmet at last.

"What the fuck?" I manage to get out, feet stumbling on the gravel as he begins to lead me up the steps to the main door. "Stop! Where the hell are we? What is this?"

There's no fucking way this is where they live. It's insane. They're based in Killrover, they must be. I can't process that this - this beautiful, old manor house - is housing a pit of snakes.

Hating the Cavanaughs is in my blood, no matter how in awe of this place I am.

"It's the clubhouse!" Sebastian says cheerily, his strong grip on my shoulder not matching the easy teasing tone of his voice. "Where we host all our balls and banquets." He puts on a stupid posh accent with the last words, and I hear Nessa snort with barely disguised laughter.

I dig my heels into the top step, the front door looming in front of me. I expect to smell blood in the air, but there's only the fresh scent of the impending winter.

I can't step inside this place. If I do, I might never leave.

I scream, thrashing in Sebastian's grip and he curses. His grip falters on me as I manage to kick at his knee, taking him by surprise. I tear away, running awkwardly with my hands bound. Adrenaline pumps through me, my ears ringing with panic.

I can't go in there.

I'll never get out.

"For fuck's sake!" Nessa shouts, and my panic climbs to new heights as I try to speed up, feeling her closing in at my back.

It's useless. I'm useless.

She tackles me to the ground and I land with a shout, face first in the gravel, unable to break my fall with my arms tied. Sharp stones dig into my cheeks, and my mouth fills with blood as my teeth bite into the soft skin of my lips, agitating the already tender skin.

They don't bother letting me walk again. Nessa simply yanks me up by my hair, ignoring my cry of pain, and drags me up the steps. I scream my protest, but they don't react, as Sebastian holds the door open for us, rolling his eyes at me as if I'm being dramatic.

The door bangs shut behind me, and I sob.

I don't want to die here.

6

Nessa

"What the *fuck* do you mean my job's not done!" I spit the words at the man who's saved my life more times than I care to admit. But I don't give a fuck about the fact I owe him right now. No, currently, I'm envisioning stabbing him in the eye.

Thomas raises a dark brow at me. His pale blue eyes are fixed on me with unwavering strength, not reacting at all to my outburst. Now that the girl's in our possession, he seems significantly less stressed.

I, however, have perhaps never been more frustrated in my life.

"Well, given the fact I'm currently trying to get my fucking son to safety, and you're the best enforcer we have, yes, the girl's your responsibility. At least until we decide what to do with her," he answers smoothly.

We're in the library, with the fire on and an open bottle of scotch. The chair I'm in is so comfortable I could fall asleep, especially after the abysmal sleep I had last night, but I'm too angry to appreciate it now. The curtains are pulled shut but through the red fabric, the sun tries to reach us. I tuck my legs up under me to avoid the desperate rays skittering across the floor.

Thomas has his feet up, the top buttons of his shirt undone, and a splatter of blood on the side of his face.

I grimace. "She started a fucking *war,* Thomas! I want fuck all to do with her. Dispose of her for all I care."

He looks disappointed as he sits up straighter, leaning forward with his elbows on his knees. "You're better than this, Ness."

I seethe. "I thought I made my disdain for babysitting clear yesterday."

He shakes his head. "Think about it without the self indulgent cloud of anger," he scolds. "The Branigan asshole doesn't know where his daughter is, and he's wounded. We have the advantage here."

I still, forcing myself to breathe. Annoyingly, he's right. I am better than this. I'm a fucking force to be reckoned with. I have dealt with far worse than *Siobhán fucking Branigan.*

But *Jesus,* that girl gets under my skin. The Goddamn nerve of her to act like the victim in all of this.

"They're searching for her?" I ask, though we both know the answer to be yes.

"Heavily," he confirms, sitting back with a sigh. I shrug out of my leather jacket as I wait for him to continue. "The shoot out at Blessed Hearts gave us a head start. I managed to get you on the phone before Seamus called his dogs in. They don't know we have her, and if we play this right, they won't for a while. He's got every spare fucking pair of eyes he has looking for that girl and I'm telling you now, he'll want payback for her shooting him today."

"*She* shot him?" I can't imagine Siobhán shooting anyone, never mind her own father. I'm almost impressed before I remember who the fuck we're talking about. "It's war," I say, keeping my voice steady even when the knowledge of the danger we're in rings through my head. "Who'd you kill today?"

Thomas smirks, the left side of his lips tilting up. He's attractive for an older man, though his years as head of the Cavanaugh family have left their mark. A deep scar mars his upper lip, making his smile crooked. He was only eighteen when he fathered Oisín, and life has only gotten harder ever since.

"Branigan rats," he answers smoothly.

Rats. The word ricochets through me, and I fight to keep my expression mutual.

Fucking street rats like you lot will never be good for anything 'cept lying on yer backs with yer legs spread.

The memory rises unbidden and I take a drink of the whiskey, letting the burn soothe me. It's still early, but we've both been up all night and he didn't offer even a drop of coffee to tide me over. "How many did we lose at the wedding?"

"Just one. Daizen." Thomas says. I take another swig of my drink and bury the anger I feel beneath the burn of the alcohol.

"One too many."

He nods. "The Branigan kid has a lot to answer for. On both sides."

I exhale slowly, trying to cool my anger. "She's not very apologetic," I surmise, words clipped.

"That's alright," Thomas says with a gleam in his eye. "You're good at breaking 'em."

My brows raise at that. "You want answers outta her that badly?"

Thomas considers for a second. "Now's the best time to strike, what with the bastard's troops on the hunt for the girl in our *care.* Without the marriage, there's no chance of a deal. Not again."

At the mention of the marriage, I sit up straighter. "Where's Oisín? Shouldn't he be the lucky bastard who has to tame his wife?"

Thomas' eyes narrow at the mention of his son. "He won't be around for a while. Can't have Seamus getting his filthy fucking hands on 'im."

I chuckle, the sound empty and humourless. "Like we've got our bloody hands on his heir?"

Thomas snaps his fingers. "Exactly," he says with enthusiasm. He's got this unsettled energy around him, like does when he's excited. "The princess is our most valuable asset, and you, little Ness, are the dragon guarding her."

I sneer at the analogy, deciding Thomas must've had too much to drink today. He's talking shite and I'm too fucking tired to listen.

"Got it," I say as I stand because there's no arguing with him when he decides something. He wants Siobhán kept hidden, fine. But the first chance I get, she's the one in the line of fire. The bitch got one of our men killed, and fuck knows how many injured, with her runaway fantasy. She deserves to bear the responsibility.

Then again, she's a Branigan.

She's used to the blood on her hands.

I storm through the house, exhaustion and anger churning my stomach. I need to eat, punch something, and sleep. In that order. I forced Sebastian to watch her door while I went to speak to Thomas, considering he actually got to fucking sleep last night. He hadn't even argued with me, the situation is that dire.

The smell of coffee lures me to the kitchen. Someone's left a half full pot on the counter and I beeline for it, snatching my usual *don't talk to me until this is empty* mug out the cupboard. The kitchen is sprawling, all shiny black worktops and dark wooden cupboards. The scent of bacon and toast lingers in the air making my stomach grumble. Dirty cups and plates have been abandoned in the sink, and the stove is still warm.

Not all of us live here, but most of the enforcers and Thomas' right hand men do. Thomas has been head of the family for years, and though Oisín is heir, he probably won't take over for another good few yet. Not while Thomas has such a strong hold on the gun business and the cocaine coming in from the docks is practically sold before it can even hit our warehouses.

It's been years since Thomas found me, since I began working for him and as long as he doesn't cross me too severely, I'll stand by him.

I sip the hot coffee, cringe, and dump sugar into it as I pull my focus back to the present. My gaze wanders to the window, watching the wind whip the leaves on the trees into the air. It's getting colder, and the knowledge that I'll be warm all winter never fails to feel like a luxury.

A loaf of bread has been left out, and I snatch two slices, popping them in the toaster. I fight the urge to grab more food to stuff my pockets with. It's muscle memory, and half the fucking time I don't even realise I'm doing it until I find a melted chocolate bar or a bruised apple in my pocket hours later. Vaguely, I wonder if I should take something down to the Branigan, but the thought makes my anger flare to life again. Spoiled brats like her have never had to want for anything. She'll survive for a few more hours, and I'll make Sebastian give her dinner later.

I think if I see her now, I'll end up with bloody knuckles.

7

Siobhán

My hand hurts like fuck from pounding uselessly at the door. If Sebastian is still waiting on the other side he doesn't answer. Fear curdles my stomach as I stare at the slab of wood keeping me trapped here. My throat burns from shouting, and my cheeks are wet with frustrated tears.

God, my da was right.

I don't know anything. Couldn't even survive by myself for more than a few hours before I was dragged back into the clutching hands of the gangs.

I scream again, but the sound is broken and cracks on its way out my throat. I try to force my emotions under control, to find that same cold demeanour Nessa seems to master, but it's useless. *I'm* useless.

I squeeze my stinging eyes shut, pressing the heels of my hands over my eyelids. My breath stutters in my lungs as I try to slow my hyperventilating.

I already know there are no other exits in the room, not so much as a window to break, but it doesn't stop me from searching again anyway. With my panic subdued, I pry my eyes open again and manage to stop the urge to throw up as I face the locked door.

Turning away, I take in the rest of the small space. It's dark, given that there are no windows, and the bare lightbulb in the centre of the room is half arsing its one and only fucking job. In one corner, there's a toilet and sink that I refuse to contemplate using. There's a small, single bed against the left wall, with a thin mattress and a rickety metal frame. Thankfully, there's a blanket at least, though given that the bare stone walls are providing absolutely no warmth, I doubt it'll do much to keep the cold at bay.

Maybe that's their plan. Leave me here to freeze to death, alone and afraid, in this old mansion where nobody will find me.

Gritting my teeth as I ball my hands into fists, my nails cutting perfect crescent marks into the palms of my hands, I ignore the stinging pain there as I realise that there's fuck all else for me to do but wait.

I inhale shakily as I slide down the back wall, facing the door. The cold seeps through the stone and my shirt, making me shiver. I want a shower, a hot meal and the chance to sleep without nightmares, mine or someone else's, chasing me awake.

I glare at the door for so long that I'm sure I must be hallucinating when it opens.

Sebastian appears in the doorway, frowning down at me as he locks the door behind him. He leans against it, one knee bent, his foot pressed against the wood, with his arms crossed over his chest. He squints in the low light.

"Fuck me, it's darker than Nessa's thoughts in here," he

mutters and I fight the desperate urge to punch him in his pretty face.

I wonder if he'd look as good with a broken nose. Probably. Something tells me he's one of those bastards that could make the blood look like a fashion choice.

Prick.

"That'll be the lack of windows," I deadpan back at him, gesturing to the bare walls. He has the nerve to act like he's contemplating.

"Guess we didn't do much decorating in here either, huh. Why don't you give us a review after your stay and we can take your suggestions on board," he says, his dark brow raised at me.

I sputter. "What, was your last prisoner not open enough about their interior design preferences?"

Sebastian grins, looking slightly feral. "They tend not to be able to speak long enough to give us their opinion."

Bile rises in my throat. He must see the expression of fear on my face because he waves his hand through the air like he's dismissing my panic entirely. "Don't worry, princess, we're not gonna kill ya. Not for a good while yet anyway."

The sick feeling worsens. I clench my hands to stop them trembling.

"Aw cheer up, sunshine!" he tries again, features softening as he realises just how fucking terrified I am. This is quite literally my worst nightmare come to life. I tasted the sugary sweetness of freedom, only to have it replaced by the coppery tang of blood.

I don't think I'll ever be able to wash it from my mouth.

Or my hands.

"Things could be worse ya know," Sebastian continues when

I don't answer. "Yer da could've found ya first. Doubt he'd have been as nice to give you a safe room and bed to sleep in."

I blink at him, mouth hanging open. "Safe?" I utter, rage seeping into the word. *"Safe?"*

His brows draw together as his mouth turns down a little at the sides. "Sure. Nothin' can hurt you here. Nobody can get close enough to even sniff you out."

"*You* can hurt me here," I correct, pressing myself closer to the wall.

"I've already told you we won't," he says. "I'm a man of my word, Siobhán."

"Why even bother to bring me here then?" I ask, finding my tongue again. "Why not just let me leave?"

He cocks his head at me like I'm stupid. "You're pretty fucking valuable currency right now, sunshine. And you've pissed off a whole lotta powerful people. You can't seriously think you'd have managed to outsmart them all?"

Shame burns my cheeks at his rhetorical question. "You have no idea what I'm capable of." I refuse to let him believe I'm as pathetic as I seem right now. I refuse to let myself believe it either, no matter how useless I feel. I won't survive this if I just roll over and let them gut me.

I find that anger deep inside me and clutch it until my knuckles whiten.

If there's one thing I'm good at - it's surviving.

Interest flares to life in his blue eyes. Even in the shitty light, I recognise his curiosity. Like a kid that just got handed a new toy.

"I think I just might learn to like you," he announces, nodding at me once.

My eyes widen. "What?"

"You've got some fire, I can see it. That'll piss Nessa right off. I can't fuckin' wait." He has the gall to laugh like he finds this hilarious. All I can do is stare at him, wishing I had a weapon or something to defend myself with if he decides to change his mind.

Seeing as I'm empty handed, I might as well use his apparent liking to me to my advantage. "Can I get a shower then at least?" I try, grimacing at the feel of sweat and blood lingering on my skin.

He winces. "Not unless you want to stick your head under the tap," he says, pointing to the tiny sink. "I'll do you a favour and get you a wash cloth though. But I'll have to watch you. Can't leave you alone with anything you could use to hurt us." After a beat, he adds, "or yourself."

I gape. "What the fuck am I going to do with a wash cloth?"

Sebastian shrugs. "Strangle me with it. Strangle *yourself* with it. Use it as a gag-"

I cut him off before he can continue his horrifying list. "I won't do any of that."

He shrugs again and turns for the door before pausing, key in the lock. He glances over his shoulder at me, seeming to decide something. "How do you take your coffee?"

For a second, I'm too shocked to speak. When I manage, the words come out jumpy and tight. "Just milk."

Sebastian flashes me a grin and leaves, locking the door behind him.

I shiver as cold water drips down my neck. The smell of citrus floods my nose as the soap washes grime down the drain. Sebastian, true to his word, reappeared half an hour later with a yellow wash cloth, a bar of soap and a cup of coffee.

I'd jumped at the wash cloth and soap, hesitant of the drink. For all I fucking knew, he'd drugged it. But now as I finish my makeshift bath and stand shivering in the corner, the hot coffee is nearly too tempting to pass up.

I hurriedly dress again in my dirty clothes. I'm clean of the sweat and grime from the inn and the journey, but the feeling of blood on my skin remains, haunting me.

Sebastian turns back around, frowning as I lose my stare off with the mug on the floor. He'd stayed while I washed, but had enough kindness to turn away from me and give me an ounce of privacy. It was more than Nessa would've done, I'm sure of it. If I had to choose, so far I'd say that he's my favourite of my captors, and it isn't exactly a close race.

"Is it offending you?" he asks with a chuckle, gesturing to the cup.

"For all I know, you've poisoned it," I answer, restraining another shiver. It'll take me hours to warm up again without the coffee in my system.

He sighs heavily before striding over, picking up the mug and taking a sip. Dramatically, he spreads his arms wide in triumph. "See? No poison."

I concede to his logic, and take the coffee from him when he offers it back. I sip it, groaning a little when it warms me from the inside. It's strong and in a big enough cup that it might save me from the impending hypothermia.

Gingerly, I perch at the edge of the bed, greedily clutching the cup in my hands as the warmth seeps into my frozen fingers.

"What's going to happen to me?" I venture, hoping that he'll give me any information to work with.

"Nessa'll be here this evening," he tells me, yawning as he slides down the wall, back against the door. He's always blocking the exit, I notice with a pang of sadness.

The feeling is quickly doused by my anger, burning its way through me. "I don't want to see her."

Sebastian snorts. "Don't have a choice there, I'm afraid."

I'm silent as I finish my coffee. The small seed of hope that the gesture of kindness had planted in me shrivels.

Sebastian glances at his watch then pushes himself to his feet. He grabs the wash cloth and soap from the sink, reaching in his pocket with his free hand.

He holds out two granola bars to me, and I take them without hesitation. They're still wrapped and sealed, so I figure they're safe enough. I don't know where my bag ended up, and the small amount of food stored there has disappeared with it.

Sebastian picks up my now empty mug in exchange, offering me a sympathetic smile before he's unlocking the door again, preparing to leave me here alone.

The thought makes my eyes sting once more.

I'm angry at myself for the sadness that won't stop rising in me like a tidal wave, angry at my father for landing me in this shitty situation, and at Sebastian for being nice to me after what he's done.

But mostly, I'm angry at Nessa.

I'm going to figure this out, I promise myself. And then I'm going to find a way to make Nessa feel as helpless as I did when she pulled me away from my one chance at a life.

A real life.

Because I may not be dead, but this - locked up at the hands of the enemy - is worse.

8

Siobhán

It's been two nights. Two nights on the mattress so thin I can feel the metal slats of the frame through it. Two nights of fitful, fear filled sleep. Two nights of wondering if I'd wake up to the barrel of a gun.

Instead, I've woken to Sebastian unlocking my door. He brings me coffee and the wash cloth, and today, he's even come armed with toast. It's cold, but I swear to God it's the best thing I've ever tasted.

The hunger isn't the worst part of all this. Nor is it the fact that my clothes are filthy and it's making my skin itch. No, the worst part is the waiting.

Waiting for someone to come, waiting for the plan to be unveiled, waiting to be killed or, worse, sent back to my father for judgement.

The pain of it is eased a little by the fact Sebastian has brought his entire jigsaw inside this morning, the pieces scattered now over the concrete floor.

"Don't you have something better to be doing?" I ask him, fiddling with the edge piece in my hand.

He looks up from the puzzle, and in the dim light, I almost miss the dark circles under his eyes. "Nope." He pops the *p* and grins wickedly at me. "It's all very boring ya know. Nessie and I are under orders to stay here. There's a whole *war* going on and we're not even allowed to kill anyone."

He sounds genuinely disappointed and my stomach twists. I must make a face to match because he just laughs at me.

"You're awful soft for a mob boss's daughter, sunshine," he comments, sliding a dark green piece into place. The jigsaw is a wide landscape - all green grass and tall trees. It's a fucking nightmare to do, if I'm being honest, but I have literally nothing else to keep me occupied.

"You say it like it's a bad thing," I mumble back. In truth, I know it's a weakness. My desire for soft things, for dresses and makeup and pink painted walls, were never in line with my father's blood soaked world. I have tried, so fucking hard, to harden myself and yet, twenty-five years later, I'm just as soft as ever.

Sebastian hums like he's thinking. For a minute, we sit in silence, each of us trying to find pieces to fit.

"I can't imagine Seamus as a Da," Sebastian muses finally and I can't help scoffing.

"Neither can I."

His eyes narrow on me, head tilted. "That bad, huh?"

My laugh is brittle. "Worse."

He gives another nod as he snatches the piece I was fiddling with and slots it into place along the border of the woods. "What about your ma?"

"Dead."

He's determined to get information out of me, the curiosity in his blue eyes burning. I don't give a shit what he knows, I have nothing that would help him. Da never trusted me with any secrets, and anything I could tell Sebastian would be shit he already knows.

"Damn," he says. "Life really kicked you in the balls."

"You have no idea."

He frowns at that, dark brows drawing together. "I might. You got any other family, or just good ol' Seamus? Friends? Boyfriend?" He looks up. "Girlfriend?"

My heart twists the mention of partners. Images of Conor flick through my head, of his sandy blond hair and deep brown eyes. Images of his blood. "I'm bisexual, if that's what you're asking," I give in to his questions. It's more friendly conversation than I've had in years. "But no. No partner, not now. Think Seamus takes kindly to anyone getting close to a Branigan?"

Sebastian's lips press together in thought. "Not now?" he repeats, cocking his head to the side like a puppy learning a new trick.

I don't want to tell him about Conor. About how it took him a year after being assigned my guard to admit he liked me. I'd managed to persuade him to take me out to a bar, for the first time in my life. One shot later and a whole lot of courage, I was hooking up with a girl in the bathroom. Her hair got in my mouth and our elbows and knees bashed together in the tight space but I'd never felt more *alive*.

I didn't even know her name, but when Conor had taken me back home, he'd done it in angry silence. Two days later, it was his mouth on mine, his hands on my naked skin, desperate admissions of *this is a fucking terrible idea but shit Siobhán, I can't stop*, in my ear.

We were so fucking careful. But even being *friends* was

reckless. And he was right, in the end. It was a terrible fucking idea.

I don't answer Sebastian. I can't. Guilt tears at my heart, ripping the hastily stitched seams.

"What happened to them?"

He just doesn't fucking know when to quit. I snag a new puzzle piece and twist the cardboard in my hands until it's mangled.

"What do you think happened to him, Sebastian?" I snap at him, and to his credit, he doesn't even flinch. His eyes darken a little, but other than that, he continues solving the jigsaw like I haven't just admitting my father murdered the only boyfriend I've ever had.

"I heard you shot him," Sebastian says, and I bristle. "Seamus, I mean."

I exhale slowly, releasing the ruined piece, and nod.

"You missed his heart," he states, tone even.

"Yes."

The unsaid question hangs in the air between us. *Why?* But he doesn't voice it and I don't answer. The idea of killing one more person, even the man who's abused me my entire life, is more than I could live with. I barely bloody sleep knowing that I have myself to blame for Conor, without waking up, sure I can feel Jackie's warm blood on my skin.

"Nessa'll be coming down soon," Sebastian sighs as he stands and begins to gather the pieces. I snatch up the mangled one, cup it in my palm.

"What is she going to do to me?"

He stops, freezing with a handful of jigsaw pieces. "Well, she's far less talkative than I am, so probably fuck all."

The *probably* is not reassuring.

I want to scream at Sebastian not to leave. I want to beg him not to lock the door. I want to sob and tell him that I'd rather they just shot me already.

But I don't. I close my fist around the jigsaw piece and watch him tidy up, pick up the box, and leave without another glance back.

Sebastian may be acting like my friend, but I know better than to trust it. He wants information, that much is clear, and that's where his interest in getting to know me ends.

Loneliness throbs in my chest.

I can do nothing about that, either.

9

Nessa

I'm just as angry when I wake up as I was before I went to bed. Two days have passed and I still want to strangle the girl. I keep my visits to her room short, ignore the sadness she wears like a cloak, the way she looks at me like she's begging me to just hurt her already. I ignore the way that every part of my body is urging me to do just that.

I shower under cold water in an attempt to cool the rage pulsing in my veins. I need to calm myself the fuck down. As much as I want to storm into Branigan's room and demand apologies for the chaos she's started, I know for a fact it won't work.

Thomas had been very clear when he said we needed her. And though I hate it, I can agree. Reluctantly.

I'll find a way to use her, even if it's the last thing I do. One way or another I'll ensure the Branigan bitch is worth the effort it takes to keep her here.

Like fuck did I track her down and drag her back here for nothing.

The freezing water helped to clear my brain and now, as I

towel off my wet hair, images flick through my mind. A plan threads itself into existence, images of the blood of my chosen family fuelling my need to punish the girl who ruined our one chance at peace.

Sure, we fucking hate the Branigans on principle, given the fact they'd come into the territory we'd held for years and disrupted all of our supply lines with their own. But this marriage was a peace treaty of sorts. They'd stop trying to weasel their way further into our territory, and we'd stop blocking their routes. It was business, packaged up in a nice white ceremonial bow.

Seamus is looking for her, Thomas' voice echoed in my head. Sooner or later, he'll figure out we have her.

I need to use the advantage we have, while we've still got it.

I dress quickly in black baggy jeans and a black tank top, grab my favourite knife off my side table and hurry out of my room. It's a simple blade with a heavy black handle, but it has sentimental value and I refuse to replace it. I take my time moving through the house to the basement level where the girl is being kept, reluctantly grabbing a plastic cup of water for her on the way.

"Oi, Nessa!"

I clench my jaw as I turn on my heel. I'm on the staircase, halfway to the ground floor, but the man's voice behind me makes me pause.

"What do you need, Anji?" I snap. I have no time for him today.

His black hair is pulled back into a bun, and his eyebrows are raised at me in mock shock. "All right, no need to bite my fucking head off," he says, hands raised in surrender. "We just wanted to know what the fuck is happening with the Branigan brat."

I exhale sharply, fighting the urge to shoot him just to make him leave me alone. Given that I am the head enforcer for the Cavanaugh's empire, it doesn't surprise me when the others ask me for shit.

But it still annoys the fuck out of me.

"Leave it to me and Seb," I tell him, giving him a withering look. Clearly, he's used to my shit because he doesn't even back up a step.

"We lost Denizen," he says, and I notice the way his jaw ticks as he says his brother's name. "Because of her."

Briefly, a pang of pity shoots through me. I shut that the fuck down, forcing my resting bitch face back in place. I can't afford to show weakness, not when they need me at my strongest. Like hell am I going to let down the only family I have.

"I know, Anji," I murmur, the water sloshing in the cup as my grip on it tightens. "She'll get what's coming to her."

He nods briskly, lips pressed together like he's trying to resist saying anymore. I don't give him the option, interrupting him mid thought, "Anji? Do me a favour will ya?"

"What's up?"

"Find me a way to contact Seamus. *Discreetly.*"

His eyes widen a little, but his shoulders straighten and his eyes light up with the challenge. Seamus is a notoriously difficult person to pin down and though I'm sure Thomas has ways to contact him, there's no way he'd tell me. I know Anji likes a challenge, and I secretly hope having a purpose will help him through his grief. Plus, he's the best we have at finding information. There's next to *nothing* he can't get his hands on.

Daizen was nothing short of a complete and utter prick. He was vicious and cruel, but he was damn good at getting his job done.

I barely spoke to him on account of his personality, but his loss would hit the business hard. Anji turns at the top of the stairs and jogs off in the direction of his room, and I continue my descent to the girl.

"Fucking bitch," I mutter under my breath as I make it to the ground floor, veering sharply to the left and through the door under the grand staircase. I'm sure it was used as a servant's entrance years ago, but now the dark, hidden staircase leads to our holding rooms.

"Nessie! A sight for sore eyes," Sebastian cries as soon as I come into his view. The corridor down here consists of a low ceiling, old brick, three doors and a musty, earthy smell.

It's grim.

He's set himself up with a small table and chair outside Siobhán's door, and his gun rests on the surface next to a half finished jigsaw puzzle. The sight throws me for a loop so badly I wonder if I'm hallucinating.

My face screws up in confusion and he grins. "What the actual *fuck*, Seb?"

"What?" he asks in mocking shock. "I was bored. And I think sunshine needed a nap."

I force myself to exhale slowly. "Right. Jigsaws are the *obvious* answer to that."

He nods enthusiastically, standing up and grabbing his gun but leaving the key and puzzle. "I'll be nice and leave it for you to finish up."

I glare at the stupid jigsaw pieces forming a half finished forest on the table as Sebastian leaves, his heavy footsteps echoing on the stairs. Snatching the key off the table, I unlock Siobhán's door and prepare to restrain myself from murdering her.

She's curled up on the bed in the corner, blanket tangled around her. Her knees are tucked up to her chin, her arms wrapped around them like she's trying to make herself small even in her sleep. Her long red hair is splayed over the thin pillow, and her brows are pulled together as she dreams. Her breathing is rapid and laboured, and a whimper falls from her mouth.

She looks like she's in *pain.* Her fingers clutch at the blankets around her, but she doesn't kick, doesn't lash out. Just lies there, taking whatever hell she's reliving in her mind. I can't make myself look away.

I hate her for it. For the feelings that watching her stirs in me. Some part of me, the still beating, not yet calcified part, *understands*. It knows all too well what it's like to want to be invisible. To hide in the darkness and wish it would swallow you whole. I know the pain of facing the monsters that lurk in the shadows, because they cannot be outrun. I know what it's like to be trapped and how it feels to find yourself at the mercy of others, with no escape in sight.

I want to wake her and tell her that nothing can touch her, that she's safe. But it would be nothing more than a lie.

I shake any sympathy from my head. We are not the same. We never will be. She's the girl who starts wars over her own selfishness. And I'm the monster in the dark.

So instead, I shout, "Wake up!"

10

Siobhán

I flail in the sheets, panic ripping through me as a shout forces me awake. Nessa's sharp voice cuts through my sleepy haze and my heartbeat skyrockets, trying to convince me to get up and run, *run, run, run* far away from the danger.

I have to remind my heart that there's nowhere I can go to outrun myself. And, as long as my father is alive, I will be hunted. I can never escape.

"Jesus, fuck," I gasp as I finally free my legs from the damned blanket. I'm on my ass on the floor, staring up at Nessa, wide eyed. She stands in the doorway, her blond hair damp around her face, her green eyes dark in the dim light. In one hand, she holds a cup and in the other, a knife.

She looks demonic. No, that's not right. She looks like a fallen angel - both terrifying and beautiful.

I hate her.

"I brought you water," she says, still staring at me. Under her inspection, I shiver as I dart to my feet. My mouth is dry and my throat is scratchy, so when she offers the water I down it.

It doesn't go unnoticed that the cup is plastic. Clearly, I'm not to be trusted with glass.

That's fine. I wouldn't know how the fuck to fight someone like Nessa anyway.

I watch as she steps into the room, shutting the door behind her before leaning against it. Not once does she turn her back towards me. I know it's not because she sees me as any sort of a threat, but because she can tell just how much having her gaze focused on me unnerves me.

I hate her for being able to read me so easily.

Desperate for a distraction from her unwavering stare, I tilt the cup back once more, hoping to catch the remaining drops of water with my tongue. My throat feels better than it did just moments ago, but a second cup of water wouldn't have gone astray.

I keep a watchful eye on her over the rim of the cup as I bring it back down, and silently curse myself when I catch my eyes zeroing in on the way her arms flex as she folds them across her chest. I crumple the plastic in my hand, allowing myself to let some of my anger dissipate with the move.

Locking my eyes with Nessa's, I drop it to the floor and force myself not to smile as she sneers at me for my show of disrespect

We stare at each other for an immeasurably long time, neither one of us willing to be the first to speak. I swear I can feel the seconds slipping by and, quickly, I grow tired of the game.

I break first, turning to face the bed, and pick up the tangled mess that is my blanket from the floor. Out of habit, I place it on the bed, and do up the sheets in an attempt to draw some sort of comfort from my old routine. With that done, and nothing else left to distract me from the reality of the situation, I collapse onto the bed, a sigh leaving me as I give in to the knowledge that I hold no power here.

It's a familiar feeling, and there's an odd comfort in it. I know what I am. I thought it would change when I shot my own father, but clearly, I was wrong. Here I am, powerless and waiting for the anvil to drop, like I always have been.

"What do you want?" I ask, my voice devoid of any emotion.

She doesn't answer. My heart gallops inside of my chest as she tilts her head, the knife in her hand twirling end over end between her fingers.

Swallowing dryly, I shift uncomfortably on the thin mattress and pray that if she's here to kill me, she'll at least do it quickly.

"Nes-"

"Don't fucking say my name, Branigan."

Ice floods my veins as it sinks in just how angry she is with me.

I'd assumed that she was still pissed, hell, I'm guessing that will never change, but the switch in attitude in a few short minutes has my head spinning.

"Okay," I croak, hoping to appease the monster inside of her.

She narrows her forest green eyes at me, cautious of my agreement.

I can't blame her, if I were in her position I'd be sceptical of me too.

"What do you want?" I try again, and gulp as the hand brandishing the knife lowers to her side.

Nessa smiles at the fear that must be evident on my face, and I look at the ground, ashamed of myself for not being stronger. For not being the tough mob princess my da always wanted me to be.

"Tell me something," Nessa purrs, and I shiver as her voice caresses my skin. She's much closer to me now, having moved silently across the room while I'd been staring at the floor.

My nipples peek at her nearness, and I grit my teeth as the thin shirt I'm wearing brushes against them. I mentally curse my body for being such a traitor, barely resisting the urge to curse her out loud for making me feel this way.

"What do you want to know?" I ask, my own voice shaking.

I hold my breath as she lifts the tip of the knife to my face. Every muscle in my body freezes as it reaches my temple, tucked just beneath the strands of hair that tangled in my sleep.

This close I'm certain she can see the way my pulse jumps in my throat.

The cold steel kisses my skin as she moves my hair from around my face with the knife, tucking it behind my ear. I don't breathe again until she's pulling the weapon away from my face.

"What were you dreaming about?" Nessa asks, and I choke on air.

Suspicion clouds my mind as she hunkers down, meeting me on my level.

I don't move my gaze from the knife in her hand. Her grip is loose as she twirls the black handle in the palm of her hand, the tip resting against her index finger. I watch, mesmerised by the level of control she exhibits as she does it with ease, all the while not marking her skin even slightly. I feel like I've fallen into a trance by the time I remember that she's asked me a question.

Squaring my shoulders I promise myself that I won't be so easily distracted again, no matter how deftly she uses her fingers in my presence.

"Nothing," I answer her, hoping that she can't hear how breathless I am.

Nessa scoffs. "You're as good at lying as you are fighting."

I baulk at that, my face heating. "I said it's nothing."

She rises from her position in front of me and turns to move back toward the door.

Disappointment floods me, and I hate myself for that too.

I shouldn't want her to be here. Shouldn't want her to stay. Fuck, just two days ago I was cursing the idea of ever being in her presence again. But something about her draws me in, and it takes everything in me to fight it.

I have to get over whatever the fuck it is, because I'm barely surviving as is. Wanting her is sure to end me. This isn't just playing with fire, this is dousing myself in gasoline and waiting for the dropped match. I know, without a doubt, she'd light me up if I let her.

The worst part is, I think I'd like the burn.

Nessa nods slowly, her eyes boring into mine as she reaches for the handle. "I heard. The problem is, I don't believe you."

Confusion ripples through me and I hide my frown by burying my head in my hands. I am hollowed out, exhausted despite the sleep, and weary from the mind games Nessa plays.

I watch helplessly as she pulls the key for my door from her pocket. The fragile hope I'd collected like treasure over the years crumbles in my hands.

Why the fuck did I ever think I'd get out of this? Why did I ever dare to want a life for myself?

Anger barrels through me and I rise from the bed before

I can stop myself. I march across the room, and latch onto her arm, knowing that I'll probably pay for that later, but too pissed to care. My rage is a lifeline and now that I have it, I refuse to let it go.

I pull her back, and curse as she dares to look down at me, as if I'm nothing more than an annoyance to her.

"What do you want from me, Nessa? Do you want the sob story about how I was forced into a marriage I wanted nothing to do with? That I have done *despicable* things and that every fucking time I close my eyes, I can only see a version of myself that terrifies me? Do you want to know how I've been abused for years, Nessa, is that it? Would it make you feel better to know that my da would rather I'd not survived my own birth?"

I'm breathing heavily, but I can't stop.

"Do you want to know that I'm miserable, and that I don't remember how to be anything else?" I gesture wildly to the knife in her hand, taking a trembling step toward her. It's been years since I've dared to speak back to my father but Nessa stands there, straight faced, not moving as my voice grows louder. I should stop talking, but I can't, I can't and *fuck* it feels so good. "Go on, stab me then. You want to anyway, don't you?"

Nessa's hand flexes on the handle of the blade, and I watch the way her fingers tighten to within an inch of their life. "You have no fucking clue what I want to do to you right now."

She moves so fast I don't stand a bloody chance. My back hits the stone wall hard, my breath leaving my lungs in a gasp. The cold press of steel meets my neck and on instinct, my body freezes.

My concentration is so focused on not breathing too hard for fear of the blade that it takes me a second to realise her face is only inches from mine. I can feel the warmth of her breath on my cheek, and smell the deep, fruity scent of her shampoo. It's so at odds with the violence that seems to run in her blood it holds me captive.

My whole body shakes, and a bead of warmth drips down my neck. I can't even begin to worry about the blood, because Nessa is right *there* and fuck she smells good and I *hate her, I hate her so much-*

I repeat the mantra over and over in my head but then she kisses me and nothing can save me.

11

Siobhán

Her teeth nip at my bottom lip, demanding my response, angry and brutal and unforgiving. I gasp against her, both terrified and desperate, heat flooding my body. It's been *so long* since I've been kissed. The last person to touch me like this was Conor, but I can't let myself think about him now.

"Fuck you," Nessa hisses against me and I can do nothing but moan uselessly against her. I don't let myself question why I'm allowing this to happen. Why her touch makes me spiral out of control like this. I hiss as the knife is still at my throat digs a little deeper, the metal growing warm with my body heat. Her other hand grips my waist roughly and I groan at the feel of her fingers gripping me so harshly through the thin material draping my skin.

At some point, my shirt has slid up, the stone behind me snagging at the fabric, and her hand meets my bare skin. The contact is somehow so much worse than her kiss, and I shudder, anger, confusion and arousal settling deep in my gut.

"Nes-"

"I said don't say my name, Branigan," she murmurs, breathing heavily. "I won't survive if you say my name right now."

Fear forces my arousal to burn hotter and I shudder. I feel horribly exposed like this, with her knife at my neck and my life in her hands. Still, my body arches towards her, needy and unconcerned with the fact that it's my enemy's hands on me. The only thing it wants is to feel the caress of another human being. To lean into it, no *chase* it, and find the euphoria my body craves. My mind twists with wrath, promising revenge for the way she's turned my body against me.

The callouses on her palm scratch at my skin as she shoves my shirt up higher and higher, until she's cupping my breast and groaning. The sound is warm on my lips, and though we're not kissing anymore, somehow this is more intimate.

We both know this is a terrible idea. The hatred is so thick between us that I can't breathe.

Or maybe that's the lust.

I'm beginning to think that they're one and the same.

She pinches my peaked nipple between her finger and thumb roughly and I can't stop the ragged moan that leaves my mouth. She grins, showing her teeth, all feral demand, and I'm helpless against her.

"I could kill you," she whispers, continuing her torture on my breast. My brain is short circuiting. "So easily."

"I know," I pant, head hitting the wall. Her blade leaves my neck, dragging the sharp tip lightly down my skin to my collarbone. It's not enough pressure to cut me, but the scratch and the threat have my pussy clenching with want. At the back of my mind I recognise just how fucking twisted this is, but I can't find it in me to care. As long as she's touching me I doubt I'll be able to focus on a single rational thought.

She exhales sharply, that knife continuing its descent down my body. It snags on my shirt, tearing through it at the bottom and splitting the hem.

Before I can process it, her other hand is at the waistband of my leggings, tugging them down, and the blade is tracing its way over my hip bone.

Nessa drags her gaze down my body, her eyes fixed to her knife. I swallow thickly and bite my lip, trying hard not to jolt. My leggings are pulled down past my ass, and that fucking knife scratches the sensitive skin of my inner thigh.

"Nessa," I gasp as the steel moves just inches from my wet underwear, and I hear her low groan.

"I fucking *told* you not to say that," she warns, and in the next second, the thin material covering my pussy is cut free from my body. The knife slices through one side then the other, her knuckles lightly brushing against my pebbled skin. I do my best to hold still, desperate for the slightest touch as I feel the way my cunt responds to her brand of violence.

I can't tell if the pounding of my heart is from my need or terror, but I know I don't want it to stop. I don't want *her* to stop.

I open my mouth to say something more, but the flat of the blade meets my heat and I snap my mouth closed.

I grit my teeth as I wait for her to move, unsure of how this is going to go. One flick of the blade is all it would take. One wrong move, and I'll be bleeding out from my femoral artery.

Nessa traps me against the wall with her free hand beside my head, a warning not to move. I couldn't even if I wanted to. I don't seem to have control of my body anymore.

The flat of Nessa's knife drags over my pussy, coating the

blade in my arousal. I fight the part of me that tries to grind against the barely-there pressure, but the tight coil of want in me is almost too much to resist.

I fucking hate this woman. Why am I *soaked* for her?

Fear and arousal fight for dominance as I push back against the wall.

"Please." The word falls from my lips before I can stop it. I don't know what I'm asking for, for her to stop or to keep going.

Nessa's nails scrape against the stone next to my ear, and she raises the now wet blade between us. I watch with wide eyes as her tongue darts out, licking my arousal from her knife.

I swear I'm dreaming. The only problem is I can't tell if this is a good dream, or a nightmare waiting to unfold.

"Please *what*?" Nessa asks, her voice sharper than her knife. The fucking blade is mocking me, the way she licks her lips tormenting me. No matter how hard I try, I doubt I'll ever be able to get the image out of my head.

"Touch me," I manage to force out, my voice shaking.

Nessa pulls back, shaking her head like she's trying to clear her mind. Her breaths are coming in heavy pants, but her features have twisted into an expression of disgust.

"You don't deserve it."

She steps away from me, her strides long and sure, and wipes the blade off on her jeans. I watch her, leggings rolled around my thighs and the taste of her on my lips, as she heads straight for the door.

She doesn't look back at me as she leaves.

12

Nessa

"Fuck, fuck, fuck, *fuck!*"

I pace my bedroom as Sebastian perches on the edge of my bed, watching me with undisguised amusement.

"Chill, Nessie," he says with a laugh. "It's not like you fucked."

I glare at him. Sure, I stopped my act of stupidity before it could go that far but, Goddamnit, I can still taste Siobhán's cunt on my tongue.

I shudder as the memory of her breathy voice whispering *please* replays in my mind.

I catch my tongue sneaking out to chase the taste of her from my lips. Anger rises unbridled in my chest. I hate her. I hate myself for being attracted to her. For the weakness she draws out in me, for the way she makes me forget myself.

"We need to get rid of her," I snap, shaking my head. She's thrown me off balance and I can't stand it. Anji hasn't gotten back to me with the contact details I need either, and after the shit show in Siobhán's room earlier, getting her the fuck out of here is more urgent than ever.

Thomas wants to use her, and I'll make sure she's worth the

hassle we went through to get her here. But if I kill two birds with one stone, so be it.

"Scared you'll fall in love?" Sebastian teases, his voice thick with fake sweetness. The bastard has the audacity to flutter his dark lashes at me and grin.

"Jealous?" I fire back, sick of his shit. "In case you forgot, Seb, I'm not into men. You've no chance. Go practice batting your eyes at someone else."

He laughs, head tipping back. "Get fucked, Ness. Fucking you would be like fucking my sibling. I'm into some fucked up shit, but incest is too far, even for me."

I throw a book at his head. I'm faster than he is, and he doesn't duck in time. The spine of the hardback hits his forehead with a satisfying *smack*. It's enough to cool the urge to stab him. He shouts at me, gripping his head, as he sends the book crashing to the floor.

It lands on the rug unharmed, and I smile as I pick it back up and tuck it away on its shelf. Serves him fucking right.

"Look, I have shit to do today," Sebastian starts, still frowning at me even as he relinquishes his grip on his head. There's barely a mark, he's just being his usual dramatic self. "So you're gonna have to go and see her again whether or not you want to."

"What *shit* are you doing?" I ask, suspicion heavy in my voice. I know for certain that Thomas has other members out on the streets in Killrover searching for Branigan rats and thinning the ranks trying to swarm our territories, but he's yet to call on me again. I'm eager to do literally anything else apart from the babysitting he's assigned me, and my anger is riding me hard.

"Classified, sorry," Sebastian says, and from the way he looks away from me, I can tell it's not official business.

I make a mental note to keep an eye on him. I trust him with my life but he's a sneaky bastard. He has a knack for getting himself in messes that are damn hard to clean up and it's only going to get worse with Oisín gone. Without him here to keep Sebastian in check I worry he'll do something he'll come to regret.

The three of us grew into adults together. From clumsy, eager sixteen year olds to outright murderers. Sebastian is still the same over eager boy chatting the ear off anyone he meets. Oisín has always been quieter, but there's a new calculated air to him that came with adulthood and the responsibilities as Thomas' son by blood. And I've always been rough around the edges, refusing to let anyone dull the sharp bits even when they cut those I loved.

"She needs new clothes," Sebastian continues despite the fact I haven't answered him. "And a proper shower. Her clothes smell like sweat and blood and frankly, it's rank. Good old Thomas doesn't give a fuck what we do with her as long as she doesn't die or leave the house. Let the girl out to shower and lend her some clothes at the bare minimum."

I stare at him in shock for a minute. Granted, Sebastian is naturally far friendlier than I am, but I didn't expect him to go soft for her so fast. I shouldn't be surprised. Siobhán has that doe caught in headlights thing going for her that Seb can't stay away from.

But I had expected him to hold onto his anger for a little longer.

At least he's not trying to get in her pants.

I'd have to cut his dick off.

"She looks about your size," he keeps fucking talking. I

wonder if he'll predict me throwing the book at him again. "Maybe a little smaller, given the fact you're jacked. I'll grab some stuff on my way back tonight. But I'm serious, Nessie, it's obvious you want to fuck the girl. Let her out of her room and maybe she'll get on her knees as a thank you." He winks and I can't stop the way I advance on him in anger. The bastard only laughs like a maniac and rolls backward onto my mattress, deftly avoiding me.

"Prick," I tell him, his words going round and round in my mind. I don't have to like the girl, but he has a point. Even if she somehow escaped this house, there's nothing but fields on all sides of us. She'd get lost in seconds and then I could drag her sorry ass back and have an excuse to let her rot in the basement.

If only it was that easy.

"Fine," I decide, much to Sebastian's delight. I run my hand down my face in defeat. "I'll let her out of her cage for a bit after you bring her clean clothes. Maybe I'll teach her how to throw a proper punch."

She was abysmal at fighting.

It shouldn't bother me as much as it does, but at least teaching her to fight is better than nearly fucking her.

Sebastian grins widely at me. "Knew you had a heart in that tin chest," he jokes, darting up and out of my room away from my anger.

I go to follow him, muttering about murdering him under my breath, only to find Anji taking up my doorway. I hate people being in my space, so I step forward, forcing him to step back, and close my bedroom door behind us. We're in the hall on the topmost floor, and I can hear a few of the others in their own rooms but none of them are within earshot.

"Anji," I greet him, my tone dry.

He holds out his hand, a crumpled piece of paper falling into my palm. "Number," he says, voice low and dark brows raised in expectation.

I know better than to ask how he got this or from who. I learned years ago that asking questions leads to trouble. So instead, I nod my thanks at him and he turns and walks away with an unreadable expression on his face.

I wait until he's gone before slinking back inside my room and reaching for my phone.

I un-scrunch the scrap of paper in my fist and dial the number.

13

Siobhán

It's been two days since *the knife incident*. That's all I let myself think of it as. I try, valiantly, not to think about it at all but my brain refuses to stop playing the memory on repeat.

I'm a mess of anger, shame, and need, and I hate it. I've not left this fucking room since I was forced in here and, clearly, being isolated has made me crazy.

There's no other explanation for why the nightmares of my years under my da's roof have made way for the nightmares in which Nessa pins me beneath her and finishes what she started.

I want to call her a coward. I want to tell her to woman the fuck up. I want to scream at her that I fucking hate her and I hope she rots in hell.

I want to beg her to fuck me.

But I can't say any of those things because I haven't seen her since.

Sebastian has been the one bringing me cereal, pasta and plastic cups of water. Two days ago, he arrived with an armful of new clothes for me. For the most part, they fit, though I did curse him out for buying me lacy black thongs instead of comfortable underwear. Still, the pile of jumpers, t-shirts, leggings, even a few sports bras and tracksuit bottoms, was enough to make me want to sob with joy.

He *is* good company, and his initial hatred of me seems to have softened. I don't know what changed, but fuck does it feel good to be around someone who doesn't wish I was dead for once.

I don't remember the last time anyone treated me with that sort of kindness. Conor, probably. But that was three years ago.

"I'm going to die of boredom in here, Sebastian," I tell him seriously, sipping my coffee. It's become a sort of routine between us, a strange sort of domesticity. I'm not attracted to him, despite the fact he's handsome as fuck, because apparently I only like violent, crazy assholes. But despite the fact I'm literally his prisoner, I'm counting him as a friend.

"I'm offended," he shoots back, clutching at his heart. His own coffee sits at his feet and, like usual, he's on the floor with his back to the door. "Am I not entertaining enough, sunshine?"

I throw a glare at him, but he just levels me with a stare. "How long am I to be locked up here? Can't you do whatever the fuck you want to do with me in the kitchen or something? Literally *anywhere* that has windows." I'm clean from my supervised baths in the damn sink but I would *kill* for a proper shower.

His expression softens. "Best I can offer ya is the gym with Nessa."

I freeze, my heart rate picking up. "What?"

Sebastian shrugs, faking innocence. "She's your keeper, sunshine. And when she's not following Thomas' instructions, she's training. You can't tell me you didn't notice how fit that girl is."

"Don't make me throw this fucking mug at you."

"You wouldn't."

He's right. I need the coffee too much to waste it.

"Are there showers at the gym?" I hedge.

"Sure are, sunshine."

"Fuck it," I mumble, admitting defeat. I need out of this shithole and if I have to work out with the girl I both want to murder and kiss until I can't breathe, then so be it.

On second thought, maybe I'd rather rot in here forever.

"She'll be overjoyed," Sebastian says, voice dripping with sarcasm. He snags my empty mug right out of my hand before I can aim it at his head. "I'll be back in an hour to take you up."

I step over the threshold leading into the gym. Sebastian pats me on the back and shoves me a little further into the room. The sour smell of sweat assaults my senses and my nose scrunches in disgust but I do my best to ignore it. It's late, and the place is nearly empty.

There's one man jogging on a treadmill who looks as though he's running through his cool down. A fine sheen of sweat on his skin and his laboured breathing tells me he's been at this for a while. A woman who looks about my age is stretching on a yoga mat in the corner, weights stacked to her left. Her curly black hair is tied into a large bun, and she glances up at me while she wipes sweat from her deep brown skin with the back of her hand. There's curiosity in her dark eyes and the weight of it makes me shift from foot to foot. It's eerily quiet, and despite the fact there's barely anyone here, I feel exposed.

"She'll be here soon. Nobody here will give you any bother, or I'll cut their balls off." He raises his voice with the last few words and out of the corner of my eye, I see one of the men nod his head in acknowledgement.

Still, the sting of bile rises in my throat as fear ripples through me.

"Where are you going?" I hiss at Sebastian as he takes a step back towards the door.

"Shit do to, places to be, people to charm," he drawls, continuing out the door while I glare at him. "Wait right there for Nessa, don't move a muscle."

I gape after him, both exhilarated to be out of my room and terrified to have been left here to wait for the woman I'm scared to see.

At least there's a window. It's dark outside, but I can catch the soft glint of stars through the leaves of the trees. My heart rate calms slightly at the sight.

I look around trying to spot Nessa but the lights gleaming off the mirrors lining the wall directly across from me makes it hard to see. Ignoring Sebastian's command, I skirt the edge of the training mats, stopping to appreciate the sight of the two guys there, grunting as they rain punch after punch on each other. I might learn to like the gym after all if this is what it has to offer.

"You're here."

Nessa's voice catches me off guard and I yelp, spinning on my heel to find her. She's standing in the doorway, leaning against the frame, arms crossed over her chest as if she doesn't have a care in the world. It immediately pisses me off.

Her blonde hair is tied up in a loose ponytail, strands escaping around her face and softening her features. She's dressed in a tight workout top and bike shorts and I force myself not to look at the tattoo on her thigh.

I hate the way my breath hitches at the sight of her.

"You're late," I answer, more venom in my tone than I'd planned as Nessa steps into the gym.

She arches a perfect brow in response to my snarky attitude before unfolding her arms. That look spells trouble, but I don't care. I like pushing her. My heart rate spikes slightly as she takes measured steps in my direction. The confidence I felt when she first appeared is quickly waning and on instinct, I take a step back for each one she takes forward.

I feel eyes on me once more, but I pay them no mind. I'm too focused on Nessa to care about anything else.

"Have you warmed up?" she asks me, still sounding far too fucking unbothered for my liking. Like I'm boring her.

I shake my head. "I just got here."

"I guess that makes both of us late then." I see the corner of her mouth twitch and I baulk at the idea of almost getting a smile out of her. It unsettles me as much as it thrills me.

"Yes, but not as late as you," I quip, wondering if I can push my luck further and encourage her to lose control again. The laugh she gives me is rough and short, but, fuck, I feel it all the way to my bones.

I take another step away from her for good measure, needing the distance between us. She is not my friend. She can't be *anything* to me.

Noting the space I've created, she nods before locking her emotions away. I watch as the physical shift happens. Her face hardening into a blank mask, her shoulders rolling back as she plants her feet shoulder width apart.

"Stretch, then ten minutes on the treadmill," Nessa instructs, turning away from me to stick her water and bag in one of the empty cubbies lining the back wall.

I obey with a sharp nod, copying her movements as she returns to hide the fact that I don't fucking know how to do any of this properly. Pressing my hands against the brick behind me, I lift my legs up, one after the other, cupping the heel to stretch out my thighs before pressing my toes against the wall and stretching out my calves. The last thing I need is to get a cramp and fall flat on my arse in front of Nessa. Happy that my body won't revolt and lock up, I take up residence on the treadmill beside the man I'd spotted earlier.

I don't push her by arguing, so I turn the devil machine to a punishing pace and force my body to keep up.

By the time I finish my sprinting session I'm gasping for air and my hair is stuck to the nape of my neck. Sweat rolls down my spine and my skin feels too hot. I can barely see, stars clouding my vision but I try my best to hide it. The low chuckle that escapes Nessa lets me know I'm doing a shit job of it. I hadn't noticed her standing behind me between struggling to stand on shaking legs and silently begging for death to claim me.

"Jesus Christ, you're a mess, Branigan'. Pick yourself up. We're just getting started."

Nessa's gruff voice washes over me and ice coats my veins at the realisation that I'm not going to survive today's training session. How can I? I can barely run for ten fucking minutes, meanwhile she looks as unaffected as ever.

I knew I was out of shape, but I'd never cared before. I hadn't needed to. When you grow up with bodyguards for shadows there's very little reason to work out. Not when you know someone else is already doing the work for you.

Dragging my legs off of the treadmill, I shoot a weak thumbs up in her direction before waiting to see what form of torture she's planned next.

"Show me what you know," she says, taking a place in the centre of the training mats. The gym has emptied now. On one hand, I'm glad there'll be less witnesses to my incompetence, on the other, the fact that we're alone only fucks with my heart rate even more.

"Uh," I stutter, wiping my hand over my forehead. "That would be nothing."

"Nothing?" she echoes, brows furrowed. "Nobody taught you to fight?"

I shrug, embarrassed. "I was more of an accessory than an enforcer," I say, feeling my face heat. God, I'm a mess.

An unreadable expression flits across her face as her stern features soften slightly.

"Let's change that."

Shock races through me. My brows furrow as I try to understand why she'd want me, her prisoner, to learn how to fight but I nod a little, my feet moving forward of their own accord towards her. She motions for me to copy her stance, feet shoulder width apart with my left leg forward. I raise both my hands, forming two fists. I put my right fist up by my jaw, and my left is tucked close, but far enough away that I can reach out to hit when needed.

Watching me carefully, Nessa steps closer to assess my position.

"Thumb over the knuckles, not under. Unless you want it broken, that is."

I cringe at the thought, ignoring the way Nessa smirks at my reaction.

"I've got it," I grunt, hating how inadequate I feel right now. The feeling is my oldest friend, and one that refuses to leave my side.

"Alright, no need to get your knickers in a twist," Nessa says with an eye roll before stepping away. She picks up two pads then retakes her stance before me and holds them up in front of her.

"Hit them, as hard as you can."

"What? I've never hit anyone or anything before in my life, and you want me to hit them? What if I miss and accidentally hit you instead?" Images of my fist connecting with her skin flit across my mind, and I shiver at the idea of marking her.

"Unlikely, Branigan. Just aim for the pads."

It's not lost on me that she refuses to use my first name. I force a deep breath into my lungs and shove down the burning embarrassment. I want to learn, I do, but the idea of making a complete fool of myself in front of this woman has me wanting to dig my own grave.

Still, I step forward and throw my right fist out, landing a pathetically soft punch at the edge of the pad.

I watch for Nessa's reaction, but she gives me none. "Again. With your weight behind it this time."

I refuse to meet her gaze, staring straight at the cracks in the leather of the pads and aim for the centre. It feels better this time, but still clumsy. Weak.

"I'm not going to stand here all night," she says after a few attempts. "Harder."

"I'm hitting as hard as I can. I told you, I've never done this before."

I go to walk away, frustrated that I can't seem to do better and ready to give up trying. Sitting alone in my cell sounds better than humiliating myself. But before I can reach the edge of the mat I feel Nessa's hand wrap around my arm. I freeze at the contact, unsure of how I should react.

I turn slowly, steeling myself against her cold gaze.

I don't know why I expected anger, or even amusement to line her face, but instead all I find is a mask of indifference. For a brief moment I wonder if Nessa's even capable of either emotion. She seems completely unaffected by everything around her at all times aside from when she's angry. Yet, seeing her this relaxed, this calm, quietens some of my nerves.

Shockingly, she doesn't mock my lack of knowledge, or how pathetically unfit I am. She waits patiently, her eyes fixed on mine and I suddenly feel ridiculous for the pity party I've been throwing for myself.

"I know you can hit harder than that, I've seen you angry. Just take a deep breath, and resume your position."

"Clearly you haven't pissed me off enough today," I murmur under my breath, shaking off her touch.

Nessa scoffs. "Hit me, darlin'. You know you want to."

14

Siobhán

I watch in stunned silence as she unstraps the pads from her hands and sets them to the side. The nickname rings around my head, consuming all my thoughts. *Darlin' darlin' darlin'.* My stomach flips, a horrible spark of heat settling low inside me.

Her stern expression leaves no room for argument. She takes a step back and waits, completely at ease. I frown at her as I resume that balanced stance she showed me before, not quite as shaky as last time.

I've watched enough fights in my life to know how fast you have to be. How fast Nessa must be. The fact that she's not doing the same lets me know just how well trained she is.

She lets me get the first punch in, the solid muscle of her shoulder meeting my fist. It shocks me so much I stumble, the force behind my fist driving me forward. She catches me, one hand on my shoulder, the other on my waist, stopping me from going head over heels.

"I take it back," she says, a tinge of amusement sneaking into her voice. "Less weight behind it this time. And maybe don't aim near my face?"

"I was aiming for your stomach," I mutter, glaring at her.

The full body laugh that leaves her shocks the shit out of me. I watch in awe as her head tips back, exposing her neck to me and I can't suppress the blush that shoots from my chest to my hairline.

Holy fuck.

She takes advantage of my distraction, stepping forward so fast I don't register her movement until my legs are out from under me and I'm falling, *hard*.

My back meets the mat and the air flies from my lungs.

"Lesson number one…" I can feel Nessa's words on my skin, her breath coasting over my shoulder as she holds me under her. Her arm is trapped beneath my back, clearly there to soften my landing, and suddenly my breathlessness has nothing to do with the fall. "There's no such thing as distractions when your life's on the line. Focus."

I can't fucking speak. She shifts, pushing off the mat with her hands and straddling my waist. Her knees are pressed into the mat on either side of my hips, her hair hanging over her face as she stares down at me like she's conquered me.

How the fuck does she expect me to focus on *anything* like this?

"Right, yeah, focus," I breathe, licking my lips and staring at hers.

Shit, there's no way she's not gonna kick seven shades of shit out of me if I don't get my head screwed on right.

Grunting, she stands up straight before extending her hand out towards me. I stare at it for a second before holding my breath and grasping it. I can feel the calluses on the palm of her hand grazing against my smooth skin. I don't breathe again until she lets go.

My skin feels like it's burning and I can't blame our sparring session since all I've managed is a few measly punches so far. It's her. It's always fucking *her*.

Angry at her for making me feel like this rises hot and fast to the surface, competing with the burning flush.

"Show me how you did that," I surprise myself by saying as Nessa goes to resume her stance.

"You want me on the ground that badly?" she replies dryly and I gape at her attempted humour. First laughing, and now this.

I won't survive this.

She saves me from answering by stepping one foot forward and instructing me to wrap my leg around hers to throw her off balance. She's steady as fuck while I do it, patient as I try to find the right angle. I refuse to let myself think about the fact I can feel her body heat through my thin leggings.

"You need momentum, especially because I'm bigger than you," she tells me, untangling me from her and stepping back. "Come at me faster and try again."

I do. This feels far better than punching her. I feel like less of a twat.

"Now grab here." She takes my hand in hers and guides it to her back. I hope to God she can't feel the way my pulse jumps at the contact. "That's right. Good."

I can't look at her. I don't trust myself to speak, not when I can feel the soft skin of her back where her t-shirt has ridden up, when my leg is balanced between hers. Not when her words of praise make my head fuzzy like good whiskey. *She's just helping you be less useless,* I remind myself, but my two working brain cells have apparently left the fucking building.

"And push," Nessa says.

I hesitate for only a moment before I do. There's nowhere near enough force behind it, but she cups her hand around my neck and drags me down, helping me pin her to the mat.

"Well done," she praises from underneath me. She's on her back, having landed with practised skill, her blonde tresses escaping her hair tie and splaying out behind her. Her hand is still cupping the back of my neck. My thigh is pressed between hers and I don't know how the fuck I got this close to her but I know I can't move.

I have to move.

I can't let myself be so distracted by the woman I hate. I've already given her too much of my body. The *knife incident* cannot happen again.

I'm dragged out of my head as Nessa spins us. I suddenly find myself pressed into the mat with my arms pinned above my head. She eases her thigh between mine and I freeze at the feel of her pressed against my core.

Oh God. Oh fuck. *Do not squirm.* I plead with my body to behave, hoping like hell that she doesn't realise just how turned on I am right now. No one's ever handled me like this before. Not even Conor, who spent the entirety of our *friendship* treating me like I was going to shatter if he touched me too hard. It's hot as fuck.

Clearing my throat, I look up and find emerald eyes boring into mine.

"Do you need a repeat of lesson one?"

Yes, I think desperately, *I'll take whatever lessons you want to give me.*

Instead, I say, "No."

"I'm not so sure 'Branigan, you look a little preoccupied.

Tell me, what has you locked up tighter than a nun's cunt right now?"

Shit, shit, SHIT. Don't focus on how her voice sounds when she says the word cunt, Siobhán.

I work to relax my body as quickly as possible but the moment her hand flexes around my wrists, I stop moving. I'm pretty sure I cease to exist entirely for a split second, but somehow my body remembers how to betray me as I gasp at the feel of her thumb stroking my pulse point. That shouldn't feel as good as it does.

"Use your words, darlin'," she goads, and I feel my stomach bottom out.

That fucking nickname.

Gaping sheepishly at her, I wrack my brain trying to find a plausible excuse for my behaviour.

I don't want to lie to her, but fuck. How am I supposed to tell her that the reason I'm currently dying a slow painful death is because with every breath she takes I hope it pushes our chests together? Or that I'm begging for her leg to slip closer, to press against me just a little harder? That the feel of her rough thumb against my wrist sends delicious shocks straight through my nipples? That I want her, no, *need* her, as desperately as the air I was begging for earlier?

Choosing to feign ignorance instead, I set my lips into a thin line before saying "I don't know what you're talking about."

She raises a brow at me for what feels like the millionth time tonight, and I can't help but squirm a little under the weight of her stare.

I'm so fucked.

Bending lower, Nessa closes the distance between us. I hold my breath until she narrows her eyes. I look anywhere but at her then, knowing that having her this close to me is dangerous. *You can't fuck her. You shouldn't want to fuck her,* I remind myself, but it's no use. My traitorous body is practically waving a white flag and begging for a piece of her at this stage.

"So there's no reason why you're shaking?" Nessa goads me, voice lilting in a way that makes me suspect she knows exactly why I'm fucking shaking.

"Tired from working out," I stutter, cringing at the lie as it leaves my lips.

"We've barely even started," she answers quickly, too quickly, and for the briefest second I swear I can feel her lips brush mine.

I'm not strong enough to deny my body anymore.

I close the tiny gap between us, my self control fizzling out to nothing when my lips touch hers. She freezes above me for a second, and I panic, pulling away.

Nessa's mouth is on mine again before I can even begin to feel the sting of rejection, her kiss insistent and searing. The second her tongue sweeps the seam of my lips, I open for her, desperate for more, for everything, for whatever the fuck she'll give me.

My common sense fled the second she landed on top of me.

"Tell me, Branigan," she whispers, pausing to bite my bottom lip so hard I squirm, face flaring hot with embarrassment. "If I reach down between us will I find you wet for me?"

If I was turned on before, it's nothing compared to now. I tighten my thighs, blinking up at her as though, if I just shut my fucking mouth, she'll never know how badly she affects me. How thin the line is between my hatred of her and my lust for her.

Her knee presses against my legs where I've clamped them shut, forcing them open. I try to fight it, but she's far stronger than I've ever been and my half hearted protest is useless.

Her hand trails up the inside of my thigh, leaving fire in its wake and I squeeze my eyes shut so I don't have to see the look on her face when she realises just how wet I am.

"God," she groans as her fingers skim the seam of my leggings, finding the damp spot I know I've left there. "Is this for me?"

I turn my head to the side, keeping my eyes tightly closed. Her hand leaves my thighs only to grip my chin and force me to face her. My eyes snap open to meet her green stare, her pupils blown wide. *Fuck.*

"I asked you a question," she says slowly, her thumb tracing my lips. My breath hitches.

I nod, swallowing the shame.

"Use your words," she tells me, voice dark and demanding.

My lips thin into a narrow line, and I can't help but glare at her a little.

Smirking, she lowers the hand that was tracing my lips back down between us, stopping just before my waistband. My hips jerk slightly at the contact, and I can't stop the whimper that escapes me.

"Fuck, yes, okay, *yes*. It's for you," I groan, and I can't help but gasp when her hand immediately cups my throbbing cunt over my leggings.

"Good girl," she praises, and I flush at the sound of the praise leaving her lips. She's not as angry as she was when she kissed me a few days ago, her dangerous, feral side carefully controlled. I'm terrified to see her like that again; I'm *dying* to see her like that again.

I grind against her hand as her fingers delicately trace the seam of my leggings, teasing me. I need more. She's driving me wild and she knows it if the fire in her eyes is anything to go by.

"On your hands and knees for me, darlin', I want you facing the mirror." Nessa's voice sends a wave of heat through me, and I scramble to follow her order.

I search for her face in the reflection of the floor to ceiling mirror, and a shiver runs down my spine when I see that she's just as affected by this as I am. Her eyes are hooded as she stares down at me, and I can hear how hard she's breathing.

Her hands trace the band of my leggings before her fingers gently curl around it. Slowly, torturously so, she pulls them over the swell of my ass.

I push my hips back in her direction as she takes in the sight before her. I know that the material of my thong is soaked, and that there's no fucking way I'll be able to hide just how badly I want her any longer.

She inhales sharply as she drags her finger over the delicate lace, her eyes meeting mine in our reflection. I can't help the way my hips rock against her hand, my body hopeless against her soft touches. It's not enough, not nearly enough to soothe the ache.

"Nessa," I gasp, my voice breathless and needy. I've given up denying the desire building by the second inside me. I'm driven by the resolute need to know if she's as talented with her fingers as she is with her filthy fucking words. My gaze drops to the floor as her touch stills, lip caught between my teeth to stifle my whine.

"Need something?" she teases, her free hand trailing up my spine to fist in my hair, forcing my head back. "Watch what I do to you, Siobhán. You look away, I stop, do you understand me?"

I've forgotten how to breathe. That's the only explanation for the way my body tightens at her words, and how easily I agree, fixing my eyes on the mirror.

"So obedient," she muses, finger hooking the damp fabric and tugging it to the side. She traces the centre of me so slowly I want to scream, before gently pressing against my entrance. "So pretty like this for me."

I shift a little, sure I'm about to lose what little sanity I have left, but the complaint dies on my tongue when she thrusts her finger inside me. I groan at the friction, longing for more.

"Please," I beg, my hips thrusting against her a little more desperately now.

She tuts. "I've barely started with you and you're already pleading. Are you desperate already, thinking about fucking your enemy?"

Fuck me, I am, and it takes every ounce of effort I have not to let my eyes close. She's moving too slowly, with far more patience than I have.

Then, she stills completely and I think I might cry.

"When I ask you a question, Branigan, I expect you to answer."

I glare at her in the mirror. She slips her finger out of me and I break. "Jesus fuck, yes okay? I'm desperate!"

She grins, and it's feral, her eyes darkening until I feel like a doe caught in headlights. I know that in the end all she will do is hurt me. But Christ, she's beautiful and I can't find it in myself to move away.

Catching the glimmer in her eyes, I brace for the crash.

I welcome it.

Nessa rewards me with two fingers, curling them as she enters me, pressing against the spot inside me that makes my eyes roll back. I gasp and my lungs forget how to take in air. Pleasure threatens to make me collapse against the training mat, and my arms shake as I struggle to keep my eyes locked on our reflection.

The image of us, me with my leggings shoved down my thighs, legs splayed enough for Nessa's hand to fit between them, and her, fully clothed and brutal, is enough to make me clench around her fingers.

Adjusting her position, Nessa reaches between us with her free hand, finding my clit. My moan fills the empty air of the gym as she fucks me hard with her fingers, circling my clit with her other hand. Pleasure coils inside me embarrassingly fast, and I can feel myself get wetter around her. My thighs tremble slightly as my orgasm nears, my head falling forward as I groan.

Nessa's hand leaves my clit to grasp my hair, tugging my head up roughly. My scalp screams as my hair is used to guide my gaze back to the mirror, the sting of pain sending a full body shiver over me, fuelling the need still simmering low in my stomach.

"Watch me make you fall apart for me," Nessa demands, her voice harsh and low. "Watch yourself come for your enemy. Such a filthy fucking girl, daddy would be so ashamed if he could see you now, wouldn't he?"

Shame makes me shudder, and her fingers pick up speed, fucking me hard and fast. My orgasm rises again quickly and I watch, helpless, as I come for her. My mouth opens on a scream as I clench around her fingers, Nessa's teeth sinking into her bottom lip as she looks down between us. I can feel my release coat her hand, and the satisfaction and embarrassment washes over me in waves too strong to resist.

Before I can recover, Nessa flips us so I'm on my back, staring up at her with wide eyes.

I watch, bleary eyed, as she brings her fingers to her mouth and licks my cum from her skin.

"Someone as dirty as you has no right to taste so sweet."

15

Nessa

I stare down at the woman splayed beneath me. Siobhán's dark eyes are wide and glassy with pleasure, her quick breaths echoing between us. I lick the taste of her cunt off my fingers, and suppress the urge to strip her completely so I can taste every inch of her. As it is, her leggings are bunched around her thighs and hair is a wild mess from my grip.

My pussy throbs with need, and Siobhán blinks up at me, teeth scraping over her full bottom lip.

She should hate me more for what we've just done. For the words that left my mouth, yet all I see is desire burning in her gaze.

Licking the last dregs of her orgasm from the tip of my fingers I watch as her pupils dilate once more, and her nipples pebble beneath her top.

"I'm starving," she groans, her voice raspy from the way she just screamed for me. It sends a shiver through me and I grasp for control. "Let me taste you."

I swallow the curses rising in my throat and sit back, allowing her to rise to her knees. My hand cups her neck, not enough to hurt her, but enough to guide her lips to mine and kiss her with all the hatred I feel towards her fucking family.

I'm going to wreck the Branigans in more ways than one. Defiling their princess seems like a good place to start.

I drag Siobhán down on top of me, my fingers threading through her fiery hair. She braces herself above me, balancing on one arm as she tugs my sports bra down to free my breasts. Her mouth is on me instantly, tongue swirling around my nipple, tugging at the sensitive flesh between her teeth. I groan at the feel of her, my head pressing against the cushioned training mats as my fingers tighten in her hair.

Her lips trail down my stomach, tongue darting out to lick a line from my belly button to the waistband of my shorts. She sits back on her heels, her fingers slipping under my waistband, tugging my shorts off my body. I shift slightly, helping her, too turned on to give a single fuck about how bad of an idea this is anymore.

Siobhán throws my shorts to the side, and my underwear with them. For a long second, she stares at me, her eyes dark with desire, her mouth parted slightly as her gaze trails down my exposed body. I prop myself up on my elbows, watching her face as I part my thighs, spreading my legs wide for her.

"Are you going to sit there and stare at me all day, Branigan? Or are you going to solve the problem you made?"

Her eyes snap to mine, a fire in them that only rises the heat in my veins. She moves so fast I'm almost impressed, sliding down between my legs and gripping my thighs tightly. She's not strong enough yet for it to hurt, but the sharp press of her nails into the muscle of my thigh heightens my anticipation.

She doesn't tease me.

Her mouth is on me, eager, warm and hungry. She *devours* me, the flat of her tongue sweeping from my cunt to my clit in one long lick. She moans against me, pressing closer, her tongue dipping inside me.

I swear, my hand still in her hair, pleasure spreading quickly through me. Siobhán focuses her attention on my clit, and I can't stop the moan that escapes my lips.

She's undoing me rapidly, and when she presses two fingers inside me, my orgasm crashes over me with no warning.

"Fuck," I gasp, holding her close as I come on her tongue. She continues to lick me, taking everything I give her.

She doesn't stop until I'm limp on the mat and I've released my grip on her hair. She pulls back, lips glistening with my cum, her eyes bright and slightly panicked.

We stare at each other in silence, the weight of what we've done heavy between us.

"Shower," I say eventually, standing quickly and grabbing my discarded clothes.

I try not to think about the way her shoulders drop slightly at my cold tone, or how she immediately ducks her head and avoids eye contact. I try not to think about the fact that her response sends a pang of sympathy through me, an emotion I haven't felt in years.

I block it out, block *her* out, and lead her to the shower block attached to the gym. Members that live in the city but come here to train use these showers, but it's late and they're completely empty. I find a fresh bottle of body wash, shampoo and conditioner for her and gesture to one of the stalls.

I don't shower. It's stupid to let her out of my sight, even just for long enough to get clean. I'll wash before I sleep, in my own bathroom, but I'm not cruel enough to send the girl back down to her shitty bed, sweaty and freshly fucked. I don't want my scent on her as she sleeps. She's not mine to mark like that and fuck I don't want her to be.

This was a mistake, that's all. A stupid fucking mistake.

I wait for her to emerge, naked and wet, and force myself to not react to the sight of her. She's all soft, flowing curves and freckles, pale skin slightly pinked from the steam.

I find an excuse to tear my gaze away, grabbing her a spare towel off the rack. Somehow, seeing her like this feels more intimate than when we were fucking.

Gentler. Less explosive.

Far more unsafe.

I say nothing to her as I take her back to her room. Not even when she whispers my name as she redresses and perches on the edge of her shitty excuse for a bed.

I turn around and leave, ignoring her and the way she makes my stomach twist.

She's no good for me.

I realise it now more than ever. Outside of her room, I dig my phone from the pocket of my shorts and hit redial on the last number I called.

He answers on the second ring.

"It has to be soon," I say, before hanging up and throwing the phone on Sebastian's puzzle filled table.

Soon.

Soon.

16

Siobhán

"Gooood morning, sunshine. It's coffee time!"

I feel my heart leap out of my chest as I crack an eye open to find Sebastian hovering over my head. Blinking rapidly I try to figure out how the fuck he got in here without me waking. Usually I notice the sound of the lock turning, but I must have been dead asleep for him to not only unlock the door, but come through it, set my coffee down somewhere, and lock it again.

"What do you want?" I ask, the words falling thickly from my mouth. I try to push up in the bed but before I can even so much as fully lift my head from the poor excuse for a pillow Sebastian wraps his huge hands around my arms and drags me upright. Spots dance in my vision at the sudden movement and I have to close my eyes to steady myself.

Holy fuck, what kind of a wake up call is this?

After a couple of seconds, I gingerly open my eyes to find Sebastian staring at me, amusement dancing in his eyes. I can see a hint of a smile playing on his lips, but I don't bother questioning it. There could be any number of reasons for that smile. A new victim at his disposal, a solid cup of coffee, a quick fuck, or even just having gotten the chance to annoy Nessa over breakfast.

Choosing to ignore him instead as I wait for an answer to my earlier question, I reach for the coffee placed at my feet. I take a sip and allow myself to relish the warmth of the mug in my hand and the rich taste as it passes my lips.

"You my dear, are getting out of this room today. So do me a favour would ya and hurry the fuck up."

What?

I choke on the coffee as I beg my mind to replay the words he's just said.

The only other time I've been out of this fucking prison cell is when I'd trained with Nessa. And even fucking her on the gym floor hadn't been enough to grant me anything but a rushed shower and her dismissal. Even that was three days ago and the glimpses I've seen of her since, neither of us have brought it up. Shame, I think, keeps me quiet. The only flickers of emotion I've seen on her face since, when she's checked that I'm alive and brought me enough food to keep me alive, have been anger and disgust.

I haven't done anything to deserve leaving this room, unless they've finally decided they've had enough of me.

Oh fuck... what if *I'm* Sebastian's latest victim? Shit, shit, *shit*.

My pulse climbs higher as I think about it more.

I'm nothing but a burden to them. The longer I stay here the more money and resources get wasted on my existence.

Sure, they think they can use me to get back at Seamus. But what if they've finally learned the truth? What if they've finally come to realise that Seamus would no sooner pay a ransom for me than see me dead.

Fuck.

Gripping the cup tighter, I do my best to keep my face neutral.

"Why?"

The word falls from my lips strong and steady and I silently send up a prayer in thanks for how unbothered I sound. Lifting my gaze, I note the confusion flit across Sebastian's face before he can cover it.

"What do you mean *why*? I thought you'd be jumping at the chance to escape this shithole."

Gritting my teeth, I bring the cup to my lips and force myself to swallow another mouthful before I sigh. There's not enough coffee in the fucking universe for a conversation like this first thing in the morning - or at least I think it's morning. I only have Sebastian's word to go off of given the lack of natural lighting down here.

"Am I to train with Nessa again?" I ask, hoping that my line of questioning will lead me to some proper answers.

"What, you don't want to see your new girlfriend?" Sebastian teases, lifting his hand to his mouth in feigned surprise. I glare at him in return while shifting uncomfortably on the bed. The idea of Nessa being mine makes my jaw clench.

"She's not my fucking girlfriend and you damn well know it," I snap, growing tired of his games. "Just tell me why I'm suddenly allowed out of the room," I plead, the edge in my voice nowhere to be found now.

"I've been ordered by a certain someone that I'm to show you around the mansion," he chimes as he seats himself on the end of my bed.

"So... you're not here to kill me then?" I ask, surprised

at myself for how bold I'm being. But against my better judgement, I can't help but feel that, in some way, I can trust Sebastian. At the very least, I can trust him to feed me, to ensure that Nessa doesn't cross a line she can't come back from, and to not kill me without at least being given the order to do so first. And given the situation I'm in, that's the best I can hope for.

"Ha! No. Listen sunshine, I know this hasn't been your most pleasant experience," his begins, but the way his eyebrows wiggle suggestively makes mine furrow. There's no way he's implying that there's been pleasure here. I refuse to believe it. The idea that he knows what mistakes I've made with Nessa has the shame threatening to drown me. "And that you're probably used to duck feather pillows and being waited on hand and foot. But you're not going anywhere and you need to accept that fact," he continues before resting his head back against the wall behind him.

Pressing my lips into a thin line, I decide that if I'm going to be forced to stay here any longer I may as well take the bit of freedom he's granting me.

"Alright then," I sigh, accepting my lot for today, and chug the remainder of my coffee. Stepping out of the bed, I grab the closest pair of leggings to me and drag them up my legs without bothering to check if Sebastian's watching. "Lead the way, pretty boy."

As we reach the top of the steps, I ball my hands into fists at the sound of people talking coming from the right of us. Almost as though my body is on autopilot, my feet widen into the fighter's stance and my shoulders tense. My mind quickly flicks through the limited training Nessa gave me, but I have to hope that it'll be enough for me to cause some damage should someone decide to test me today.

"Relax, nobody's going to touch ya with me beside you sunshine," Sebastian murmurs as his eyes trail over the two men currently glaring at me. Hatred simmers in their stares and I can tell exactly just what they think of me as the one on the left folds his giant arms across his chest. Part of me wants to lower my head in submission. To fall into the same docile nature that kept me from being slaughtered at the hands of my father.

But I won't do it. I won't allow myself to go there again.

Not when I've done so much to escape that, to become someone else.

Instead, I lift my chin, daring them to make a move. The shorter guy on the right bares his teeth in disgust at me as he notices the change in my attitude but when they swing their eyes in Sebastian's direction they quickly avert their gaze and find somewhere else to be.

Huffing a breath, I look to my left and narrow my eyes at Sebastian, unsure of how true his statement is.

I know, if given half the chance, any one of the bastards roaming through this house would level me without a second thought.

Pushing the reality of my situation to the side though, I try to relax my body as Sebastian points down the hall the two men just turned towards.

"The living room and the kitchen are that way, but I think we'll take a wander down the opposite end for now," he states, his tone thick with annoyance as he glares at where the two men previously stood.

"Sounds good to me," I murmur. My eyes rake over the hall

we're currently standing in. It's much warmer up here than it is down in the basement, and I can feel the heat seeping into my bare feet with each step forward I take.

I hadn't bothered grabbing shoes before leaving the cell since I'd figured I wouldn't be allowed outside anyway, and for once I was glad for it. I cherished the warmth defrosting my toes.

"Heated flooring?" I question, as I lift my head to take in the walls around me.

Large floor to ceiling windows line the hall and I can see how dull it is outside. A shiver skates down my spine at the realisation that I'm standing in natural daylight for the first time in days.

"Yeah, Thomas had it installed when he first moved in. Said he couldn't stand the feel of cold tiles."

Nodding my head in understanding, I step closer to the window and try to take in our surroundings. Nothing but grassy hills and sprawling fields at every turn.

Looking up toward the ceiling, I spy the crown moulding lining the edges and trail my eye around it. A gaudy gold chandelier hangs from the centre of the ceiling, light dancing off the hundreds of crystals hanging from it. Bringing my eyes back down, I catch sight of an antique vase, and a couple of paintings, though none detailed enough to hold my interest.

"C'mon, let's take a look at the library," Sebastian hums and the corner of his mouth tilts upwards at the shock on my face.

"A library?"

Excitement bubbles in my chest at the idea of a room filled with books. Maybe if I play my cards right I can convince him to let me borrow one of them. I need *something* to keep me occupied. To focus my thoughts on anything but Nessa, my father and the nightmare that was the night of my twenty-fifth birthday.

Quickly following him down the hall, I come to a stop as he pushes open the two large wooden doors directly in front of him. Standing on my tip toes, I do my best to see over his shoulder but given that the man is a giant, I'm at nothing. I huff a breath as I focus on keeping my balance. Spotting my struggle, he steps to the side and waves his hand forward, motioning for me to step through the entrance with a barely concealed smirk twisting his mouth.

As I walk through the doors, everything else fades into the background. Light creeps through thick red curtains from the windows lining the wall on the right hand side of the room, highlighting the books encased in thick wooden shelving. Glass doors seal them in, a lock on the middle of each one. I step closer to them though, desperate to read the titles on each and every book. Sebastian steps up beside me and I can feel him watching my reaction, but I pay him no mind as I move further into the room. Warmth seeps out of the fireplace nestled in the back wall, and a comfortable looking arm chair lined in a smooth red material and gold embroidery rests beside it. I catch sight of the art work hanging above the mantle and gasp when I realise that something like this must have cost a couple of million at least. It's a notorious piece, something I'd seen in a book once a long time ago.

"Ya know, half the art work hanging in the museums you'd read about scattered around the world aren't even housing original works. If anything they're cheap imitations of pieces like this one," Sebastian murmurs, his eyes narrowing on the painting. I hadn't pegged him for an art connoisseur but I'm learning that the man is full of surprises and I don't bother to call him on it.

"Yeah I'd read something about that once in the paper I think," I half heartedly comment, hoping that he can't see just how uncultured I am when it comes to things like fine art and its history.

Nodding his head once, he smiles softly at me before settling into the chair beside the fire. Taking that as my invitation to keep looking around, I continue to work my way around the room and look at the rest of the books.

Hours pass as I leaf through the pages of a few books that have been left abandoned on the mahogany table in the centre of the room. I startle as my stomach rumbles, pulling me back to the present and away from the fairytale I'd been reading.

Embarrassment courses through me as my stomach groans again, cutting through the silence.

"Jesus Christ, did somethin' die in there or what?" Sebastian laughs, and I can't stop the blush staining my cheeks.

"Just hungry," I grumble, as I cross my arms over my stomach.

"Let's feed ya then," he nods, and I follow after him like the good little prisoner I am.

17

Siobhán

"You know what you did when you ran, don't ya sunshine?" Sebastian asks, stopping in front of a truly hideous painting. The frame is giant, gold and gaudy and the paint is faded and dull now, a crude depiction of what I think is supposed to be a bunch of flowers.

After feeding me a bowl of spaghetti bolognese, Sebastian shows me the kitchen, wash room, the hall filled with endless bedrooms and, now, the living room. I can't help but feel like Thomas Cavanaugh hasn't got the knack for home decor down just yet. Everything's antique, priceless and unnecessarily over the top. The mansion feels less like a home and more like a showcase of his wealth.

I sigh, avoiding Sebastian's gaze by pretending to study the blobs of colour for a bit longer. "My head isn't as empty as you all seem to think it is," I answer, but there's no venom in my voice. The words come out as tired as I feel. I can't seem to focus on giving a shit anymore, not with the conflicting, confusing muddle of emotions curdling my stomach.

Starting a gang war didn't fuck me up as much as having

sex with a woman on a gym floor did.

Sebastian scoffs, and I can *feel* the way he's rolling his eyes at me. "You're too used to being underestimated, Siobhán. I think you're far more calculated than you're given credit for. So the question remains, sunshine, why would you do it knowing people, your own people, would die?"

I swallow the thick ball of guilt that chokes me up. It's an odd feeling, guilt for hurting people who hurt me for years.

"I didn't ask for this life, Sebastian," I begin, trying to make my voice more powerful than I feel. "Do you know how many times I'd met the man who was supposed to be my husband before my wedding day? *Twice.* And one of those times, I didn't even speak to him. For all I knew, he was a monster worse than the ones I'd learned to deal with. My options were, stay with my father in the same miserable life I'd led for the last twenty-five years, or marry a man I didn't know and have a new, equally miserable life if not worse. I don't want the sum of my life to be a pawn for your political bullshit. I just wanted *out.*"

I'm panting, and Sebastian is stock still beside me.

"I have done bad things. I know that. But I don't deserve a life of misery just to make everyone else happy."

Sebastian knocks his shoulder against mine, so briefly I'd have thought it was an accident if I didn't already know everything about this man is calculated as hell.

"You couldn't have just told your father that you didn't want to do it?"

I scoff, the sound harsh. "You've met him, right? Does he seem like the kind of man you say no to?"

I don't say that I was terrified, when he'd told me of my own engagement, that saying no would finally be the thing that got me killed. That, for years, I'd known that the man I shared blood with was just waiting for a reason to remove me from his life. That since the second he'd walked out of the hospital with a screaming newborn but no wife, he'd been dreaming of the day I'd be buried.

"You've got a point," he concedes. "Where did you want to go?" His question surprises me.

I shrug a little pathetically. "Anywhere that's not here. I've never even left the county. I saw photos of France in a book once. I think I'd have liked to go there for a while."

"You still could."

"We both know I can't, Sebastian. Don't try and placate me with false hope. Not after all this."

He turns away from the painting, facing me fully, and I follow his lead by turning to him. "Okay, no France for now. But you don't have to be miserable here."

My brows hit my hairline. "I'm just trapped in another gang house. New people, same shit."

"But your father's not here," he says, waggling his eyebrows. "And you and Nessa-"

I cut him off with a death glare. What the fuck does he know about me and Nessa? No, there is no me and Nessa.

He laughs, head tipping back, and I realise he can see every thought written on my face.

"She's not the monster you seem to think she is, sunshine." I frown at him in obvious doubt. "Not that she's shown it, I know. But she's loyal as fuck, and beneath the many, *many* layers of assholeness, she's all soft and gooey."

It's all I can do to stare blankly at him.

"You know better than me how *sweet* she can be," he taunts and I feel my face flame.

"How the fuck do you know about that?" I shriek, horror shooting through me. Did she tell him? I didn't think she would. She'd be too ashamed of it to admit it. Too ashamed of wanting *me*. Maybe he saw? Or heard? Fuck.

I want the ground to open up and swallow me whole.

"I didn't until now," he grins, pointing at my bright red cheeks.

"Oh fuck you," I snap, earning myself a laugh and another nudge on the shoulder. The brief, friendly contact shouldn't make my stomach twist with longing. But I've never had a proper friend. And I want one. I want him to be one.

Stupid, stupid Siobhán.

"Fuck Nessa you mean," he wheezes back. "It's obvious you both want to keep banging each other's brains out. Hate is the best aphrodisiac after all."

"You're such a prick."

"That's just part of my charm."

18

Nessa

"...but I don't deserve a life of misery just to make everyone else happy."

I pause, my heart thudding loud in my ears as her words reach me. The raw truth of her admission cuts me, the way her voice is somehow both strong and shaking.

My first instinct is to bristle and grit my teeth at her selfishness. But then I hear the fear lingering in her words, imagine the longing on her face, and I deflate.

I'd always thought of Siobhán as the Branigan princess. Holed up in the tower of her father's stronghold, spoiled and needing for nothing, never having to struggle or work a day in her life.

Too spoiled to need to fight, using the mob like bodyguards.

Never had I had the thought that perhaps she hates her father, her life, the way I do.

I shake my head, frozen to the spot. I know if I turn the corner, Siobhán and Sebastian will know I've heard them. For some reason, I don't want them to know.

I don't know what to do with it all.

"Does he seem like the kind of man you say no to?" Siobhán says, her voice quieter now, and an unfamiliar feeling settles in my gut.

It's cold and clawing, and I don't understand why it feels as though I've been punched in the stomach.

I retreat, feeling like a Goddamn coward, hands pressed over the ache in my abdomen. For the first time in *years* something akin to regret sinks into my skin.

My phone is a heavy weight in my pocket as I turn and walk away, ignoring the fact I needed to pass them to get to the kitchen. I'd rather starve than look at Siobhán right now.

I shouldn't harbour any feelings except hatred for that girl and yet somehow she's managing to make me *retreat.* I am not the kind of woman who turns from confrontation and here I am, pressed against the wall, my breaths coming faster than normal and my thoughts racing.

I've dreamt about the way she panted for me, the perfect moans that fell from her parted lips, the soft warmth of her around my fingers.

Sebastian was wrong when he told Siobhán that I was nicer than I was making it seem. I am every bit the monster I've shown her, unapologetic for my claws and fangs and bloodlust. But fuck, if she's not the only person I want to sink my teeth into now.

I don't think I'm capable of giving her anything less. Reality beat the softness out of me before I even had the chance to hide it.

Memories of running barefoot in the rain rise in my mind, feeling the cold seep through the still soft skin, ice travelling through my veins until I swore it pierced my heart. Being *gentle* gets you nowhere.

I don't even have the heart to warn her. My kindness was abandoned on the streets along with me.

I'm not unfamiliar with dickhead parents. I mean, given the whole abandoned by my mother at age eight thing, I'd argue that I'm extremely qualified in that particular trauma.

But I only wandered for a few days, calling out my ma's name, before I realised she wasn't coming back for me. I only had to lie through my teeth to a few men who wanted me to come home with them so I'd "be safe" before I started hiding in alleys and the less busy parts of town. My life with my mother had prepared me for this, adulthood as a child.

Now, I think that perhaps she died. Or that the drugs finally wore away at her brain like the ocean carves out the cliffs, and she forgot she had a child entirely.

The word "mother" no longer fits in my mouth.

And I could never pronounce "father" at all.

I find myself outside Thomas' office. My hand raises to knock, before it falls to my side again. Today is a day for cowardice, it seems. The fact burns a hole through my stomach and I press my hand over my gut, shocked when I find no wound.

So I stand outside the room of the only person who's ever come close to the title *parent* and find uncertainty curling from my throat like smoke. For the first time since I was an eight year old too big for her boots, I don't know what the fuck to do.

19

Siobhán

Everyone in this house hates me, except maybe Sebastian. He took me on an entire tour yesterday, and every time we saw someone else, they immediately reached for their guns. Or knives. Or just fisted their hands and glared at me so hard I was sure I could *see* all the ways they were imagining killing me reflected in their eyes.

The feeling was mutual, though, except I had significantly less weapons.

The pile of dirty clothes in my room is growing worryingly large, and I planned to beg Nessa to take me to wash them when she brought me lunch. It's hard as fuck to keep track of time down here, given the whole no windows thing, but my captors are decently good at remembering to deliver me three meals a day, which helps.

Still, I feel like a dog begging for scraps, jumping at the chance to do anything, to go anywhere that isn't here. I'm lucky, I know that. Unharmed and looked after, and honestly probably safer than if my father had found me.

The thought of his wrath if he'd gotten to me first makes

me shudder.

The door opens and I'm on my feet in seconds, an eager hope spreading through me like fire, faster than I can put it out.

"Nessa."

I don't know why I say her name. I can't help myself. She's dressed in a loose fitting black t-shirt and grey joggers, her hair hanging around her face. With her arms crossed over her chest, the muscles of her arms are on display and I try to hide the way my mouth waters.

I want her to devour me.

I blink and realise she's speaking to me.

"...to the gym again?"

My breath catches in my throat. Could I handle going into that fucking space again, knowing what happened last time?

I know for certain that there's no way I can work out without wanting a repeat.

I can't even curse myself for it anymore. Nessa is fit as fuck and the danger that emanates off her just makes me want to push her more.

"Or you could take me out on a date," I say, not catching my words before they push past my teeth. "Since you've already fucked me. I'm pretty sure that means you owe me dinner now."

The words hang between us, heavy and sinking. I hold my breath. This, without a doubt, is the worst idea I've ever had in my life. But at the back of my mind, a small part of me is insisting that this is good- that if she takes me out of here, I can find a way to escape. I know my way around the place now thanks to Sebastian.

Despite this though, I need to know what I'm facing beyond

the fields outside this fortress if I ever want to make it further than a few feet from the Cavanaugh grounds.

But as the silence continues to stretch between us, the smarter, more logical side of me knows that I won't leave, even if I get the perfect chance. Because, whether I like it or not, this is the safest place for me to be.

As I glance back at Nessa, I cringe as I note just how genuinely shocked she seems by my suggestion. Shame heats my cheeks as embarrassment sweeps through me, hot and uncomfortable. I open my mouth to take it all back, but Nessa beats me to it.

"You can't run," she says.

I stare at her, wide eyed. A laugh sneaks past my lips, the notion of me outrunning her fucking hilarious to me. But fear creeps up my spine as I realise just how easily she was able to read my mind. A darker thought follows quickly, one that has my stomach clenching with desire. "Maybe I'd like you chasing me."

Her eyes flash, her jaw clenching as she takes in my words. "You're terrible for me, Siobhán."

I can't argue with that. I am, and she is perhaps the worst choice I've ever made.

Nessa curses sharply, running her hand through her hair. A pang of jealousy shoots through me, desperation to know how her hair would feel with my hands tangled in it again.

"Why couldn't you have been a raging bitch? Why couldn't you have been anything but my fucking type? Why did *I* have to be the one to find you?"

I can't tell if she's insulting me or despairing because she likes me. I hold my breath. I'm not sure which outcome I want. I don't *like* her, per se, but every inch of my body wants to be pressed against her bare skin. It wants to find every single spot that makes her gasp, wants to memorise how to make her come so hard she sees stars.

I want her again, so badly it hurts.

Maybe I'm just touch starved. It'd be like this with anybody, right? Even as I try to convince myself of it, I know it's not true. There's something infuriatingly enticing about this fucking girl.

"Fuck it," Nessa says finally, seeming to come to a conclusion. "Get up, get dressed. I'll be back in ten minutes."

She leaves, locking the door behind her, but instead of the sinking feeling I normally get with the snick of the lock, I feel buoyant with hope. I change into a clean pair of leggings and a tight top. I have few options to choose from, certainly none that are even close date attire, but they're clean and that will have to do.

I buzz with excitement as I pull the shirt on and rake my fingers through my hair to tame it. My pulse quickens as time flies by and I try to tell myself that I'm excited at the possibility of leaving, but really, it's the possibility of leaving *with Nessa*.

It's a stupid notion. I know that. But I was never very good at keeping my hopes low. Years with my da should have taught me better. But even as I was walking down the aisle to marry a man as part of a fucking peace treaty, I still hoped that he would look at me with love. Still longed for him to see my worth.

He never will. He isn't capable of it. But I don't think that silly little flickering dream will ever really die.

Nessa comes back in without knocking, a hoodie in her hand. She throws it at me and I scramble to catch it, nearly knocking myself off balance in my haste. She watches me stumble with a raised brow, a smirk on her lips. My heart beats faster.

"Put it on and pull the hood up. Look at the ground and don't speak until we're out of here, got it? Disobey me and there'll be trouble."

My brows raise. "Trouble?" I ask, my voice huskier than I intended.

Her eyes are bright again, her tongue darting out to wet her lip. I want to trace its path with my own. "Unless you want to get up close and personal with a gun this time, you'll do as I say."

The words spill out before I can even think to stop them. "I liked the knife. Maybe I'll like your gun, too."

Nessa goes very still. I can hear her ragged breathing as I tug the hood up over my head. The hoodie is slightly too large, but fits nicely enough and smells like her. I want to tuck it under my mattress and never give it back. I want to rip my own brain out for even having that thought.

I'm so fucked.

"Don't speak like that, darlin'," Nessa warns, her voice tense.

I take a step toward her, fuelled by some ridiculous notion of confidence. I don't think she'll hurt me, though I almost want her to.

"Why? Are you picturing it?"

I swear to God, I can hear her teeth grinding together as I twist my hair between my fingers. My heart is pounding so loud it fills my head. I don't know if I'm scared or excited but the adrenaline is the same. I like the feeling. I like not having to think about the fucking state I'm in. Fucking with Nessa, *fucking Nessa*. She has a way of making me feel like nothing else exists except her. Us.

She demands every ounce of my attention and I give it. Fuck, I give it gladly.

I can almost hear Sebastian's voice in my head chanting *daddy issues*.

"Go, now, or we're not leaving this fucking room for the rest of the night," Nessa hisses, and for a second, I don't move. Then she grabs me by my arm and hauls me out the door after her, making the decision for me. My heart sinks a little.

"Ness-"

"You wanted to go out. We're going out. Don't push your fucking luck with me, Branigan."

Her sudden change of tone is like being bathed in ice. I don't know what I did wrong. What I said to make her hate me like this again.

For a second there, I thought she maybe wanted me too.

"Sorry," I whisper, angry at myself for saying it, for sounding so pathetic. For becoming the woman I ran from. I shake myself, and square my shoulders, refusing to cower anymore. "Actually, I'm not. You were the one who fucked me on the gym floor. If you don't want me, you've got a funny way of showing it."

Nessa continues walking up the stairs and I follow, anger burning away the coldness of her apparent rejection. But she's still taking me up, up and out the front door, walking so fast I have to run after her like a dog being dragged on its leash.

"You fuck with my head," she hisses under her breath.

"You fuck with mine!" I nearly shout it, barrelling out of the front door after her. I don't see anyone else around us, but that doesn't mean someone won't hear us talking. "I don't understand."

Nessa says nothing, shoving a helmet at me as she dons her

own. Her bike's waiting on the drive, the sleek black paint shining in the afternoon sun. She straddles the seat, looking back at me over her shoulder. My mouth is dry as I stare at her, thighs parted over the saddle, hands resting on the handlebars, helmet obscuring her face.

Heat pools between my legs.

Fucking hell.

The seconds drag on too long before I break myself from my trance and rush towards her. Clumsily, I climb on behind her, unsure what to do with my hands.

"Hold on to me. Tight," she instructs as the bike comes to life beneath us. The thrum of the engine vibrates through me, and I do as she says, leaning forward and wrapping my arms around her waist.

I press my eyes closed and try not to think about the fact I can feel her muscles through her shirt.

I think about not thinking about it the entire drive. The countryside passes in a blur and I'm not sure what the legal speed limit is, but I've a feeling Nessa is definitely doubling it. I press closer to her, feeling the wind whip my hair into knots and wishing I'd asked for something to tie it up with.

The longer we drive the more I focus on the road. I don't think about her body heat seeping into me. I don't think about the way she smells, like smoke and cherries. I don't think about the fact that my underwear is wet and my cunt already needy.

She stops harshly, and my eyes fly open. I thought she'd take us back into Killrover, but instead I'm greeted with an old building surrounded by fields. The air smells of hay and horses, but the gravel car park is surprisingly full.

Nessa parks, then helps me off the bike. My legs shake

beneath me and I try to hide it. The way she stares at me tells me I'm no good at hiding anything from her. Her stare snags on my hair and she shakes her head, setting her helmet on the seat to open the top box.

I see the glimmer of steel stored inside and my breath lodges in my throat, but she only pulls out a hairbrush. A laugh bursts from me as I take it.

"Comes in handy," she says with a shrug. "Tuck your hair inside the helmet next time. Wind's a bitch when you're out in the open like this."

I make quick work of tugging the brush through my hair, the stinging pain of pulling the knots out centring me as I try not to fixate on the words that fell so casually from her plump lips. *Next time.*

Done, I hand her back the brush and pull my hood up, inhaling her scent. My pussy throbs and I swallow harshly. I'm sure she hears it, but I press forward and act as though I'm not secretly begging for her to bend me over her bike and fuck me right here, right now.

"Where are we?" I ask, fighting to keep my voice even. I turn away from her to take in the building - old red brick, the roof missing a few tiles, and a warm glow from the windows. It's one story, but decently large, and looks like it was once a farmhouse. There's a faded sign above the door that reads *The Hen's Roost.*

It's...charming. And not at all a place I could picture Nessa in.

"Closest pub and inn. Filled with farmers and travellers and nobody from Killrover. Food's decent and nobody will bother us here."

A small smile tugs at my lips, my shoulders dropping as

tension leaves me. Here, I don't have to be a Branigan. Here, maybe, I can just be Siobhán.

My smile grows wider, and I can feel the heat of Nessa's eyes on me. Her shoulder grazes mine as she stalks past me in the direction of the inn, giving me her back.

It should be an insult. After all, you don't turn your back to anyone dangerous. It'd be like offering yourself up for the knife. But she doesn't view me as a threat, and the knowledge makes my stomach sink a little. In all honesty though, it just makes me hope she'll teach me to be as deadly as she is.

I want her to watch her back around me. I want her on edge, walking the tight line between *will she kill me or fuck me.* I want her to have a taste of her own bitter sweet medicine.

There are so many things I desperately want, and still I can't make sense of the tangled mess of my desires.

I rip my gaze away from the pub and follow her, catching the door just before it swings shut in my face. It's heavy, and my shoulder aches a little with the impact. A rush of warmth engulfs me as we enter, the scent of beer and chips thick in the air. The low chatter of the other customers greets me, one man's laugh loud and rich as it overpowers everyone else's conversations. Some part of me is soothed by it. The familiar drunk revelry is comforting.

The walls are the same old red brick, peppered with photos of horses and chickens. It's not particularly clean, muddy boots marking the floors, and dirty glasses left on the table that Nessa sits us at. She shoves them all to the edge in a clear hint to the bartender to collect them.

The table she's chosen is near the door and away from the main crowd at the bar. It's not too busy, but the group of men who were laughing lean over the bar, talking over each other and spilling beer. There's a few other customers keeping to themselves, and I imagine this is as full as it must get out here.

"Are you hungry?" Nessa asks, stretching her legs out under our table. I feel her foot graze my ankle, the barest contact sending sparks shooting through me.

"Yes."

There's an ache in me, a cavernous one, that's *starving*. I don't think food will ease its hunger.

Above the bar, there's a blackboard with today's menu scrawled on it. The font is barely legible and I have to squint to make out the list. Steak pie, fish and chips, soup, burgers. After the protein bar, cereal and pasta diet Sebastian and Nessa have had me on lately, my mouth waters at the idea of fresh food.

I don't want to push my luck with Nessa. I suspect she's only brought me here because she's sick of my whining and maybe, maybe, a tiny part of her sympathises with me.

Regardless of her reasoning, I'm going to take advantage of it. I reel off my order to her and she nods once, telling me in a sharp tone to stay put, before she heads up to the bar to order.

I look around the pub, inhaling the warm air greedily. I know Nessa will lock me back in my room when her kindness reaches its limit, but if I have to be locked in a basement once more, at least I'll have tasted fresh air. Well, *fresh* might be a stretch, considering that this air is tainted with beer and spirits, but I'm not fussy.

Someone sits across from me and I snap my head up, expecting Nessa to have returned with our drinks.

Instead, I find a man. He's older than me by about ten years, with shaggy brown hair and a dopey grin. His eyes are heavy lidded and creased at the sides as he smiles at me.

The smell of liquor wafts off him and I tense.

"Not seen you round 'ere before, love," he says by way of introduction, waving his hand about. "Name's Paulie."

I raise a brow at him, unimpressed by whatever the fuck he's doing. I didn't come here to talk to strange, drunk men. "Hi," I say blandly in return, refusing to answer his unspoken question of who I am.

"Not gonna give me your name, huh? Playing hard to get, I like it." Paulie winks, and my stomach ties itself in knots.

"I'm here with someone," I tell him, tone harsher this time. I need him to leave. I don't want to be seen here, for my whereabouts to somehow make their way back to my father. I tug on the edges of my hoodie - Nessa's hoodie - and refuse to give him my name.

"That's alright, love," he slurs, leaning across the small table. He's face is too close to mine now, and I press myself against the back of my seat, trying to create distance. "I don't mind a challenge."

Anger rises hard and fast. "What part of *I'm not interested* are you not getting?"

Paulie reels back, a sneer replacing his drunk grin. "Bitch. I should teach you some fucking manners. You'd like that wouldn't ya? Being put in your place."

"Please leave," I try, biting at the words in my rush to get them out. I look around frantically for Nessa. This guy is bigger than me in every way and as pissed as a cut cat. I don't know if I could fight him. I don't want to have to.

"Come with me, and I'll fuck that attitude right outta ya." Paulie stands and grabs my arm. I yelp, unable to stop the sound. I open my mouth to say no, but another voice cuts in before the word can get past my teeth.

"She's not going anywhere with you." Nessa's voice is dark, angry but carefully controlled, that feral part of her back in its cage. "I suggest you let her go before you lose your hand, *Paulie.*" She hisses his name like it's a curse, and the drunk's face grows redder with rage.

"Who the fuck are you?" he spits, turning to her and letting me go. I breathe a sigh of relief, though fear is still oily in my veins.

"I'm hers," Nessa tells him with a deadly grin. My heart beat skyrockets, a needy ache coming to life between my legs as she claims me. Declares she's mine. My body doesn't care if it's just a front for the sake of this man. It sounds so good on her tongue.

Paulie laughs and it's a cruel sound. Nessa's eyes spark and my own widen as she grabs the man by the scruff of his neck like a misbehaving cub and drags him outside.

None of the others in the bar stop her. They just turn back to their drinks and meals, ignoring us altogether now.

I wonder what usually happens at this place in order for them not to even bat an eye at a woman threatening to cut a man to shit.

Unwilling to be left alone at our table again, I rush after Nessa and into the cold.

20

Nessa

The snivelling excuse for a man falls on the gravel. I've dragged him round the back of the pub, where there's nothing but fields and cows to witness his whimpering.

And Siobhán, who stands shaking against the brick wall, arms crossed and face stony.

"You made a mistake, Paulie," I say in a slow voice, leaning down like I'm speaking to a toddler. "You touched my property."

The man spits onto the gravel as he pushes himself back to his feet. "You crazy cunt-"

He shuts his mouth when he sees my knife. This is why I never walk around unarmed. You never know when you'll have to teach some prick his place.

"The fuck are you doing?" Paulie shuffles backwards but the drink has made him slow and he trips, landing on his arse. I hear Siobhán's unbridled giggle, and warmth pools in my stomach. The familiar rush of adrenaline heats my body as I advance on him, blade held comfortably in my hand.

"You can't stab me! I'll call the Guards, I'll report you, both of you crazy cunts!" To emphasise his point, he fishes his phone out his pocket and holds it up like he's brandishing a weapon.

I tip my head back and cackle. "Go on. Call 'em. Tell them Nessa fucking Tobin has you. See what they do, Paulie. See what they do."

He frowns, a crease forming between his bushy brows. The Guardí won't do fuck all. They stay the fuck away from both the Branigans and us. Seamus and Thomas have bribed them to hell and back. Even if they caught me with my knife buried deep in this prick's bollocks they'd sooner turn their heads and close their eyes than even attempt to slap me with the cuffs.

Too many Guardí have gone missing trying to put a stop to our business for them not to know better.

I watch the confusion contort Paulie's face for a minute before I put him out of his misery. "You heard of Thomas Cavanaugh, Paulie?"

He pales drastically, eyes widening. His throat bobs as he swallows. I hear Siobhán shift on her feet, the crunch of gravel under her, at the mention of his name.

"That's what I thought," I surmise, giving him a wink for effect. You'd have to be living under a fucking rock not to have heard of the two men who own the Goddamn city. "So you're not going to call anyone. You're going to take your punishment, and then you're going to crawl home to lick your wounds, that is if I even decide to spare your pathetic life."

Another gulp. Sweat beads on his hairline.

"Do you want the honour, darlin'?" I call over my shoulder at Siobhán, glancing back at her just in time to see her shaking her head.

I shrug, turning back to the man only to find him scrambling away on all fours. The gravel shifts and scatters under his clumsy limbs and I click my tongue off my teeth in disappointment.

"A coward and a rapist," I say, loud enough for him to hear me. "Which hand was it you grabbed her with? The right, was it?" I know it was. But the look of utter terror on this fuck's face is worth me drawing this out.

"Yes," Siobhán fills in from behind me.

I grin down at Paulie. "Stay nice and still now, won't ya? Or you might lose more than a hand."

He screams but there's no one to hear it, no one to care. I stand on his right hand, flattening his palm against the gravel and holding him in place.

My knife is large, but it still takes a few good *whacks* to sever the hand from the arm entirely.

He's screaming. Siobhán is silent. I'm grinning so hard my face hurts.

"Stop, fuck! Okay, I'm sorry please, *Jesus Christ, stop!"*

Blood spurts from the stump of his arm, pooling around the severed hand. The gravel is soaked with the stuff, and he's pale as fuck already from pain and blood loss.

I'm honestly impressed he hasn't passed out.

I kick the severed limb away from me, disgusted by it and him. "Fuck off out of here before I decide to stop being so kind."

Paulie sobs, clutching the ruined arm to his chest, soaking himself crimson. I wait until he's made it round the front of the building, vaguely hearing another voice cursing before the hum of an engine fills the air. Someone has taken pity on him, it seems.

I feel Siobhán's breath on my neck and spin, finding her so close to me our chests brush together. I steady myself, watching her shiver. I can't tell if it's from the cold or the sight of me spattered in blood.

"You didn't have to do that," she whispers. Her pupils are blown wide, her lips holding the indent of her teeth.

I meet her eyes, cleaning my knife against my thigh before tucking it back into its holster.

"Yes, I did. Nobody hurts you but me."

21

Siobhán

My breaths come in short pants as I watch Nessa tuck the knife back into its holster. I'd rubbed my eyes at the sight of it at first. In all honesty though I shouldn't have been as surprised as I was. I'd yet to see a single person from the Cavanaugh clan unarmed, never mind Nessa, aside from at the gym.

But truth be told, I'd been too preoccupied by the need pulsing through my veins to care much for my surroundings on the drive over. And after the claim she's just made, it'd be a lie to say that that has changed any bit at all.

The idea of being her's is something I want far more than I ever should.

I shouldn't crave her touch. The feel of her lips pressed against mine. The warmth of her hands on my body. The way her voice turns smokey as she's moaning my name.

I shouldn't dream of all the ways I want to make her mine.

My pulse races as our breasts brush together once more, each breath pushing them closer. I fight with every bit of strength I have not to let my eyes drop past her face. To watch her chest rise and fall in rhythm with mine. Her tongue sneaks out to wet her lips, and I feel my own copy the motion, as though it's desperate to chase the taste of her.

Wrapping my hand around Nessa's, I quickly pull her back in the direction of the wall I'd been leaning against earlier.

"We don't need to hide in the shadows, Branigan. It's not like anyone gives a fuck what happens to a spineless bastard like him," she grunts as I quicken my pace.

"We're not hiding because of that," I choke out, my eyes flinging towards her wildly. I give her what I hope is my best sultry smile and pray like hell that she won't think me too crazy for what I'm about to do.

I want her to want me as much as I want her.

I want her to be so caught up with the thought of me that she loses all sense of her surroundings. I want my name to be the only word to pass her lips. My taste to haunt her and my lips to be the last thing she feels before the night is over.

Turning us quickly, I press Nessa against the wall. Taking the clean knife from the twin holster at her back, I bring the sharp edge of it up, resting the tip at her collar bone. The steel glints in the evening sunlight and I feel myself smile wider.

It feels good in my hand, the heavy wooden hilt perfectly balancing the weight of the blade.

Standing here with Nessa pressed against the wall and the knife in my hand I feel powerful. Strong. Like I could take on anything the universe dares to throw at me.

Lifting my gaze I stand statute still as I look at Nessa. Her pupils are blown, barely a hint of her emerald green irises to be found. A light flush stains her cheeks and I can't help but wonder if it's from the cold evening air, or the effect me brandishing a knife is having on her.

Her hair is sleeked back into a perfect pony tail, and all my mind can focus on right now is how much I want to fuck it up.

To fuck her.

"Want a slice of me, darlin'?" Nessa jokes, but as the words hang in the air with no response from me, I catch her brows furrowing. It's almost as if she's genuinely considering whether I'm a threat to her safety or not.

The fact is, she's not wrong.

I do want a piece of her, but what's worse is I want more. I want all of her. I'm just not willing to admit that to Nessa. To say it out loud and confirm the truth.

Because doing so could destroy me.

She's the enforcer to the gang I've been taught to hate. And I'm nothing more than a means to an end for her. A way for her to destroy the Branigans, or so she thinks.

And even though she has the potential to ruin me, and despite all of the weapons training Seamus forced on me, I'm not a threat. Not to her.

Nessa fucking Tobin has gotten under my skin and it seems there's nothing I can do about it.

Ignoring her question, I slowly drag the tip of the blade down from her chest bone to the collar of her shirt. My free hand rises to rest on her hip as I press her firmly against the wall. She moves, but only because she allows me to move her, and for that I'm grateful.

Christ, I shouldn't be feeling like this.

Thankful for being let out of my fucking prison cell.

For being *allowed* to brandish a weapon against my enemy. Against the woman who took me from the life I was trying to build for myself. From any chance of freedom I'll ever have.

And yet as I bring the knife further down, over the lip of her shirt to rest it right above her heart, there's not a single bone in my body urging me to end it. To press the steel between her ribs, clean through to her heart.

Nessa's hand flies up, her fingers deftly curling around my wrist, halting my movements and pulling me from the mess that is my thoughts.

"What do you need, darlin'?" she whispers, her breath caressing my cheek and I shiver at the feel of it.

I swallow dryly as I contemplate how I want to answer. Do I tell her the truth? Do I give her the power to wreck me?

Or do I walk away? Do I dig deep inside of myself to find the hatred that was burning there only days before?

Blood wells as the knife slips by a couple of millimetres and my pulse climbs higher.

My mind whirls with fantasies of Nessa coated in her own blood. My hands slippery from the feel of it and my name carved into her chest.

I feel my pussy flutter and my chest tighten with longing. I know then that I'm in deep shit. Because no matter what happens next, I don't think I can walk away from her.

Come hell or high water, I'm Nessa's and I'm sure as fuck going to make her mine.

22

Nessa

The small cut Siobhán's just marked me with stings slightly, but I ignore it.

I tilt my head to the side as I watch her carefully. Her chocolate eyes are blown wide, her copper curls are tangled again at the back of her head, a few loose strands framing her heart shaped face and an unbridled smile twists her lips. If I didn't know her as well as I do thanks to the days I've had to watch her, I'd say she looks unhinged.

But the glimmer in her eyes tells me a different story. It shows me just how much she's enjoying this. The power she feels at having me pinned against the wall with my own knife pressed against my chest.

The fact that she chose the twin blade to the one I'd used to hack off Paulie's hand hasn't escaped my notice either. It was a calculated move on her part and it's one I can appreciate.

I keep her hand steady as I wait for her to answer me. For her to finally admit what we both know is true. She's been mine from the second I took her. From the moment she ran from that church. As soon as Thomas set me on the hunt to find her there was no escaping me.

Every muscle in my body is pulled taut as the silence stretches between us. The longer we stand here like this, the more turned on I become. Some part of my brain recognises just how fucked that is, but I can't bring myself to care.

If we're going to do this, then she has to answer me.

I need to hear the words. For the words to tumble free from her fuckable lips. For her to give herself to me without restraint.

"You. I need you, Ness," Siobhán whispers, and as her eyes lock onto mine I snap.

Squeezing her wrist, I twist her until her back is pressed against my chest, the knife she'd wielded against me now flush with her throat. I groan as she presses her ass against me, my pussy fluttering with need.

There's no fucking way I can walk away from her. Not like this. Not when she's doing everything she can to drive me insane.

As soon as the thought flits through my head, my mind ungraciously reminds me of the shit I've pulled. Of the call I made to return Siobhán to the Branigans. My stomach twists with distaste as I remember that soon enough I'll have no choice but to leave her.

But it sure as fuck won't be tonight.

Dragging my free hand up, I rest my hand against her throat and smile as my fingers squeeze there beneath the knife. Her pulse sky rockets and I feel it flutter against the pads of my fingers.

"You need me darlin'? Fine. You've got me."

I squeeze her throat once more and feel her sharp inhale at my words.

Christ, she shouldn't be able to mess with me so easily. But just knowing she's wet, needy and dying for me to be the one to make her feel better is enough to undo me.

Moving the hand with the knife in it away from her throat, I holster it against my back while keeping Siobhán firmly pressed against me. My left hand slowly roams downward toward the hem of her hoodie, and I hiss softly as I sneak my fingers beneath it. Her skin is warm, flushed with the same desire driving my every move right now.

Lifting my hand beneath her clothing, I graze my nails against her skin until I reach the swell of her breasts. I groan when I find her perfectly pert nipple, pinching it harshly. A whimper escapes her and I rock my hips forward unconsciously, desperate for any bit of friction I can find.

The seam of my jeans presses against my clit and it takes everything in me not to moan.

"Show me how wet you are for me darlin, I want to see your cum coating your fingers," I hum, my words vibrating against the nape of her neck. I roll my eyes as she shivers, but I'm quick to return my focus to her as she deftly slips her hand inside her leggings.

Her legs buckle as her fingers move beneath the clothing, and my clit pulses, as though it can feel the movement.

"That's it darlin, fuck your hand," I groan as her hips rock forward. Her hand slips further inside her leggings and my right hand circles her neck, squeezing once more. I pinch her nipple again and I can't help the flush that further dampens my underwear as she presses her chest outward, pushing her breast against my hand a little more.

"Show me how soaked you are," I growl, my voice hoarse as she rides her fingers. Mewling softly, she releases her fingers from her pretty pussy and lifts them high enough for me to see.

Her fingers glimmer in the late sunlight and all I can think about is how much I want the taste of her coating my tongue. I want her dripping down my chin, begging for more.

"Let me taste you," I demand. I need her like I need air.

Turning to face me, she brings her fingers up to trace against my lips and my tongue sneaks out immediately lapping up each drop she gives me.

I drag the flat of my tongue along her index and middle fingers, sucking at the tip, chasing every single bit of her arousal.

Christ, she's the sweetest thing I've ever had the pleasure of putting in my mouth.

Her cheeks flush as I suck her fingers a little deeper, and I can't stop the hum of satisfaction that leaves me.

"Strip," I command, my hands bunching in her hoodie. Before she can comply though, I'm dragging the top over her head. Her chest is flushed and her breasts swing softly with each inhale. Her skin pebbles as the cool evening air surrounds her, but if she's feeling anything like I am, it won't do anything to tame her.

She shimmies her leggings and thong down and they tangle around her ankles until she kicks her legs free. Standing there I feel my breasts grow heavy at the sight of her standing naked before me. I graze my knuckle against her hips and delight in the shiver that snakes up her spine at the gentle touch.

"Tell me what you want, darlin'."

"You. Your fingers buried in my cunt. Your cum coating my tongue. Your moans to be the only sound I hear," she replies easily, her voice clear and strong despite how breathless she is. And there isn't a single part of me that can deny her any longer.

Our lips meet in a clash of teeth and tongue, a war for dominance and I immediately press one hand between her legs while cradling the back of her head with the other. My head tips back as I drag my finger through her slit, the slick heat of her coating my hand. *Fuck*, she's dripping. Her knees fold but I caution her with a look as I relentlessly shove two fingers deep into her greedy pussy.

I feel her spasm around my hand and I grin as she lets out a low moan at the pressure. Pumping my fingers in and out, I drag them against her inner walls, hitting the spot I know drives her mad, struggling to keep my control as my underwear grows uncomfortably wet.

"Fuck, don't stop, please don't stop," she begs and I couldn't stop the swell of hunger building in my chest if I wanted to.

Her mouth opens into a perfect O shape as the heel of my hand presses against her clit, grinding it against her. It doesn't take long until she's gyrating against me, lifting her leg to wrap it around my hip.

Moans climb up her throat and I swallow the sound of them as I devour her.

Her cunt tightens and I feel my pulse become erratic as I watch the pleasure contort her features.

Her eyes squeeze shut, her brow pinched with concentration as she chases the high only I can give her and I grunt as her nails dig into my shoulders, but I just move my hand faster.

"Come for me darlin'," I command, dying to see her fall apart for me.

Her lips part on a silent scream as pleasure ravages her body.

Her cunt clamps down on my fingers and I wrap my free arm around her waist as her legs buckle, unable to withstand the orgasm violently coursing through her. Her head tips forward, resting against my shoulder as she heaves in ragged breaths, her nails buried deep in my skin, but I don't stop.

Circling the heel of my palm against her clit, I use the aftershocks of her orgasm to my advantage, pushing her higher and higher. Using her leg wrapped around my hip she drags me closer, and with my arm trapped between us there's nothing I can do but let her wring every drop of pleasure from her body. I move us until my back is firmly planted against the brick wall once more and watch with heat burning in my eyes as she rides my hand. I scissor my fingers once, twice, three times and she falls apart with a scream, my name hanging in the air.

23

Siobhán

My body trembles as I work to withstand the force of the back to back orgasms Nessa's just given me. I'm a whimpering mess as she cradles me against her. Standing in front of her now, completely naked, my cum soaking her hand as she's pressed against the wall I feel completely spent. But I refuse to stop. I won't. Not until she's in the same state as me.

Dropping to my knees, using my discarded leggings as padding against the gravel, I quickly unbuckle her jeans and roughly drag them down her legs. They rest at her ankles, right above her boots, but I make no effort to undo those. I want her caught in my trap, incapable of moving.

I reach forward and tenderly press my lips against the deer skull tattoo, following the lines of the antlers until I reach her bare hip bone. Stretching up, my hand climbs higher and higher until I'm squeezing her breasts through the thin lace material of her bra beneath her shirt. I stroke my thumb over it, feeling the peaked bud beneath, and I feel myself getting wet again. My thighs are coated after the two explosive orgasms

I've just had, but just knowing Nessa is a hot needy mess for me is enough to set me off again.

Grabbing the edge of her underwear with my teeth, I drag my nails down her abdomen as I pull the material between her thighs down.

"Jesus Christ," Nessa curses as her hips raise from the wall to let me pull the thong past her ass. I hold her hips in place with my hands as my teeth let go of the damp material.

Burying my nose in her pussy, I inhale the fresh scent of her arousal. My fingers move to grab the swell of her ass. Pressing myself firmly against her, my tongue peaks out to circle her clit and her hips buck in response.

I look up at her from beneath my lashes and smile as I catch her biting her lip. Sucking her clit into my mouth, I roll my tongue over the sensitive bundle of nerves and moan as she begins to fuck herself against my face.

Her cum drips down my chin and I chase the taste of it, burrowing deeper between her thighs. Gruff moans escape her and I accelerate my pace.

I lift one of my hands from her ass and rest it at her opening, teasing her with feather light touches.

"Fuck me, darlin'. Do it," she commands and I follow her order like the good girl I am.

I bury two fingers in her pussy, and give her no time to adjust to the feel of me. Jackhammering my fingers inside her, I increase my efforts and nip and lick her clit, swirling my tongue like she's my saviour and I'm on my knees worshipping her the only way I know how.

Her pussy tightens around my digits and I know that she's close to coming, but I don't want her to yet. Not until she admits that she's mine.

I pull my fingers free from her cunt and smirk at her when she groans with disappointment. I press a gentle kiss to the swollen bud in front of me before resting back on my heels.

"What the fuck are you doing?" Nessa snarls, her anger heightened by the need driving her.

"Say you're mine and I'll let you come," I order, my voice thick with power. I've never felt stronger than I do now, controlling her pleasure. Not even wielding her knife against her earlier compares to this.

"Jesus Christ, Branigan," she hisses and I feel her muscles lock as she starts to move but I pin her in place with my arms.

She might want to run, but I've got her trapped in my snare. The only way free is for her to fucking admit the truth.

"No."

Without a second thought, I raise my hand and slap her pussy. The resounding *smack* lingers in the air between us and I arch a brow when I see her sink her teeth into her bottom lip.

I soften the sting from the blow by pressing gentle kisses to her flushed skin, moving closer and closer to her clit once more. I hover above her pussy, blowing cool air against her pebbled skin.

"Say it Nessa, or I'll leave you like this. Writhing in need, clawing for my touch, a mess between your thighs," I coo, my lips trailing open mouthed kisses along the smooth skin on the inside of her thighs.

She shivers as I reach the apex of her thighs and lick once along her slit.

"You wouldn't dare." Anger burns in her eyes but I just chuckle.

Every move I've ever made has been decided by someone

else. By my father, his men, and now Nessa. Each one got to decide when I sleep, when I shower, when I eat, hell even when I breathe. But this? Her pleasure? My consent? These are mine to control.

Sensing how serious I am she drags the knife from the hilt still tied to her back, and points it in my direction. If she thought it would serve to scare me, she's wrong. There are many things about Nessa that terrify me, but her brandishing a knife in my direction isn't one of them. Not anymore. Not when I know that she needs me alive. Could she physically hurt me? Sure. But I'll survive it, and nothing she does to me with that knife could ever hurt more than the way she's going to inevitably break my heart.

"Tell me you're mine," I try again, my hand lifting to wrap around her wrist. The irony of the situation isn't lost on me. Just minutes before she was the one halting me from harming her with the same sharpened steel.

Releasing the knife, Nessa curses beneath her breath and I feel my smile widen. The handle falls perfectly into the palm of my hand and I clutch it firmly.

"I'm yours." I barely hear her words as she whispers them between clenched teeth, and if I hadn't been watching her I'm not sure I would have ever noticed her speaking.

She might not want to say it aloud, with her heart behind it just yet, but she will soon. I'll make sure of it.

Taking her defeat for what it is, she rests her head against the brick wall and exhales shakily.

"Good girl," I praise, my free hand soothing her now shaking legs with a firm massage working its way upward.

With a far more gentle touch this time, I ease a finger back inside her swollen cunt. I move it in a *come hither* motion and watch as the line between her brow relaxes and her mouth loosens with relief. I swallow reflexively at the sight of her cum coating my fingers and drop my lips back to her clit. I press delicate kisses there, my tongue caressing her with each brush of my lips.

"Please don't stop again," Nessa pleads, her hips rolling to match my movement.

"Keep being a good girl and I won't," I promise, adding a second finger to her dripping pussy.

"Oh God," Nessa hums, her hips moving faster as I pick up the pace once more. When I feel she's finally relaxed enough I pull my fingers free and replace them with the handle of her knife before she can complain.

"Jesus fuck, are you nuts?" Nessa shouts as she realises what is now placed between her thighs. If I didn't know Nessa liked to live on the edge I'd never have the balls to do this, but the silky tone of her voice tells me she loves it as much as I do.

"No crazier than you. You had no issue pressing a knife to my pussy not too long ago," I say, pushing the handle deeper inside of her. I hold the blade firm, careful not to cut my hand on its edge as I pull it free slowly before pushing it back inside of her.

Her knees widen as she tries to spread her legs further apart, but her jeans stop her before she can stretch them completely.

"Fuck, that feels good darlin'," she hums, licking her lips as she swallows thickly.

My hand slips as she gruffly grabs my hair and presses my face flush against her pelvis. I hiss at the swell of blood now dripping down my palm from the stinging cut, but I don't stop.

Licking her from clit to slit, I stop at the feel of the hilt and circle my tongue around it as I pull it out.

"Christ, you're going to make me come if you keep doing that," she breathes and I shiver at the thought of her exploding on my tongue. Fuck yes.

With renewed vigour I press my tongue inside her, stretching her further and pushing her closer to her breaking point.

"Come for me Nessa. Let me make you mine," I command before pressing my tongue deep inside her. It takes a little manoeuvring so as not to cut my face with the blade, but even if I did, it's a scar I'd wear with pride. Shit, at this point I want her name fucking branded on me.

I freeze slightly at the thought. I can't allow myself to think like that.

While we both know that we want each other, that there's more brewing between us than explosive sex, I can't let her have any more pieces of me than I'm willing to give. And her branding me is far more than I can afford to let her have, at least not until I know that I can truly trust her.

Brushing my thoughts to the back of my mind, I return my focus to Nessa, giving her every ounce of my attention. I lick her fully again, sucking at her sensitive flesh I go and continue to fuck her with the handle of her knife.

"Oh fuck, oh God, I'm coming, I'm-"

"Say my name Ness. Let me know who you belong to," I demand, my words crisp in the fresh air.

I watch with rapture as her mouth parts and she screams my name. Her head tilts back, her breasts press forward and her whole body spasms with the force of her orgasm. I wince slightly as she tugs at the roots of my hair, but I ignore the pain and focus on seeing her through her climax. When she starts to tremble violently, I slow my movements and let her come back from what's sure to be one of the hottest fucking things I've ever seen.

Nessa angry is a sight to behold, but Nessa coming is a fucking work of art.

"Holy shit," Nessa gasps and I feel pride bloom inside of my chest.

Bringing her hand down to meet my face, she caresses my cheek while slowly dragging her thumb across my chin, collecting the mess she's made on me. My tongue flies out for a final time, lapping at the taste of her as she brings her thumb up to my lips.

I stand on shaky legs, gritting my teeth as my knees click. Red, stone shaped indents cover them despite the barrier of my balled up leggings but I don't mind. My knees very well might be black and blue by tomorrow and my palm scabbed and aching, but it'll be fucking worth it for hearing the two words I'd hunted.

I'm yours.

There's every chance that she said it without believing it, but Nessa Tobin will be mine before this is all over. Because this woman has buried herself in my chest so deep she's become a part of me. And whether she likes it or not, I'm not willing to lose any more of myself.

24

Nessa

My phone rings and I start, then curse myself for being so unfocused. I dart into the nearest bathroom, considering the house is busier than usual with Thomas calling a meeting, and in here, I can lock the door. I was purposefully *not* invited to the meeting, and part of me wants to break something in retaliation.

Everything Thomas does is calculated. As his best enforcer, I should have been there. As his best enforcer, I should be doing more than babysitting Siobhán. I can't fathom what I've done to make him exclude me from the briefing.

The idea that he knows what I'm planning, or - worse - what I did to Siobhán, makes me want to be sick.

There's no way he knows. He never said I couldn't train the girl, and there was nobody in the gym or at the back of the pub when I fucked her. It was reckless, stupid, and yet I can't bring myself to regret it.

As for the plan I set in motion...I'm counting on him being too distracted to snoop on me, as well as banking on it being too late if he does find out before I pull it off.

I force my mind to clear as I swipe *accept* on the call. It's an unsaved number, but I recognise it immediately.

I say nothing, choosing to wait for him to speak.

"The little traitor doesn't want to talk?" His words rumble deceptively with laughter.

Anger clogs my throat, the sound of his voice making my teeth grit. I despise this man to my very core.

I'm not a fucking traitor. I'm doing this *for* my family. I'm doing this because Thomas is acting like a fucking idiot.

But I don't say this to Seamus. "What do you want?"

The laughter is gone entirely when he answers. "My daughter."

I inhale deeply, trying to keep my breaths even. Until now, I've spoken to his rats, but clearly they've decided the reward of their lost princess is worth the risk of me speaking to their beloved asshole.

"Let's say, hypothetically of course, that I have her. What would you be willing to give me in return?" I hum, pushing his buttons as much as I can. We both know I do, in fact, have Siobhán, but without proof he's up shit's creek without a paddle. There's no way he can order his men to barge into our holding. Not when we're killing them like flies already. Every business they have has been shot to shit in the last few days. A couple of the rats managed to sneak into our warehouses last night, but before they could even think of taking the guns we run, we caught and killed them too.

Like flies with honey they just keep coming, and there's nothing sweeter than the feel of Branigan blood staining my hands.

"Listen here you little cunt. I don't owe you a fucking thing. Tell me where she is so I can handle the bitch myself. I'll skin her alive for causing this mess."

Words fail me as I listen to the venom spew from his mouth and out the receiver of my phone.

"I'm just trapped in another mob house. New people, same shit."

Siobhán's words hit me like a tonne of bricks as I suddenly remember the conversation she had with Sebastian not too long ago. A renewed sense of rage boils my blood and I clench and unclench my free hand in an active effort not to slam the phone against the wall.

Fuck, I'm no better than this bastard. I've treated her terribly since we caught her. I locked her up and threw away the key only to use her like she's my personal plaything anytime we've been around each other.

But I had no choice. I still don't.

I cannot allow Thomas to continue this war. Good people are dying, and all because he wants to play the long game. I can't allow it. Half my job as the enforcer is to protect this family. To ensure that nobody fucks with us. To stop the damage from spreading any more than it has to, and if I have to be the one to cause the damage to stop the carnage, then so be it.

I can't stomach the realisation that I'm turning my back on Thomas, not after all he's done for me. But the thought of letting him burn us from the inside out is even worse.

"What's to say she's even alive?" I goad, desperate for him to feel even a hint of the rage that's consuming me. I move the phone away from my ear and roll my eyes to the heavens as a string of expletives comes bursting through the speaker. No wonder Siobhán wasn't happy, the prick is unhinged.

"Jesus fuck, settle down would you. I've got the girl, but if you want her you're gonna have to do something for me first,"

I hiss, keeping an eye on the bathroom door. Anxiety coats my skin with a thin sheen of sweat as I lower my voice and ask him for the one thing I never thought I'd need.

"I need information on Thomas Cavanaugh." The words taste like bile. They burn coming out, but I have to know what he's planning. He's shut me out for so long now I can't help but feel like something horrible is heading my way, and I refuse to be unprepared. I can't live like that again.

I can't spend every second of my day looking over my shoulder wondering who's going to stab me in the back next.

It's different this time. You're not helpless anymore, I remind myself while taking a deep breath as I settle my nerves. Fuck, I hate Thomas for doing this to me. For making me feel like the lost little girl I was when he found me on the street corner digging through rubbish for food. Every inch of me was coated in grime and God knows what else. I'd spent countless nights sleeping beneath park benches or behind restaurant dumpsters, too afraid to be left completely uncovered. Too aware of the monsters that lurk in the dark.

Years of adults walking past me with disgust on their faces as they looked at me. Horrified by my presence, as though I'd set out to purposefully ruin the view of the city they claimed to love. Not once did any of them ever approach me to see if I was okay with good intentions. To ask if I needed food, water, medical treatment or even a couch to crash on. I was alone. Left to fend for myself, and defend myself against the men who deemed themselves worthy of owning my body without my permission. Who took pleasure in using me against my will. Over and over again, until Thomas.

He was the first man to approach me in years and not immediately assume that my body was for hire. The first man to respect my boundaries. To give me a chance. To teach me to grab life by the balls and make it my bitch.

I owe him my life.

And yet, I feel like this is the only way to stick by the lessons he taught me. Betraying him to save him is my only choice.

"What do you want to know?" Seamus asks, dragging me back from my memories. My skin crawls with disgust at the onslaught of memories I've just faced, but I push it down and press on.

"Everything. I want to know what he's planning, the skeletons hidden in his closet and hell if it helps me, you can even tell me each time he fucking shits. But you're not getting the girl until you give me this."

Laughter hits my ears, echoing off the walls outside the bathroom door and I curse myself mentally for being stupid enough to have taken the call inside the house.

Twisting behind me I turn the gaudy gold tap on the sink until the pipes rattle and water gushes out. I pray the sound will be enough to cover my voice.

"Are you done?" I snap, fed up with this bastard.

"Ahhhh Nessa Tobin, Thomas' right hand, turning coat. Never thought I'd see the day. Christ, Thomas would have a fucking conniption if he heard 'bout this," Seamus chuckles and it takes everything in me not to scream.

It's one thing to fight the knowledge alone, it's another to hear your enemy say it out loud.

"Give me what I asked and I'll get you the girl," I spit, desperate to finish this godforsaken conversation.

"Done. You'll have what you want in the next hour, rat."

I see red as the final word drips from his lips. Like fuck am I one of his lackeys. But I simply hang up, too angry to respond.

My knuckles whiten as my grip on the phone tightens. My pulse echoes in my ears and I can barely catch my breath. I need to get the fuck out of here before I break. I need to get to the gym, hit the bags and burn off the rage coursing through my veins.

Settling the phone on the counter, I flex my fingers, desperate to shake off the violence calling to me before cupping the icy water flowing from the tap in my hand. I rinse my face with it a few times before I settle enough to take a full breath. Turning off the tap, I dry my hands and head towards the door. Twisting the lock, I swing it open and startle as I find Sebastian on the other side.

He towers over me, his brow lowered and his arms crossed over his broad chest. Shit, how long has he been standing there?

"We need to talk," he hisses, his words clipped and laced with anger.

Fuck.

25

Nessa

My life would be so much fucking easier if I'd never met Siobhán fucking Branigan.

A heavy, writhing sensation has taken up residence in my stomach as Sebastian glares daggers at me, anger radiating from him. In the ten years we've been friends, I've never seen him this upset with me, and I don't like the way it's making my skin crawl.

After leaving the bathroom, he'd followed me back to my room, hissing insults at me the entire fucking way. The second the door was closed though he'd let rip. He hadn't been short on letting me know just how much of a *fucking idiot* I am, or how he hopes like hell I have my ass handed to me for being thick enough to betray the family like this.

"-even think about what kind of shit this would bring down on the rest of us? You're such a selfish fuck-"

Sick of his shit, I cut off his tirade with a harsh glare.

"What the fuck was I supposed to do, Seb?" I snap, throwing my arms in the air.

"Listen when Thomas tells you to *watch* her not *give her*

back!"

"Why do you care?" I have to restrain myself so I don't shout. The last thing we need is someone overhearing us. "This is the best thing for us. They get their princess back in return for leaving us the fuck alone!"

"It's not your deal to make!" Sebastian's voice rises before he clenches his jaw and lowers his tone. "And fuck knows what her father will do to her."

"She'll be fine. She needs to leave." The words taste like ash, and no matter how much I like her, it's still the truth.

"Why, Nessa? Tell me, why are you so fucking desperate to get her out of here when you have no idea if she'll even survive Seamus after what she did?" His eyes bore into mine, the blue burning into me."Oh, I know, you're fucking terrified that you care about her. Would that *really* be the worst thing ever? For you, the almighty Nessa fucking Tobin to give a shit about someone?" Sarcasm drips from his words. He knows how I feel about her. Sometime in the last few days he's managed to figure it out. But I can't afford to say it outloud. Not to him.

"I don't give a shit about her." My throat aches with the lie.

He laughs, but the sound is cold. "Do you often cut off the hands of men for touching people you don't give a shit about? 'Cause if so, you sure as fuck didn't give me the memo on that!"

I freeze, chest rising and falling rapidly as I try to regain some sense of control. "It's done, Sebastian. Leave it be."

"For fuck's sake, Ness! Listen-"

"It's *done.*"

"I'll tell Thomas."

His words land like a blow and all I can think to do is hit him. I get as far as raising my hand before I pull back, stumbling a few steps away.

Glaring in his direction, I assess how serious he is about this. He wouldn't. He fucking *can't*. Thomas can't know that I've gone against him. He'd slaughter me just for thinking of it and Sebastian knows that.

The threat hurts though. I refuse to admit it.

I meant what I said. It's done and there's no way to reverse the damage that's already been made. There's someone on their way for her. Obviously, I didn't give them our location, but when they'd emailed me the file on Thomas I'd sent them coordinates for the drop point. If I don't turn up to meet them then no doubt the war will only worsen.

We've already had the Branigans slaughter fifteen of our men, some of them in ways even Sebastian wouldn't go so far as to do. We can't lose any more. I can't lose any more.

"Sebastian." I don't know what else to say. His name is just the first thing to come to my mind when I need someone.

"Talk to Siobhán, Nessa. She doesn't deserve this. You know that. I know that. Get your head out of your arse and think about someone else for once."

I reel. "She doesn't need to know. She's a prisoner, for fuck's sake, not a guest."

"Jesus fucking Christ," Sebastian despairs, and I want to grab onto him and make him see sense.

"I'm doing this for our own good!"

"*Your* own good!" he counters, tugging at his hair in exasperation. "I love you, Nessa. But you can't chase away your feelings by getting rid of the girl."

My fists clench at my sides. There's a hundred words in my throat but none of them are right. None of them mean what I want them to.

How do I say that I'm angry and guilty and fucking *disgusted*. How do I say that the thought of Siobhán staying here for any longer makes me want to dig my heart out of my chest just to make it stop begging for her.

How do I say that I hate myself, that I don't know what the fuck I'm even fighting for anymore but I can't stop fighting nonetheless.

"Tell her what you've done, Nessa, or I'll tell her. You can't do this."

"Don't."

"Go. I'm not bluffing, Ness."

I know he's not. Sebastian doesn't bullshit anyone. He commits to every bloody idea inside his head with his whole being. He doesn't know how not to fall in love with everyone he sees. He doesn't know how to hold any part of himself back.

I also know that he's right.

He steps into my space, hand on my shoulder, and pushes. I let the momentum guide me backwards, until I'm turning and walking away, leaving my best friend glaring daggers at my back.

I don't intend to go to her room.

I find myself outside her door anyway.

"Nessa?" Siobhán's voice is surprised and sweet as I push the door open.

She's sitting cross legged on her bed, the sheets pulled up over her lap, and a book in her hands. I recognise the title as one Sebastian was reading a few months ago, and the knowledge that he's gifted it to her makes my stomach tighten.

There's a pile of folded clothes at the end of her bed, and a few scrunched up in a corner that I assume are dirty. Her hair is loose around her face, and the dim lighting makes it look darker than it is. Her red brows pinch together as she waits for me to say something.

I can't.

The door falls closed behind me. Siobhán sets the book down and tilts her head, pursing her lips as confusion crosses her face. Fuck me, does she have to be so damn *gorgeous?*

"Nessa?" she repeats, pulling back the covers and stretching her legs out. "What's wrong?"

I'm striding towards her before I can stop myself, the heat in my blood rising and rising until I swear I'm going to burn her when I grab her and pull her to me.

She gasps, her lips opening and eyes widening as she falls against me. I tighten my grip on her, one hand on her neck, the other on her waist and before she can ask me anything again, I kiss her.

I kiss her like she can fix the mess I've made of myself.

She kisses me back like she just might.

26

Nessa

"Tell me I can fuck you," I murmur against her mouth, shaking with restraint. I'm trying to be good. I'm asking nicely.

Siobhán chuckles, her tongue darting out to trace my bottom lip. I swear to God I almost lose it and shove her against the shitty bed and bury my face between her legs right then.

"How nice of you to ask," she teases, her hand slipping beneath my shirt. She leans closer and her lips skim the shell of my ear when she whispers. "Fuck me like you hate me, Nessa."

My self control vanishes. I grab her, lifting her by her ass and making her wrap her legs around my waist. Immediately, she melts against me, sighing into my mouth as her lips meet mine desperately. Her tongue meets mine, the soft, silky warmth making me groan. I move, pressing her back to the stone wall so I can touch her better. Her thighs tighten around me and need pools in my core. I want those thighs around my head. I want her grinding against my face. I want her cum on my tongue.

I want to drown in her. I want to forget everything else exists except her taste.

I begin to slide my hand under her hoodie, and the second my skin meets hers, she pants, pulling away from me just to tear her clothes off. The hoodie falls to the floor in a heap, and I think I die when I realise she's bare underneath. With her braced against me like she is, I have perfect access to them. I cup one with my free hand, tracing my thumb over her nipple, squeezing her sensitive flesh as her head hits the stone on a moan.

Leaning down, I trace the path my thumb had taken with my tongue, catching her peaked nipple between my teeth. She arches sharply, pressing herself closer and I repeat the motion, harder this time. Her hips buck against my waist.

"Little pain slut," I mutter against her chest, adjusting to give her other breast the same treatment.

"I'm so wet for you," she says, voice needy. And fuck me, so am I. I'm too desperate to tease her, tease us, anymore.

"Legs on my shoulders," I tell her, dropping to my knees in front of her. She bites her bottom lip, her hair a red, tangled mane from my hands, her cheeks flushed. I don't think I've ever seen anything as beautiful.

Siobhán terrifies me.

I'm addicted.

She pushes her waistband down, and I grab the fabric and tug it off the rest of the way. Then she's naked in front of me, and I forget how to breathe. The pale, thick expanse of her thighs makes me want to bite her, to dig my fingers into her flesh and see how prettily she'll bruise for me. I skim my palm down her soft stomach, feeling her shudder under my uncharacteristically kind touch. My hand reaches the patch of curls between her legs, then lower, dipping between her thighs to find her dripping. She bucks against my hand like a needy little slut.

"Legs on my shoulders. Don't make me tell you again."

I want to ruin her and I want her to beg me to do it. I want to touch every inch of her body, want to make her come until she can't remember her own name.

This time, she obeys, hooking her knee over my shoulder and exposing her glistening pussy to me. I grab her ass again to support her weight as she repeats the motion with her left leg, trapping me between her legs.

I'm practically fucking drooling as I take her in.

She looks down at me with a wariness in her eyes that I hate. I glare up at her in warning before giving us both what we want. Self indulgently, I lick slowly from her cunt to her clit, lapping at her so her taste fills my mouth.

"Fuck me, I could get drunk on how sweet you taste." I squeeze her ass, digging my fingers in until she sucks in a sharp breath and only then do I lick her again. "Stay still for me like a good girl and I'll let you come."

She whimpers, and I can see how wet she gets at my words. She's as desperate for this as I am. I can't stop myself from devouring her any longer.

I press myself as close to her as I can get, dipping my tongue inside her cunt. She flutters around me, and I know I'm not giving her enough. I torture her for a few seconds more before the need to have her fall apart on me is too great to bear. I return my attention to her clit, scraping my teeth over the swollen, sensitive spot. Siobhán makes a strangled sound that has me moaning against her and sucking her clit between my lips.

It doesn't take long for her thighs to tighten around my face, for her to curse and the sound of nails on stone mix with our moans as she scrambles for grip on something to anchor her.

"Fuck, oh *fuck*, Ness-"

She comes with my name on her tongue and I shift, uncomfortably turned on. I don't stop, even as her cum drips from my lips. Even when she squirms in my hold and her breath catches, I can't stop.

"More, darlin'," I say, mouth still pressed to her. "Give me more."

"Can't," she gasps, her thighs clutching me so tightly I can barely hear her.

I nip at the sensitive flesh at the crease of her thigh. My words come out in a growl. "I am not done, Branigan, so yes you fucking can."

I force another orgasm from her before I set her down again and stand.

She's shaking, her eyes glassy with tears as she stares up at me. I go to move us towards her bed, because I'll be damned if I don't have her coming for me again tonight, but the sight of the single bed and thin mattress sends anger flaming through the haze of lust.

Reluctantly, I snatch her discarded hoodie off the floor and shove it over her head. She frowns at me, her red brows pulling together and her teeth find her bottom lip.

"I'm fucking you in a proper bed," I tell her, revelling in her squeal when I grab her and hold her to me. She clings to me, legs around my waist and arms looped around my neck, giggling. I adjust her carefully so her ass is covered because like fuck am I having anyone seeing her but me.

She buries her face in my neck and I fight the urge to bite the pale sliver of throat exposed by a gap in her hair.

Quickly, I carry her out of her pathetic excuse for a room, hating myself until the door swings shut with a bang behind me. The soft weight of her in my arms has warmth blooming behind my ribs.

I shift, the sensation uncomfortable. I rush up the stairs, finding the hallways pleasantly empty as I take us toward my room. I'm sure Thomas has called some other bullshit meeting that I've not been summoned to.

For once, I don't care.

I don't want to be anywhere else but here.

My foot connects with the solid wood of my bedroom door, sending it swinging open for us. I sweep us inside, giving into the temptation of her throat as I lock the door behind us. My teeth scrape against her soft flesh and she shudders in my hold.

I refuse to set her down until we're on the bed and I'm crawling over her. It's dark, given that I didn't stop to turn on any lights and the curtains are drawn, but my eyes adjust quickly.

"Stay there," I warn her and she gives me that pleading look that wrecks my self control.

"Why?" she whines, squirming and making the duvet twist under her.

"Because I want to see that pretty cunt stretch around my strap."

I hear her gasp a little as I step to the side, reaching under the bed for the bag I keep my toys in. I find what I'm looking for, standing quickly and slipping it on. I adjust the harness around my hips, securing the strap to my body.

"Fuck," Siobhán murmurs when I turn back to her, eyes glued to the toy between my legs. It's purple silicone, long and thick.

"Spread those thighs for me, darlin', that's it."

Her knees fall to the side, exposing her soaking cunt. I groan at the sight, at the glistening arousal on her thighs, at the way she squirms, sinking her teeth hard into her bottom lip.

"Are you going to be a good girl for me and let me fuck your pretty pussy?" I ask her as I crawl on to the bed, stopping on my knees between hers.

I lean forward, swiping two fingers through her centre, slipping them briefly inside her. She spreads her legs wider for me, opening herself fully, leaning up on her elbows to watch me touch her. Her breath shudders through her, her muscles shaking as she tries to obey me and let me touch her.

"Yes, fuck, yes, I'll be good, I promise," she says in a rush as I withdraw my hand again. "Please, it *aches*, Nessa. Fuck me."

I could listen to her plead all day and never grow tired of it. The way she moans my name, the way she swears on an exhale like she can't help the desperation in her body.

I wrap my hand around the strap, coating the length in her cum. Her eyelids are heavy as she watches the movement, long lashes lowered and mouth parted.

I slip my hands under her ass, lifting her hips up to angle her cunt before the tip of my toy. Her arms collapse and she falls back to the bed, head pressed into the sheets as she arches perfectly for me. I watch, fixated, as I slip it inside her. She moans, pushing back against me, and I grip her ass harder, helping her work herself onto the toy until it's fully seated inside her.

"Fuck," I curse as I stare down at her. "Look at you, taking it so well. Such a good fucking girl, darlin'."

She moans loudly, hands clawing at the sheets, as I begin to fuck her in earnest. She's on the edge in seconds, given that I'd left her wanting before, crying out as I thrust into her brutally.

"Nessa," she cries out in a sob, her legs shaking. I know that she needs to come, but selfishly, I want to keep her like this, writhing and wet and begging.

"Soon, darlin'," I promise, reluctantly letting go of her ass to hold myself over the top of her, lowering my head to suck on her peaked nipple. More perfect noises spill from her lips as I fuck her hard, biting at her breast to send her pleasure spiralling higher. She likes the pain, demands it, and I'm all too happy to give in to her.

"I need to come," she gasps, her face flushed and her skin shining with a fine sheen of sweat. I lick my way up her throat and nip at her jaw.

"Go on then," I taunt a little, reaching between us and feeling for her clit. I pinch the swollen bud between my fingers, and she sobs. "Give me one more like the good girl you are," I whisper in her ear, repeating the motion as I thrust deep.

She shatters with a loud moan, stiffening beneath me as her orgasm draws her under. I memorise the way her face scrunches up, the way her mouth opens, how her hands reach for me instinctively.

I fuck her through it, only withdrawing from her body when she's limp and gasping.

"Nessa," Siobhán gasps as I stand, loosening the straps at my waist and stepping out of the harness. I turn to her, finding her watching me, staring at my body like she's trying to commit it to memory. "Let me touch you, *please*." Her last word comes out as a whine.

I can't fucking help myself. I climb back into bed, curling myself over the top of her, my hand finding her pussy again, gently pressing a finger into her just to feel her clench around me as she tries to recover from her orgasm.

She's so fucking *soft*.

I don't answer her plea and she doesn't ask again. My head falls, my forehead pressing against hers. We're close enough to kiss, but I hold back, watching her lips open on a sharp inhale as I thrust my finger harder, curling to find her g spot. Her hips jerk, and her eyes snap shut.

"Open," I snap, fucking her harder as punishment. I know she must be sore by now, but I can't stop. "Look at me when you soak my hand."

My thumb finds her clit as she forces her eyes back open, the deep brown depths threatening to swallow me whole. Her hands clutch at my hair, holding me to her, as if terrified I'll stop.

"Too sensitive, *fuck*," she says as I circle her clit with firm strokes, but she's grinding against me, forcing my fingers further inside her. "Nessa, it's so much."

"This cunt is greedy for everything I'll give it," I answer, my voice raspy with need. "And I will decide when you've had enough, do you understand?"

She whimpers, eyelashes fluttering as she fights to obey my command to keep her eyes on mine. Her fingers tuck at my hair at the nape of my neck, and I groan at the sharp sting of pain.

Her pussy flutters around my fingers, wetness dripping onto my palm, and her hips lose their rhythm as she desperately rides my hand. I know she's close, and I sit back on my heels, grinning down at her affronted expression.

"I want to watch this pretty cunt cry for me," I tell her, pinching her clit with my free hand and continuing the furious rhythm. I should be gentler, I should be kinder, but the more I hurt her, the more she begs for it.

She falls over the edge with wide eyes, back arching off the sheets, her cunt clutching at my fingers as her orgasm rips through her. Siobhán's cum covers my hand and when I ease my fingers from her pussy, they're slick and shiny.

I raise them to my mouth and suck off her taste. She's panting, limp against my bed, thighs damp and still spread for me. The sheets beneath her are damp, the dark spot making me grin.

I could touch her for hours. I want to, I realise. My mind wars against the idea of removing her from my bed.

Ever.

But she's tired - her eyes half lidded and her body spent. So instead, I say, "come on, let's shower."

Siobhán looks surprised. "I'm tired." She says it simply, but there's a tension to her voice that tugs at something inside me.

"You can sleep after," I reassure her.

"It's so cold in the basement," she whines, and I can hear her swallow in the silence that follows.

I try to get air into my lungs but the guilt is wrapped tight around my chest like a snake. "So stay here." Then, remembering myself, I add, "just for tonight."

Her hopeful expression shutters, and she looks away from me as she nods. I pretend I don't feel like I'm dying slowly as she shuts the door to the bathroom behind her and the sound of the shower reaches me.

I wait on the bed until she comes back out, wrapped in my towel. Neither of us speaks, but I pull back the covers in a silent plea for her to get in bed. She pads over to me, pausing in front of me and frowning down at where I'm sitting.

"I don't understand you Nessa," she whispers, like she can't decide if she meant to say that out loud or not.

"I don't either," I tell her, before she sheds the towel and climbs into my bed naked.

I don't bother fighting the urge to join her. Silently, I wrap her in my arms and clutch her soft, warm body to mine. I'll tell her what I've done tomorrow. In the morning. After coffee.

Right now, I hold her like I'll fade away without her touch. I hold her like I'm not sure of anything else in the world but her right now. I hold her and I don't want to let her go.

I will. I'll let her go tomorrow. I'll tell her in the morning.

27

Siobhán

It's morning when I wake, and I'm shocked at how well I've slept. A small, persistent ray of weak sunlight has crept through a tiny gap between Nessa's dark curtains, giving me just enough light to see. I'm warm and cosy and I wonder how long I can pretend to sleep so I can stay tucked up in Nessa's tight embrace. It feels like a guilty pleasure. I'm sure she'll wake and push me away, though the thought hurts.

Careful not to move, I survey her room. It's large, but oddly cosy. The curtains are black and floor length, like she's tried to block out the outside world out completely. There's a wooden chair in the corner by the door, currently doubling as the base of a mountain of clothes. A small bookcase holding about five books and a bunch of trinkets - a toy gun that I can only imagine Sebastian buying her - and a few random keyrings and coins. The door to the attached bathroom is on the right, and on that same wall is a modest wardrobe. The only other furniture is the bedside table.

Though her room is relatively sparse, it feels like her. The rumpled black fluffy blanket that's been squished to the end of the bed, the coffee cup that reads *don't talk to me until this is empty* left on a shelf of the bookcase, even the Goddamned knife tucked into the shelf of the bedside table.

And fuck, is her bed comfortable.

The door opens with a rush and suddenly there's a man in the doorway shouting, "Morning!"

I start, and Nessa's hands slide away from me. I mourn the loss, but keep my mouth shut.

I'm not attached. I can't be attached. Fuck, *don't get attached.*

Sebastian's eyes grow wide as he takes me in and I'm thankful I'm still hidden by the covers. A sly, knowing smile pulls at his lips. Nessa groans beside me, fumbling for something to throw at him.

A laugh bubbles in my throat.

"I see we're all nice and cosy in here," Sebastian teases. Then, to a groggy Nessa he says, "I'm glad she didn't stab you. Cleaning up your blood would've been a new low, even for me."

Nessa goes very still, and confusion pools in my veins.

"Why would I stab her?" I mean sure, there's the whole kidnapping thing but really all she did was make me safer than I'd have been anywhere else. And while I don't appreciate the basement, I do understand why she did what she did. I was - am - her enemy.

And I've done a lot worse to my father's enemies before.

"Sebastian no-" Nessa starts, but he's already talking.

"Oh because of the whole selling your location to your da thing," he says so casually that it takes me a minute to process what he's saying. "But clearly you guys worked it out. Hate sex is the best sex anyway."

All the warmth seeps out of me and suddenly I don't give a

shit that I'm naked, I'm pulling away from Nessa's reach and sitting up. I snatch a pillow and hold it over my chest as dread rips me to shreds inside.

"You didn't," I breathe, and the words are so faint I worry the air will carry them away.

But Nessa's sitting up now, her pyjamas wrinkled and her hair tangled. Her eyes are still barely open, and there's a crease mark on her cheek from the sheets.

"Siobhán," is all she says.

It's the first time she's called me by my name.

And suddenly, it's all so clear to me. I have made a lot of mistakes in my life.

Trusting Nessa Tobin has been the worst one of all.

I scramble, and Sebastian curses but it sounds like he's underwater. Everything is blurry at the edges, and my fingers fumble with the sleeves of my hoodie. It barely covers my modesty but I refuse to borrow anything of Nessa's. My hair tangles around my face as I tug the hood over my head and the cherry scent of her shampoo greets me.

My stomach hurts. I might be sick.

"Tell me it's not true," I try, rocking on my feet. Nessa's frozen, nothing in her expression except defeat.

I've never seen her stripped so bare.

I don't like what I see.

I want to scream.

"Ah shit," Sebastian sighs, and I hear the floor creak a little as he steps away from the disaster he's created.

No. The disaster *Nessa's* created. The disaster I created by being a hopeful, stupid little slut. There's a ringing in my ears.

He knows where I am.

He *knows* where I am.

He knows, he knows, he knows -

"Darlin', listen to me-"

"No." I think I might be shouting. "No. Leave me alone." She reaches from me, her hand a blur of outstretched fingers and a hopeful palm. "Don't fucking touch me!"

I stumble backwards, tripping over my own two feet, the world tipping on its axis. The sky is falling around me. The floor is ripping itself apart under my feet. I can't find my balance. I can't tell which way is up.

I fumble blindly for the door. My body doesn't feel real. My hand slams into a wall, catching myself on instinct just before I fall, and pain shoots through my wrist at the impact.

I anchor onto the pain like a lifeline. Without it, I'm drowning, sinking and realising with a horrible, aching blow that I don't know how to swim at all. That all my practice treading water was for nothing. I'm out of my depth and there is no shore.

Still, I manage to find the door. Manage to tip myself out of it. Manage to find the stairs and descend without falling.

I manage. Isn't that what I always do?

28

Siobhán

It's pissing it down with rain and though I'm pressed against the ivy covered stone of the manor house, I'm soaked through. I barely feel the cold, though my breath is misting in front of my face. It's nearly winter and the weather in Ireland is a moody bitch - lashing rain and bitter wind that I should be used to by now but every year without fail, I'm surprised by its ferocity.

I considered stealing a car. I considered running. I considered finding the inn again and begging someone to get me the fuck out of here.

But I don't know how to drive. My da would never dream of giving me enough freedom to learn. And I know fine well that I'd get maybe a mile out on foot before Nessa found me and dragged me back by my hair.

I've seen how little anyone at the inn is fazed by Nessa's violence too. A part of me is more scared of a man like Paulie offering *help*.

Nowhere is safe.

My throat feels closed off, like not even air can get past the pain lodged there. Betrayal has cut me in half, and worse, I can only blame myself for feeling so betrayed at all.

Nessa has never once told me she cares for me. She's told me I belong to her, in bed, has fucked me, has let me fuck her. But it's never been anything but sex.

I am a sick and terrible liar. *Feelings* other than hate should never have been allowed to surface. Nessa has never been a safe space.

She's always been the biggest danger of all.

It's on me for forgetting that.

It's on me for forgetting myself.

It's on me for thinking I could ever get away from my father.

He's coming. He's coming for me and there's nothing I can do to stop him.

Hell, there's nothing I can do to stop any of them.

There's a pressure building in my chest. I'm still naked beneath this fucking hoodie and I'm pretty sure I'm shivering. The sky is dark, the clouds heavy and grey, spilling and spilling and spilling endlessly. Beneath my bare feet, the grass squelches, mud gathering between my toes.

Complete and utter defeat sweeps all the fight out from inside me and my knees crumple. I fall forward, hands in the rapidly muddying lawn, hair hanging around my face. I think I'd like to scream, but no sounds can make it from my chest to my lips.

So I stay there, frozen on my hands and knees, freezing autumn rain rendering me numb.

I stay there, with my closed throat and my tight chest and my muddy hands and knees, while the weather cries for me.

"Christ above, you're fucking frozen!"

A male voice breaks through the hammering of rain, and then a scorching hot hand is on my shoulder. Instinctively, I move away, but my body is stiff so all I manage to do is tip slightly to the right.

"For fuck's sake, Siobhán," Sebastian's voice comes again and this time when he grabs me, I don't get the chance to hide from his touch. He's hauling me off the muddy, ruined grass and cursing up a fucking storm as he realises just how sodden and cold I am.

He's unbearably warm and I try to tell him to leave me alone, but all that comes out is a choked sob.

"My life would be so much fucking easier if the pair of you would just *talk to each other*," he growls, but the anger doesn't seem to be aimed at me. "*Tell Siobhán,* I said. *You fucked up bad,* I said. But noooo, nobody ever listens to Sebastian."

The anger and rain have stolen all my energy so I let him have his monologue as he carts me inside. I drip rain water all over the floor, and his shoes squeak on the wood. Voices echo down the stairs, and I recognise both Nessa and Thomas' in the mix.

I expect Sebastian to take me down to my room, but he surprises me by lugging me up the stairs, taking the corridor lined with doors I know lead to member's bedrooms.

My shoulder hits the door as he opens it, and through blurry, tired eyes, I realise that this is his room. It's not unlike Nessa's but he has a fuck tonne more stuff. He has to kick at least four items of clothing out the way before he can deposit me on the bed, still shaking and silent.

"Strip," he tells me, the word both harsh and caring, before he leaves to the adjoined bathroom. The sound of running water fills the quiet as I struggle to do as he asked.

Wet fabric clings to my skin, my joints aching as I try and fail to tug myself free. Frustrated and groggy, a small whimper works its way free of my throat and Sebastian reappears in the doorway. A disappointed sadness mars his handsome features and I know when he looks at me all he feels is pity. I hate it.

"You know what she did," I manage to say as he grabs my hoodie and yanks it off me, unconcerned with my nakedness.

He says nothing as I follow him on wobbling legs to the bathroom, where the bath waits, full of steaming bubbly water.

It will hurt to sink into the warmth. I don't hesitate.

He lets me balance with my hand on his shoulder as I ease myself into the hot water. My nerves burn as they're brought back to life by the heat and the stinging sensation soothes me.

I'm not as numb as I thought.

Sebastian sits on the closed toilet lid, watching me settle. When I'm resting against the edge, head tipped back with the ends of my hair in the water, Sebastian speaks.

"Nessa is…" he seems to search for the right word, giving up then settling on, "complicated."

Despite myself, I snort. The bath has revived me slightly, and though my fingers and toes are still tingling, the ball of emotion lodged in my throat has softened slightly. "No shit."

I turn my head to see him rake his fingers through his hair. It dawns on me then how little I really know about him. Sure, I know that he's sarcastic as fuck, loyal, and more than a little dangerous. I know enough to like him as a friend. But anything deeper than surface level is pitch black and impossible to peer into.

"How have you survived being her friend?" I ask, not wanting to talk about what she's done yet. I have no idea what I'm supposed to do to help myself.

"We're a lot alike, her and I," he tells me, crossing one leg over the other. "Thomas took her in, you know. When she was barely more than a kid. Thomas, Oisín and I are the only real family she's ever had."

My heart squeezes a little in sympathy and I hate myself for feeling anything close to it right now. I want to cut myself off from the truth of her, but I've never been strong enough.

"She acts like she has no feelings," Sebastian continues. "Like she's stone cold all the damn time. But you…" he pauses to laugh, a smirk pulling at his lips. "You get under her skin and she can't decide whether to love or hate you for it."

I blink at him. "So what, she's mad that I'm not some sort of horrible troll? She's mad that she wants to fuck me? Mad enough to get me killed?"

Sebastian's smirk grows. "She doesn't want you dead. She won't let anyone hurt you but her."

Frustration boils over. "Fuck her. Her shitty ass plan is going to get me killed and she doesn't even give a shit enough to warn me!"

"I never said she was *nice*. For the record, I think this is cruel, even for her."

"What the fuck am I meant to do then, Sebastian? Huh? Hang my head for the executioner like the good little princess I am?"

He frowns. "I'm going to tell Thomas what she's done if she doesn't fix this."

Surprise has my brows rising and my lips parting. "What?" I assumed he'd hold his loyalty to her, that even though he clearly doesn't agree, he'd sacrifice me to keep her safe.

"I meant it when I said I liked you," he says. "And I may have my own invested interest in the gang's politics."

"Oh?" My interest peaks.

"If we all survive this then I'm sure it'll come to light." For the first time since I've met him, there's a genuine sadness in his eyes, and his hands flex on his knee. He looks *pained.* Then he shakes his head, and his usual smirk is back in place like nothing ever happened. "All that matters right now is keeping the heirs safe."

I remember my jilted fiancé and the look of near pride on his face when I fucked up our wedding. A smile works its way onto my face. "What's happened to Oisín?"

Sebastian looks away from me, and I frown. "He's safe. Far away from this mess." His voice is softer than normal, an ache in the words that I can't decipher.

"Okay."

Neither of us knows how to solve this. But I wash, and Sebastian keeps watch of me like he's scared I'll fall down the drain with the dirty water. By the time I'm rising and wrapping myself in a fluffy towel, the easy friendship between us has returned to normal.

The open wound in my chest still festers with betrayal and I hobble back to Sebastian's room, trying to hide the hurt behind the towel. I fail, obviously, because that damn man has to be one of the most perceptive people I've ever met.

"Sleep here tonight," he says.

"I'm not stealing your bed."

"It's not *stealing* if I offer it to you," he clarifies. "You can go back down to yours if you want but I guarantee Nessie will come looking for you. She's pissed enough at me to not check in here though."

He's right, and I'm grateful for the protection he's offering, if still a little shocked by it.

So I stop fighting, let him fetch me some joggers and a comfy top, and curl up in his fucking enormous bed. It's big enough for four people, but I make myself small beneath the covers out of habit.

He takes the armchair, sprawling his legs out onto a stool in front of him.

The ache inside me swallows me whole and I fall into the waiting arms of sleep.

29

Nessa

"Bring her, Sebastian."

"Fuck no. You've lost whatever sense you ever had," he spits back down the phone at me and I set my teeth, jaw clenching.

"I'm *serious*!" I shout, exasperated beyond belief. "I swear to fucking God, Sebastian, bring her to *Sinners*."

"I am not letting you hand her over like a fucking lamb to the slaughter house," he hisses and in the background, I can make out Siobhán's voice murmuring something unintelligible.

"I'm not going to let her go!" I finally admit, my throat burning with the words.

Sebastian is silent, and for a minute, all I can hear is the static of the line. Behind me, the man hanging from the ceiling grunts and the chain rattles.

"What the fuck are you doing, Nessa? Seriously. Because I've watched you do some fucked up shit but this is too far."

"Listen to me!" I'm begging him now, desperation seeping into my words. "Do you still trust me, Seb?"

I wait, breath held, for him to tell me no. For him to say

that I've pushed it too far now to be redeemed. For him to hang up and send Thomas my way instead.

But he doesn't do any of that.

"If you're lying, Nessa Tobin, I will cut your fucking tits off."

The sigh that leaves me is enough to make my hair flutter around my face. "I'm not, Seb. I promise."

"You've fucked this right up," he grumbles, but I can hear footsteps and then the sound of an engine revving. "Thirty minutes."

He hangs up, and I stare at the blank screen of my phone for a few seconds. Then I shut off my emotions, wrenching control back from myself, and spin to face the man.

Smith, his name is. One of Seamus' top rats. His dirty blond hair is cut short to his head, and bloody from where I've smashed his skull with the butt of my gun to knock him out.

Heads bleed like a bitch.

Scarlet has dripped over his face and puddled on the floor. He was heavy as fuck to lift into the restraints - chains attached to a meat hook on the ceiling. *Sinners* is the perfect name for this place. Nobody can ever hear screams over the pounding music and dancing.

The basement is cold, and though the hairs on my arms rise with the chill, the hot sweep of anger keeps me warm. Anger at Seamus, at Thomas, at myself.

Anger at Siobhán Branigan for making me want to cut off the hands of everyone who's ever dared to touch her.

Her father especially.

"Seamus will gut you for this," Smith groans, and I raise a brow.

"I see you've woken up. Did ya have a nice nap?" I ask,

picking dried blood from beneath my nails with the tip of my knife. The knife I held to Siobhán's neck. The knife she fucked me with.

It's my favourite now.

"Fuck you, you little bitch."

"No thanks," I answer easily, leaning against the wall and surveying the man. He's unimpressive at best, cocky and lazy. He put up a little fight when I pulled my gun on him, but he was all wide swings and clumsy dodges. It didn't take long to knock him out at all.

Restless energy builds inside of me, the urge to remove this piece of scum from the earth entirely rising rapidly.

It's my fault he's here. I know that.

But I can't lose Siobhán. It would be like losing something vital, a chamber of my heart, all the blood in my veins.

Briefly, I wonder if I've snapped whatever budding thing was growing between us, if I've trampled it into the dirt so badly that it'll never grow again.

I want to punish her for how she's made me feel. I've never been this *weak* for someone before.

Smith rambles on and on about how Seamus will murder me for what I've done and telling me how I should *"hand over the little bitch"* and maybe then he'll *"spare your life."*

I laugh at him, happily, wildly. Men always seem to think they're in control. That they have power just because they have a dick. He doesn't care that he's tied up and immobile in a basement on enemy territory.

He still thinks he's better than me.

There's a thud at the door, then the jangle of keys. Smith's head raises just as the door opens and Sebastian stomps in, dragging a pissed off Siobhán behind him.

She glares at me, hurt and anger burning in her deep brown eyes. I feel like I've been punched in the gut, all the air whooshes out of my lungs. I take a step towards her and she shakes her head, sliding behind Sebastian as if he can stop me.

"Why the fuck did you want her here?" Sebastian asks me, completely ignoring the man jangling the chains as he squirms.

They won't break. They're the strongest on the market.

"Do you know this man, darlin'?" I ignore him to ask her. Her arms fold over her chest as she stands tall, though I can still see the pain in the way she digs her nails into her arms, how she shuffles a little on her feet.

"Smith," she says to him, voice cold. She looks confused, as if she can't figure out why he's here.

"You're late you little cunt," he spits back at her. "Seamus is going to kill you for what you've done, just like he should've done when you killed Hannah."

Siobhán stiffens, her whole body freezing in place. Her breathing hitches at the name, and her fists clench.

"How the fuck are you still alive?" Siobhán grinds out, her gaze razor sharp as she narrows her eyes at Smith.

I tilt my head to the side, clenching my hand around the handle of my knife when I see him sneer.

It's obvious that Siobhán despises the man, but something else is at play here.

"Seamus decided that dragging you back and making you pay for your sins was was more important than seeing me dead," Smith chuckles, and I want to fucking gut him.

"No. There's not a chance in hell he let you get away scot-free, not after raising your gun to me in the church," Siobhán rebukes, and the reason for her confusion finally dawns on me.

"Well, he did," Smith grins. His eyes rake over my girl's body, his tongue salaciously tracing his lips, and I can't stand it anymore. My hand flies out and I punch the fucker in the nose for daring to look like that.

Blood gushes freely down his face as he curses blindly, his hands struggling to break free, and I take a deep breath as I see Siobhán nod to me in thanks.

I leave her alone for a couple more seconds, unsure of what to do, but when I hear her mumbling to herself, her fingers scraping along the inside of her wrist, I step closer.

"That means that there's no hope for me…" Siobhán murmurs to herself and I feel my blood boil all over again.

I want to hold her. To tell her all the things I couldn't bring myself to say before now, and I want to promise her that she's safe and will never have to deal with Seamus fucking Branigan again. But I don't.

Instead, I'll show her how serious I am about this. Us.

I look to Sebastian, and arch a brow in his direction when I note that he's still standing beside Siobhán. He takes the hint for what it is and nods to me once before rolling his eyes.

"Well, this seems like a you guys thing," Sebastian says, while reaching for the door. He looks to Siobhán to check that she's okay, but she's near vibrating with anger now, staring Smith down through narrowed eyes.

"Sunshine, scream for me if you need help, okay?"

She nods briefly at him in recognition and Sebastian sends a significant look my way before slipping back out the door.

"Siobhán-" I start, but she turns on me quickly, speaking through gritted teeth with an anger I've never seen from her before.

"Why am I here, Nessa?"

"Because I fucked up. But I'm going to fix it," I tell her honestly, twirling the knife in my hand before sending it flying into Smith's thigh.

Blood spurts from the wound, and I grin as Smith chokes on a scream. He swings from his arms, thrashing in pain.

Siobhán turns to me, eyes wide. "What are you doing?"

"You scare me, Siobhán," I say to her as I yank my blade from Smith's leg, getting sprayed with his blood in the process. "And I thought Thomas was making a mistake by not telling your father we had you. I thought…I thought I could fix it all by trading you…"

"Trading me for *what?"* she asks, unbothered by the screaming man.

"Information on Thomas."

She blinks, shock evident on her face. "What? Why?"

Shame floods me. I haven't even opened the fucking file, not since I decided I wasn't getting rid of Siobhán for anything. "He's hiding things from me."

She shrugs. "Don't gang leaders hide shit like literally *all of the fucking time?"*

I open my mouth to tell her that this is different. That Thomas owes me an explanation for why I've been her babysitter and not helping out in the fucking war our members are fighting in Killrover. That he needs to tell me why he doesn't trust me with whatever information he's been giving out while I've been guarding her basement door.

But I don't. There's no way she can understand and there's no way for me to say it without sounding like the spoiled brat I've accused her of being so many times.

I've fucked everything up.

I stab Smith again, just to clear my head. I'm pretty sure he's passed out from the pain, but I can't tear my eyes off Siobhán long enough to check.

"So what's your plan, huh? Stab Smith here to shit and then what?"

"Fuck you until you forgive me."

She chokes, sputtering as her eyes flick between me and her da's lackey. She doesn't say anything back, but in the dim light I can make out the rise of blush on her cheeks.

"He's not leaving here alive, is he?"

I shake my head. "Seamus sent him to get you. And I meant what I said at the start of this, I'm never letting you go."

Siobhán laughs, but it's a broken sound. "Smith wouldn't even be here if you hadn't called him to come get me. Don't bullshit me now, Nessa."

I concede to her logic, despite the self hatred that washes over me. "I'm sorry, darlin'."

That seems to shock her more than Smith bleeding out.

"Prove it," she says, turning away from me to stare the man down.

And fuck if I can deny her that.

30

Siobhán

I watch in grim fascination as Nessa breaks Smith's nose with the heel of her hand then tugs on his hair and forces his head back. Blood streams into his mouth and he gags, chokes, spits and thrashes.

This man has treated me like shit on his shoe for years. Has looked down on me as nothing more than a parasite leeching off my father. Has spat the word *girl* at me with disdain dripping from his tongue.

He has tortured, drugged and killed more people than even I know. Smith is who my father sends when he wants to send a message. Him coming for me is no coincidence.

I savour Nessa destroying this man as though it's my father she's beating. I wish I'd aimed truer on my wedding day, wish I'd killed him right then and there, wish I'd saved us all this hassle.

I think I'd do it now, given half a chance.

"Tell me, darlin'," Nessa muses, releasing Smith and laughing when he gasps for breath, bloody spit spilling from his mouth. "Did our dear Smith here ever hurt you?"

I lick my dry lips. "He didn't touch me," I start, watching Nessa's eyes narrow. "He tormented me though. Almost as badly as Da did."

That's all Nessa needs to hear. She's standing in front of him in a second, knife raised again. God, that fucking knife. Her hand is on his face, squeezing tight as he bares his pink streaked teeth at her. The coppery, thick scent of blood fills the small space, without anywhere to escape.

"Open up," Nessa taunts, scraping the point of the knife over his teeth. He resists, but he's tied up, shoulders straining so hard to carry his weight that it looks like they might slip out of place. Even if he'd been free, I have no doubt Nessa could overpower him. He might give her a challenge I suppose, but she's strong as fuck and I've seen what she's like when she has prey in her sight.

Fuck, I've been her prey. That woman is single minded when she wants something and right now, she wants him dead.

I find myself staring openly at the muscles in her back as she wedges her knife between his teeth and pries his mouth back open. She's wearing a tank top, and has foregone her gun for her knife, clearly having intended to draw this out from the start.

When I drag my gaze from her back, it's only to stare at her hand.

The hand now holding a limp, bloody tongue.

Smith is gargling blood now, making unintelligible, angry noises, the veins on his neck straining angrily.

I enjoy the sight of him helpless and writhing. Power snakes along my bones, pushing to the surface, demanding to be let out.

"Nessa," I say, and instantly, she turns, cocking her head at me expectantly.

"Yes?"

"Kill him. I want to watch the miserable life drain from his eyes."

"Anything for you," she says, her eyes locked with mine, blood spattered on her cheeks.

The things I'd do to hear her say that again. My heart thumps painfully in my chest at the words, a heavy sort of relief falling over me like a blanket.

For the first time in my life, someone is fighting for me. For a second, I feel a pang of regret for Conor, because I suppose in some way, he tried. But he hid, we hid, and it was all fucked in the end anyway.

Nessa wouldn't know how to hide even if I begged her. She is unashamedly bloody and deadly and beautiful.

She circles back to stand behind Smith so she's not blocking my view.

He struggles but the blood loss and pain have made him slow and his eyes are already half lidded, limbs hanging uselessly. Nessa's blade cuts through his throat like butter.

Blood sprays and, in my mind, a gunshot goes off and Jackie's blood sprays too. Blood pools and I'm seventeen again and scrubbing the stuff off the floor with a toothbrush. Blood drips, and it's Conor dangling there, his green eyes glassy and his mouth hanging open in pain, a love bite shaped like my mouth still on his neck.

Warmth encircles me and the smell of cherries cuts through the copper. Something clatters to the ground, and I'm being crushed against a soft chest, my head tucked under a chin, strands of blond hair tickling my cheeks.

Nessa holds me like she's holding me together. And I let her, I let her stop me falling apart, I let the girl who wrecked me pick up the pieces.

I press closer, my mouth finding her throat, lips pressing slow kisses over her rapid pulse. I don't want her to let go. I don't want her to say sorry. I don't want her to tell me why she did it. I just want to feel her skin on mine, her tongue against mine, to be made real again with her hands.

The anger is still there, still simmering, but it's inciting another sort of heat now. A deeper, darker need that pools between my thighs and makes my pulse jump.

31

Nessa

Siobhán's teeth scrape against my pulse and I still, my grip loosening a little on her in uncertainty.

"Don't let go," she whispers, breath hot on my neck as she clings to me. I'm paralysed, digging my fingers into her back, unable to deny her anything.

"Darling..." The pet name for her falls off my lips, soft and delicate in the blood scented air.

"Fix it, Nessa," she murmurs again, her tongue darting out to taste my skin, her nose nuzzling against the sensitive skin where my neck meets my shoulder. "Fix the ache."

Before I can speak again, my hand is in Siobháns, her grip urgent but soft. She guides my hand between our bodies, flattening my palm over her trousers between her legs. The warmth of her seeps through the fabric, and instinctively my hand presses against her harder. Siobhán's hips shift impatiently, her face still pressed against my neck.

I know how fear gets her off. I've held a knife to her throat, licked her arousal off its blade, had her claim me after I mutilated a man for her. But the thrill of it hasn't faded. I doubt it ever will. The fact that she's begging me to touch her, to help her like I'm the only person in the world that can make her feel the way she needs to.

It's heady, and the rush of power her submission gives me mixes with the stinging swell of guilt.

"How the fuck am I supposed to say no to you?" I say, my hand already sliding beneath her waistband. She relaxes in my grip as my fingers skim the wetness gathering at her opening. I dip one finger into her shallowly, just to feel her squeeze desperately at me, then drag her wet arousal up to her clit to circle the needy bud.

"Don't say no to me," Siobhán answers, voice thready. "Never say no to me."

And fuck me, I don't think I will.

I forget all about the dead man swinging behind us when she gasps against me. All my gentleness escapes me, and my fingers press down harder on her clit until she jumps in my arms.

"Fuck," she moans.

I tug her trousers down further, giving me better access to her cunt. Without warning, I shove three fingers inside her, making her rise on her toes and cry out.

"You like the pain, don't you, darling?"

"Fuck, yes."

I fuck her roughly, fisting her hair and holding her tight against me. She lets me, rocking against me with the force of my fingers.

"God, I'm going to come," she tells me, the words barely audible through her whimpers.

She does, biting into my neck as she cries out. She comes so hard my palm gets soaked, so hard she's shaking. So hard that when her head tips back, her mouth is open and her eyes are closed.

I slip my fingers from her pussy only to spread her cum over her clit and pinch the swollen bud between my fingers. She yelps, short nails scratching at my back.

"You're so pretty when you come for me. Let's see how many times I can make that pretty pussy gush for me before you cry for me too."

"This is so fucked up," she says, her legs shaking as I play with her clit. "Smith is *right there.*"

"Does it scare you? That I'm fucking you in the same room as death?"

"Yes," she says honestly, staring up at me with wide eyes. "But I like it."

"Such a little whore," I tell her as my cunt clenches around nothing.

"Your little whore."

Fuck.

"That's it," I murmur to her as her moans grow wilder again. "Come for the girl who just murdered your dear old da's right hand man. Look him in his eyes and show him just how much of a filthy little whore you are. Can't resist me even when I'm covered in blood, can you? So desperate to be fucked even with dead men watching."

She comes and I have to catch her as her knees give out. My own arousal is near impossible to ignore now and I groan as she pants, her hand leaving my back to fumble with the button of my jeans.

With no pretence of teasing, she pushes her hand into my underwear, uncaring that the denim traps her wrist. Her eyes are dark and glazed as she stares up at me, fingers slipping in my need.

"Yes, Nessa," she finally answers. "I am. I'm desperate for you despite the fact you're a fucking bitch for betraying me." One finger pushes its way into me and I clench my own fingers in her hair. "I'm desperate for you, feral and covered in blood." Another finger, and she scissors them, spreading me. "I'm desperate for you when you're pretending to feel nothing for me." Those fingers fuck me with short, hard thrusts that wake a deep ache low in my stomach. "Your cunt can't lie to me the way that pretty mouth does. You're mine, and I don't give a shit if that pisses you off. If I'm yours, you're mine, Ness. And there's no giving me back."

I shatter with the heel of her hand on my clit and her fingers curved just right inside me. I can't argue with her, there's a scream trapped in my throat, the pleasure she's forced out of me stealing my breath entirely.

There's nothing but our heavy breathing and the slow, creaking complaint of the chains.

I remove my hand from between her legs and suck her cum from my fingers, holding her eyes as she stares me down. She re-buttons my jeans for me, and keeps those doe brown eyes on me as she wipes my release on her thigh.

"We should go," she says, so casually I have to blink to reorientate myself.

"Go?"

"Well, I'm assuming you're not still trying to pawn me off on my da, unless that was a goodbye fuck."

There's a coldness to her voice that I don't like. "Siobhán."

She looks away from me, over my shoulder to where Smith swings.

"Siobhán, *look at me*," I snap. With a roll of her eyes, she does, eyes meeting mine as she tugs up her underwear and trousers. "I fucked up. I know I did. I haven't…I don't trust easily, okay?"

She laughs. "Nobody in the fucking mob does, Ness. The problem is, I don't think you *want* to."

"I do," I say without hesitation. "I do, darlin'. I want you to know every inch of me, and I won't stop until I know every inch of you in return. I was a coward, calling him here. Double crossing Thomas. I'm going to fix it, fix us."

"So you're admitting there's an *us* to fix?" she answers with an arched brow and pursed lips.

I grab her and tug her towards me, starved for her touch even though we were all over each other just seconds ago. "There's been an *us* since I had you pinned to the floor of that shitty hotel," I admit, satisfaction flooding me at the way she settles in my arms. "But you're right. We should go, Sebastian's waiting for us. I'll send in a clean up crew for our friend here."

She nods once, and though I can still sense the hurt radiating off her, she takes my hand when I offer it and lead her out of the torture room.

32

Siobhán

"We need to figure out how the hell we're going to handle this," I groan, my bones aching as I lift my head from the useless pillow on my rickety bed. I'm exhausted in every way after the events at *Sinners*, but I can't afford to let myself slip into oblivion until we at least have a plan.

We'd come straight back to the manor, and Sebastian had declared my cell the official meeting room, given that nobody else bothered to come down here.

Sebastian stands guard at the door like always, his back pressed against it. His brow furrows as he rakes his fingers through his hair, exhaustion etched across his face. I start as Nessa reaches for my hand, her fingers twirling around mine.

She's perched on the edge of my bed, her legs stretched out before her with her ankles crossed. She looks completely at ease as her thumb gently roves over my knuckles. The delicate move is so unlike her it shocks me senseless.

Some part of me knows that she's doing it for her own benefit. To remind her that I'm still here. Still hers. But the part of my brain that always looks for the danger surrounding me recognizes it as a warning sign. A repetitive movement done while deep in thought. Looking at how tense her shoulders are, I'm certain that that's exactly what it is.

If Thomas gets wind of Nessa's betrayal, she's fucked.

There's nothing Sebastian will be able to do to save her from his wrath, and I sure as fuck haven't got a leg to stand on given that I'm technically his prisoner.

Nessa sighs as she sinks her teeth into her bottom lip. She shifts until she's got her back pressed to the wall behind my bed, and is pulling my feet into her lap. She looks to Sebastian as she massages my calves. Neither of them say anything but I can tell that they're having some sort of silent conversation.

A few minutes pass like that, and I elect to ignore their closed off moment and focus instead on the feel of Nessa's hands touching my skin. I shift on the mattress, desperately searching for a spot that doesn't have a spring poking into my ribs, but it's useless. There isn't one.

No wonder they keep their prisoners in here, the bed alone is torture to lay on.

My eyes slip closed and I struggle to fight off the waves of exhaustion dragging me under. I feel my limbs grow heavy as they relax from the attention Nessa gives them, my calf muscles softening beneath her deft fingers.

Sebastian expels a weighted sigh and I know then that they've come to agreement about whatever it is they were discussing with their brows and eyes.

"We need to kill Seamus."

Nessa's voice hits my ears and I struggle to process the words she's just said.

"What?" I gasp, hoping like hell that I've misheard her.

Not because I give a shit about Seamus. Hell, I wish he'd been the one to die instead of my mother. But because going after him is a fucking suicide mission, and I can't let Nessa do that.

"You heard me, darlin'. It's the only way to prevent Thomas from finding out I betrayed him, and it ends the feud between the two families. It's also the only way I can keep you safe, permanently."

"Sunshine, I know that this is probably not what you'd expected to hear, but Ness is right," Sebastian coos as he moves towards me. Lifting myself up onto my elbows my head swims with a million thoughts as Sebastian planks his arse where my head was resting. Giving up any and all pretence, I lay my head in his lap. I don't have the energy to pretend I have energy anymore, especially now that Nessa and Sebastian are thinking of throwing themselves to the fucking wolves.

I smile to myself as I spot Nessa giving Sebastian a death glare for allowing me to rest my head on his lap. I tilt my head back and smother a laugh when I catch him raising his hands in the air like he's completely defenceless against my need to lay down, and smother a laugh when I hear Nessa growling at him.

"Oh fuck off Ness, it's not like she's sucking my dick! She's resting her head on my lap for Christ's sake," Sebastian exclaims and I completely lose it.

My body shakes as I let out a full bellied laugh, my lungs wheezing with the force of it. The longer Nessa glares at the two of us the more delirious I become. When I realise that Nessa is genuinely affronted by my display of ease with Sebastian I drag myself upright and lean to the left until my copper waves are spilling over Nessa's lap instead. Tucking my knees to my chest I work to keep any part of my body from touching Sebastian's so the raging jealousy rioting inside of Nessa calms the fuck down.

"I'm offended, sunshine. You just abandoned me like I'm nothing to you. Left me all alone and defenceless against the green eyed monster in the corner too!" Sebastian teases, a smirk twisting his lips as he dramatically holds his hand to his chest.

I kick out my leg and push his thigh with the sole of my foot. "Whisht will ya, that monster can hear you and I'm trying to tame her," I goad, burrowing myself further into Nessa's lap.

"Fuck the pair of you," Nessa snaps and both Sebastian and I break into fits of giggles again.

By the time we regain control of ourselves and silence has taken over I can't help but wish that things had always been this simple. This easy and fun.

The longing in my chest morphs into something hollow, something twisted and broken as my brain remembers the real reason we're here. I curse Seamus Branigan beneath my breath, wondering why the fuck someone like him gets to live when so many good people die every day.

How could any God allow that? Allow the atrocities he's done to have happened? Allow a man like him to rise in power and dictate what happens to others?

My stomach roils as my mind flashes with the endless horrific crimes he's committed.

The tortures I'd been given no choice but to bare witness to.

The deaths he's sanctioned.

The hundreds, if not thousands of people that have been affected by the years of senseless brutality that's taken place on the streets of Killrover because of this fucking feud. And all because my father wanted more than he'd had. Because he's a greedy, power hungry bastard.

Nessa's right. There's no way to escape him. He's like a dog with a bone and the longer I stay out of his reach the harder he'll hunt.

"If you're going after Seamus, then I want in." I hiss the words between clenched teeth. My breaths come in short pants the angrier I get. I'm angry that my own flesh and blood is the cause for so much misery and destruction. Pissed that I've been punished my whole life for the death of my mother. Livid that Nessa and Sebastian are now in harm's way because I dared to want better for myself.

Nessa opens her mouth to object, and I feel myself prepare to fight.

If anyone deserves to kill the prick it's me. Noting my determination she narrows her eyes at me and studies me intently instead. We sit like that for an immeasurably long time, but whatever Nessa's searching for in my face she must find it. She nods once, before resting her hand above my heart, the warmth of her palm radiating through my shirt.

I sigh with relief, too pleased with her agreement to care for examining the glee I feel over being granted permission to kill my father.

"Bás trí fhorghníomhú," I mutter to myself, a smug smile stretching my lips as I promise myself that Seamus Branigan will die, execution style, just like everyone else he's slaughtered.

33

Nessa

"Harder," I command, the sound echoing in the empty gym.

We've been here for hours and Siobhán still can't land a fucking punch right. "Keep your eye locked on the centre of the bag and put your weight behind it. A toddler could hit harder than that," I chastise, pissed that she hasn't grasped it by now.

"Easy Ness, she's trying her best," Seb calls from the other side of the gym. He's on the mats, stretching with his shirt off like the fucking brute he is.

"Her best isn't good enough!" I snap back at him and I regret it the moment I see Siobhán flinch from the corner of my eye. Fuck.

"Shit, I'm sorry darlin'. I didn't mean it like that. I'm just worried about you." I extend my hand out, reaching to pull her towards me and wrap her in my arms. Her gloved hands wrap around my back and I feel the tension in my chest lessen as she draws me closer to her.

Pressing my nose to her hair I inhale the scent of my cherry shampoo and fight the shiver climbing my spine. I want to keep her right there in my arms forever. To tie her to me so that she can never be in harm's way again without me at her side.

I hate myself, so fucking much, for the knowledge that it's me that's put her in danger now.

"It's okay, and you're right. I don't appreciate *how* you said it. But it doesn't change the fact that I can't punch for shite," she sighs as she buries her face in the crook of my shoulder.

"On the bright side I know you can handle a knife," I tease and I'm rewarded with the heavenly sound of her laughter.

She lifts her head and I smile at the blush staining her cheeks.

"I can handle a gun too, you know," Siobhán whispers, and I bend down to nip at her full bottom lip.

The idea of her holding a gun shouldn't be as appealing as it is. Especially after the destruction I know she caused on her wedding day. But the only thing I can picture is her delicate finger wrapped around the trigger, her palm cupping the butt of the gun and her face speckled with blood.

It's a sight I'd pay money to see.

Bending down, I reach for Siobhán just beneath her arse and lift her until her legs twine around my waist. I don't bother waiting until she's comfortable before locking my lips with hers again, my tongue sneaking out to taste her. Her mouth opens on a moan and I deepen the kiss, my hands moving up to grab her ass.

"Oi! Ye can shag later, we need to plot a murder right now!" Sebastian shouts and I want to fucking strangle him. I'm soaking wet and sitting here while Siobhán glistens with sweat as we discuss offing her Da isn't exactly what I want to do.

"Later," Siobhán whispers and I swallow thickly as she

presses an open mouthed kiss to the place right behind my ear that drives me nuts. My clit throbs with need, demanding attention, but I ignore it as Siobhán untangles herself from my body.

Slipping my hands down her arms I pause as I reach the Velcro on her boxing gloves. I rip it open and free her hands from them.

"Tell me about this gun handling," I tease as I gesture for her to come at me without the weight of the glove making her moves clumsy. We don't have the luxury of time on our side for her to learn *proper* ways to fight. No, I need to know she can scrap, that she can kick and claw and fight dirty.

Siobhán goes a little pale, and I can visibly see her try and collect herself. She should never have been born a Branigan. She should've been a princess in some rich, comfy country. She should never have had to be forced to violence. I can see the way it weighs on her. A weight she was never built to carry.

One she carries nonetheless.

My admiration for her doesn't break even when she says, "I killed my first man on my twenty-fifth birthday."

I hear Sebastian's movements still as he listens in.

"It's late for a mob kid, I know. And I'd been audience at many, *many* tortures and killings before then. I'd even cleaned up after them. But…" She takes a huge breath, shoulders rising. "Every time I close my eyes, I see the way he looked at me. He wasn't angry, or scared. He was just…disappointed. I swear to God, I hear his name in the shadows."

I wait without breathing as she builds herself back up, head raising to meet my eyes.

"I don't think my father's death will haunt me, though. Not

like Jackie's."

Shock ricochets off my bones. There's no way. No way.

"What did he look like?" I ask in a rush, because *Jack* isn't an uncommon name and I'm positive she can't mean the one man I've been waiting weeks to check in with me.

She blinks up at me, pain in her eyes. "Uh, I don't know…he seemed like a runner maybe? Weed, low level shit, I think. Dark eyes, shortish brown hair? Skinny, too."

I curse, dragging my hand over my face. "Stupid fucking boy."

Siobhán frowns, biting on her lower lip like she's trying to keep the memories at bay. "What?"

"Jackie wasn't your father's rat. He was mine."

Shock ripples across her face. "Thomas had a *spy* in our - my da's - ranks?"

I shake my head. "Not Thomas, me. Thomas was always too wary about what would happen if he was found. Guess he was right, considering you killed him."

She shakes her head. "Seamus didn't know you'd sent him, just that he'd been telling someone Branigan secrets. I think he suspected it was related to the Cavanaughs in some way, but Jackie wouldn't tell us shit."

I hum at that, impressed with my dead informer. He wasn't a good man, but then again none of us are. It's a shame he was killed before he could tell me anything of any use though.

"Well," I start, recentering myself after the bombshell. Behind me, Sebastian says nothing, but I can feel his eyes on me. "At least we know you can pull the trigger, and not just to injure someone, if it comes down to that."

She nods, but she's staring down at her hands like she can still see blood there. For someone who likes watching me hurt people for her, she's entirely all too caught up in her own violence. I think, perhaps, that she's never had someone willing to kill *for* her. To protect her. Someone to do all the bad things so she doesn't have to.

"We can kill him, sunshine," Sebastian speaks finally. "You don't have to."

Siobhán looks up, dropping her hands to her side and flexing her fingers. "I think I do. Besides, it wouldn't be my first time shooting him."

"Your lackey was useless," I say, voice void of emotion and phone pressed to my ear. "If you want your daughter, you'll get her yourself."

"The agreement was that you give her to Smith," Seamus seethes.

Beside me, Siobhán tenses at the sound of her father's voice. I see Sebastian wrap an arm around her shoulder, quieting her fear, and I quiet the monster rioting in my chest.

"Your asshole man threatened to kill her," I tell him, and it's not entirely a lie. It was obvious that if I'd given that man Siobhán, he'd have hurt her. Badly. "The agreement was that you got her back alive. I've upheld my end wonderfully."

The shrill sound of glass smashing screeches through the phone and I cringe. "I'll text you the address, Seamus. You meet me there and you get your daughter back. You send someone else in your stead again, and I'll kill her."

Siobhán knows I have to say it, but she can't hide the spark of fear that crosses her face regardless. *I'll earn your trust, darlin'. Just you wait and see.*

"Why would I trust a traitor not to betray me?" Seamus asks, his anger seeping into his words. I fight the urge to laugh. My hatred for him nearly overrides my good senses, but at the last second, I bite my tongue.

"I guess the question is, Branigan. How badly do you want her back?"

With that, I hang up. I do as I told him and text him the address, an empty warehouse in the east end of Killrover, right on the river. We barely use it, not since it got raided by the Guardaí on a fool's mission headed by good old Seamus himself, but it's within our territory and we need somewhere quiet for what we're about to do.

"That went well," Sebastian drawls, sarcasm coating his tongue. "There's no way he'll come now. Not after Smith didn't return. He *has* to think you're setting him up."

Siobhán shakes slightly, twisting her hair around her finger. Her voice is strong, though, when she says, "He'll be there. He won't risk me dying at anyone's hand but his. He's a prick, but he's a proud one. I doubt he'll come alone though."

I nod decisively. "We won't either, then."

Sebastian pulls a face, running his hand through his hair. "Did you at least get any information in return for this shit show?" he asks, voice tight and tired. More of that God awful guilt seeps into me. I've been a fucking terrible friend. I hadn't even considered the toll all of this would have taken on Sebastian, me causing shit with Thomas, Siobhán's arrival and Oisín's departure.

I'll make it up to him, I silently promise.

"No," I answer, shaking my head. "The file was fucking useless. I glanced over it, but there's fuck all in there that we didn't already know."

Sebastian raises an eyebrow, pulling his *I told ya so* face. He holds his hand out, wiggling his fingers in clear question. "Hand it over. You should've had Anji check it wasn't corrupted or some other techy nonsense."

I know he's right, but then again, logic has long since left me. "What and drag him in even further?" I sigh, but hand over my phone, loading up the file.

Sebastian takes it from me, scrolling quickly through the few pages Seamus had sent. It's barely a biography - basic information that any good rival should know about their enemy. Legal name, age, family-

"Children," Sebastian says and both Siobhán and I frown at him.

"What's this got to do with Oisín?" I ask. I miss him like hell but he's safe in some foreign country, living life.

Sebastian shakes his head, his eyes narrowing. His stance changes, and danger radiates from him. Confused, I push to my feet, reluctantly letting go of my girl to stand by his side and peer at the screen. Sebastian has the short biography open.

Thomas Edward Cavanaugh

Age: 44

Spouse: —

Children: 2

I blink. "What?"

The words on the screen don't change no matter how long I look at them. I don't know how the fuck I missed it before.

"Did you know about this?" he asks me, glaring at the file.

"It might be a lie," I say. "Seamus trying to cause problems."

Sebastian scoffs. "There's far easier and better ways for him to do that than making up a child."

Siobhán stands and joins us. "What's wrong?"

"Thomas."

She huffs, crossing her arms over her chest and waiting for one of us to explain.

"Oisín's an only child," I try, shock still rendering me useless.

"Apparently not," Sebastian adds, handing the phone to Siobhán and watching her eyes go wide. "So the question is, where the fuck is this second kid and why don't we know about them?"

34

Nessa

My fist meets the old wood of Thomas' office door. Siobhán's hand is in mine, fingers squeezing tight, but even her touch does little to soothe me. A nest of snakes has taken up residence in my abdomen, tightening around my ribs, writhing in my stomach. Bile is stinging my throat and there's a ringing in my ears.

The secret child shit will have to wait. First, we need to beg for his help.

I haven't felt this kind of fear since I was a teenager, clutching a piece of glass and pushing at the clammy skin of the boy on top of me.

"Who's it now?" Thomas' gruff, annoyed voice comes from inside and I barely manage to suppress the shudder that runs through me.

How do I admit what I've done? How do I admit to the man I owe my life to that I've betrayed him? Beneath the fear and raging guilt, there's a thick thread of anger still holding tight. He excluded me from the family he brought me into.

It's not fair. None of this is fair.

"C'mon, Nessie. Put on your big girl pants and lay your sins out to the big bad mob boss," Sebastian says, very unhelpfully, from my other side.

We need Thomas' help if we're going to survive this and take out Seamus. I know this. Hell, I'd hoped against all odds that we could do it without him. But given that Seamus is as paranoid as he is fucking raging, we're at nothing without Thomas. Fuck me though, asking for that help is the hardest thing I've ever done.

I push the door open and step inside.

Thomas sits at his desk, which is a fucking mess, a pot of coffee placed directly on the wood. It's late, but the dark circles under his eyes tell me he needs the caffeine. I decide not to say anything when he adds a healthy dose of whiskey to his cup and takes a gulp.

"What's wrong, Ness? Why'd ya look like you've seen a fucking ghost?"

I blink, trying to shake myself out of the clammy, nervous stupor I'm stuck in.

"We need your help, Thomas."

He frowns, running his hand down his face, and in that moment he truly does look like an exhausted father, not a brutal, vicious mob boss.

He looks to Sebastian, who's standing with his arms crossed and leaning against the door, and then to Siobhán. She doesn't baulk under the weight of his stare.

"With what?" Thomas says carefully.

I inhale deeply, force my tongue to work. "I betrayed you."

Nobody moves. Thomas sighs and sits up straighter, pushing his coffee away from him like the news has woken him up more than the caffeine could.

"With Jackie?" he asks, voice void of emotion.

"You know about that?" The words rush from my mouth and he nods like it's obvious. I fight the desperate urge to look away from him. "Yes. With Jackie. And..."

"And?" he asks, tapping his finger against the desk - the only sign he's mad.

"I called Seamus. Traded Siobhán for a folder of information."

"What information?"

"On you. Information on you."

I break and look away. Sebastian pushes off the wall and comes to stand behind me, his face betraying none of whatever he's feeling. But the point is made - he stands by me.

"I see," is all Thomas says.

For a second, nobody moves or speaks or dares to breathe. And then, Siobhán lets go of my hand and takes a step closer.

I want to reach out and pull her back. But she's already speaking.

"She fucked up," she says, pointing to me. "But evidently, did not return me to my father. In fact, she tortured the man sent to take me home. And now my father's coming for me himself. I don't know what your plans were with me, Thomas Cavanaugh, but we'd like you to help us murder my da."

I want to kiss her. I nearly do, except that Thomas' brows furrow and he stands, coming to lean against the front of the desk as he cocks his head at Siobhán.

"I knew there was a reason I didn't have you killed," he tells her, clicking his tongue off his teeth the way he does when he's come to a decision. "What, exactly, is it that you need?"

Sebastian tells him, reeling off our hastily made plan, how we need backup because surely Seamus will come armed to the teeth with his men. Thomas listens, nods once and sighs.

"I see," he says carefully. I'm holding my breath, and despite being aware of it, I can't figure out how to get any fucking air. He's not even looking at me. I want him to shout at me, to tell me how fucking angry he is. Instead, he just continues, "We need to see Aoife. We'll need her help if we're going to do this right."

Sebastian nods once at my side, and I manage to drag in a strand of oxygen. Thomas pushes off the desk, standing tall.

"Tonight is Seamus Branigan's last," he says with surety. "And when we get back, the three of you will be investigated for your betrayal. Siobhán, we need to check that you still have no allegiance to your father. If you do kill him," he sounds unconvinced, "then that will obviously prove helpful."

Investigation. I've helped at plenty of those. They're usually interrogations and end with blood. I refuse to think about it.

He'll help us. That's all that matters. We won't be walking into this alone. We just need to survive this, and then I can figure out how to survive my own mistakes.

"Are you ready, darlin'?"

We're in Sebastian's car - his favourite mustang. The second we set foot inside it he warned us that he'd kick us out of it, with zero hesitation, if we dare to get blood on the white leather seats.

Siobhán stares out the blacked out back window at the warehouse. It's bleak - a big, grey building hanging low under the sickly light of the moon. It's a cloudy night, but it's dry and this side of the city is dead after work hours.

Thomas took a separate car, as did a few of the other

members. He meant it when he said he'd help - I spotted Anji passing us on his bike. Aoife, though mildly surprised, had outfitted us all with enough guns and ammo to kill the entire Branigan gang and sharpened our blades. The entire time, she'd smiled and chatted with Siobhán like she wasn't helping us get ready for a Goddamn massacre.

Sebastian kills the engine and looks back at us. He's all seriousness - dressed in black and strapped with weapons. I hand Siobhán a gun, and watch as she sets her teeth before taking it.

"We're getting everyone out of this," I tell her and Sebastian, tone brooking no argument. "You're getting free, Siobhán."

She nods once, eyes harder than I've ever seen them. "I'm ready."

We step out and into the cold air. "Stick close to me at all times, darlin'," I remind her.

Before she can answer, a gunshot goes off.

Seamus appears at the entrance to the warehouse, silhouetted against the dim sky.

"Nice of you to join us, petal," he says to Siobhán and she pales. "Now, I think we should have a chat, just you and I."

Sebastian grunts and jumps out of my view, knife drawn, but before I can turn and help him, there's an arm tight around my own neck and I'm fighting for air.

I'm dragged backwards away from Siobhán, towards her father.

Someone screams, and though I fight, I'm at a disadvantage. Caught off guard, I struggle and kick out, but darkness is already creeping into my vision.

I hear Siobhán shout my name before the darkness swarms entirely and my body goes limp.

35

Siobhán

Nessa's limp in my father's arms. The man who knocked her out hands her over to him unceremoniously and he drags her against his chest so my shot is blocked.

The hand holding my gun shakes.

"Now that I've got your attention," my father begins, his men appearing at his back. "We have a lot to discuss, iníon."

Fuck I hate it when he refers to me as his daughter. He spent my entire life telling me how much he despised me, wished me dead. Ensuring I knew how disappointed he was to have a weak, pathetic daughter instead of a strong, imposing son.

I hate him.

"I have nothing to talk to you about," I tell him, wanting desperately to look around for Sebastian but knowing better than to take my gaze off him.

"Come now, petal. Didn't you miss me?" he goads, and I feel my finger tighten its hold on the trigger.

He watches my hand intently and I swear I see the hint of a dare flash in his eyes as he shifts Nessa up higher, blocking any chance I have of hitting him without the bullet taking out Nessa too.

Fuck, I need to find a way to get Nessa free of him, fast.

My heart pounds in my chest as I try to think of something. Maybe if I can piss him off enough he'll drop her and come for me instead.

Angering him has always been a speciality of mine.

"What kind of a coward hides behind a woman?"

Sebastian's voice washes over me and I grin. He's still got his blade drawn, the steel now coated in blood. Of all the men in the room to make a misogynistic comment, he's the last one I'd expect to do it.

But as Seamus' face turns purple with molten rage I know that it's exactly the hit we needed him to take.

I want to hug Sebastian. To sing his praises for being on the same wavelength as me.

"Yeah, Da, never thought I'd see you using one as a human shield," I push, pressing all of his buttons.

I'm terrified as he pulls a blade from his pocket and presses it against Nessa's neck, but I don't let it show.

Pissed at my lack of a reaction, he sneers at me as his fingers flex on the hilt.

Vomit climbs my throat and it takes every effort not to spew it out.

"Have you had a taste of her yet? You never were very good at keeping your hands to yourself, Conor would attest to that…or he would if he was still breathing," he chides. I flinch at his words, and his smile widens.

"You don't know shit about Nessa, or Conor," I seethe.

"Oh I know just how greedy you are. You can't help but fuck anyone that gives you even an ounce of attention and I'd bet my last breath that you've fucked this one too." His arm tightens around Nessa and I see red.

I take a step forward, but stop when at least five of his men aim their guns in my direction. But I can't stand here and do nothing. I can't stand here and pretend like this isn't breaking me apart.

My ears ring and my visions whites out as I lose all sense of control.

"Don't fucking touch her," I scream, my voice cracking with the force of it.

Before I can take so much as another breath, Seamus is digging the knife into her throat. Blood wells, and I scream as it collects at the collar of her shirt.

This can't be happening.

I can't watch as he murders another person simply because they had the balls to touch me, be with me, care for me.

Metal grates across the concrete floor behind me and I almost sag with relief when I catch the sound of measured footsteps on the floor. It's enough to halt Seamus' actions and I know then that we're not alone in fighting the Branigans anymore.

Only one man would have the gall to enter these grounds so casually.

"You fucking traitorous cunt," Seamus seethes, and my hand steadies as Thomas Cavanaugh takes his place beside me. Cavanaughs swarm the room, at least thirty of them, and I feel my breaths come more easily as Sebastian takes up position to my right.

"Watch your tone," Sebastian barks, and I smile.

"You fucking traitor. You turned your back on your own family, and for what. Some no good fucking whore?" Seamus spits, his blue eyes boring into mine. "I hope her pussy was worth the punishment you'll feel for this."

Anger boils my blood but I take a steadying breath as I feel Thomas rest his hand on my shoulder.

The weight of it shouldn't settle me like it does, but right now it's the only thing keeping me in check.

"Why the fuck would I *not* betray you?" I shout. "All you've ever done is tell me how much you wish I'd died instead of my mother. How much I disappoint you. How horrified you are by my existence!"

I take a step forward, Thomas letting me go, and I ignore the gaze of everyone in the room except for my da's.

"You've treated me worse than a fucking dog for twenty-five years. Belittling me, torturing me, ignoring me and worse, YOU USED ME AS A FUCKING BARTERING CHIP." The last words leave my mouth on a roar.

I take a deep breath and try to control myself. My arm trembles as I continue to point the gun in Seamus' direction.

"You made me watch as you brutalised dozens of men, tortured them for daring to cross you. You made me wipe the blood you spilled from the stones, then turned around and told me I was worthless. You never even gave me the *chance* to be something to you. Because the second my mother died you blamed me. And I've spent my entire fucking life paying for something that wasn't even my fault," I gasp, exasperated by all of this.

Nessa flinches in his arms and I feel all of the oxygen in my lungs leave my body. She's awake. She heard all of that.

"You took everything from me, and then you gave me to the fucking Cavanaugh's, your enemy, as if I was never worth anything to you."

Seamus laughs. His head tips back and tears blur my vision as the man who shares half of my DNA cackles over my pain.

I watch, completely spent and utterly distraught, as he struggles to breathe, fighting for air from the force of his laughter.

The only thing that keeps me from falling apart completely is seeing Nessa open her eyes.

Those gorgeous emerald eyes hold me together like a bandage over a bullet wound as my fathers grip loosens on Nessa's body. She sags to the side, her right shoulder tipping up toward the side of his throat. Clearing a space for me to shoot.

Lifting my left hand, I steady the gun and recoil as I shoot my father in the same shoulder I'd shot him in at the church.

"You fucking bitch!"

Thomas grunts his approval from beside me but I pay him no mind as all hell breaks loose.

Shots ring out from every direction and I try to run for Nessa, but an arm wraps around my waist holding me firmly against a giant body.

I struggle to break free, kicking and scraping at my captive's arm, not caring whether my hits land or not as I focus on Nessa crumpled on the floor. Blood pools beneath the band of her sleeve and I curse viciously.

"It's me sunshine, stop!"

I halt my movements at the sound of Sebastian's voice beside my ear. He drags me back into the far corner of the room, behind a bunch of old barrels, before shoving me against a wall. I gape at him as he takes up position, covering me entirely with his back exposed to the chaos as gunshots echo inside the warehouse around us.

"We need to get to Nessa." My voice breaks as my body violently trembles with the adrenaline pumping through my veins.

"She's fine sunshine, just look at me," Sebastian murmurs, and if I hadn't been watching him so intently I doubt I would have heard him over the roar of bullets ricocheting left and right.

"No, I need her! I need to know she's okay!" I scream, shoving at his chest. But the man is built like a tank and doesn't so much as rock on his heels as I throw my weight at him.

"Jesus fuck. Siobhán, stop!" Sebastian cries out as he captures my shoulders in his hands and pins me to the wall.

I contemplate kneeing him in the balls but think better of it when a bullet hits the concrete beside my head.

Christ.

I shrink behind Sebastian's body and feel like a coward in the process.

"I need to get you the fuck out of here. I don't care what Thomas said earlier. Nessa will skin me alive if you get shot," Sebastian hisses between clenched teeth and I can't help but snort.

I've no doubt that Nessa could easily take Sebastian out despite their size difference. I've seen the destruction she's capable of. The chaos she can cause when she puts her mind to it.

"I have to kill him, Sebastian."

The sound of someone choking on blood hits my ears and I can't hide the wave nausea that rolls through me.

"No, you don't. Let Thomas handle that," Sebastian says, his voice stern as he arches a brow at me.

"No. She does it. If anyone deserves to put a bullet in that prick's head it's my girl." Nessa's voice washes over me and I shatter.

I blink rapidly, desperate to clear my vision as tears stream down my face.

Dropping my gun, I push past Sebastian's shoulder and throw myself at Nessa. She wobbles on her feet slightly but I just hold on tighter as my arms tangle around her neck. My heart pounds in my chest as she clings to me, her breaths coming hard and fast.

She's alive. She's okay.

I pull back quickly, bouncing on the tips of my toes as I press my lips to hers. She moans into my mouth and I deepen the kiss, desperate to feel her.

My hands skim down her arms but I startle as I feel something wet coating her arm. I look at my palm and struggle to hold back my fury when I find it coated in Nessa blood.

She captures my chin in between her index finger and thumb while forcing me to lift my chin and look at her.

She's not okay. She's hurt. She's fucking *bleeding*.

I feel the walls closing in around me. I struggle to see as my eyes lose focus and my lungs gasp for air.

"Siobhán, focus. Look at me," Nessa snaps, and I blink past the rage consuming me. How the fuck did this happen. How the fuck were we so naive to think that we could come here, kill Seamus and face no consequences?

My eyes lock with hers and I can see the anger burning in her gaze. She's just as angry as I am, if not more so.

"I'm okay darlin', take a nice deep breath for me," Nessa commands and I follow her instruction.

"He hurt you," I hiss. I barely recognise the sound of my

own voice. I feel feral.

"Actually the blood from my arm is all you darlin'... you shot me."

My eyes widen as I process what she's just said.

No. There's no fucking way.

I swear the bullet went straight past her and into Seamus' shoulder. I'm sure of it.

I feel my chest tighten as guilt and panic swallow me whole.

I hurt her. I fucking shot her. I swore to myself that I'd do everything I could to help keep her safe from Seamus' wrath. To end the violence and chaos he brought to her doorstep. And in the process of trying to do so I fucking *shot* the woman I love.

"For fuck's sake, breathe Siobhán!" The roar of Sebastian's voice helps to ground me slightly, and as I look around I notice that fewer guns are raised and there's a lot more blood to be found staining the ground of the warehouse now.

"If we're doing this then we have to do it now," Sebastian exclaims and I watch with awe as he snaps a guy's neck. I hadn't even noticed the rat sneaking up on us, too lost in the whirlwind of emotions happening inside of me.

The body of the man Sebastian's just dealt with drops unceremoniously to the floor and I don't bother to waste my time examining who it is. Instead, I step over it as I make my way out of the corner we've been hiding in.

Soon enough I find myself surrounded by Nessa, Sebastian, and Aoife as three more of my da's men are placed on their knees in the middle of the room.

"Kind of you to grace us with your presence once more, Branigan Brat," a man spits as I pass him. His dark hair is shoulder length and a few strands have stuck together with sweat and blood.

Within seconds Nessa has him trapped beneath her boot, the heel pressing his cheek into the unforgiving concrete floor.

"Speak to her like that again Anji and it'll be the last thing you ever fucking say. Got it?"

I gulp as I hear Thomas' dry chuckle, but I don't take my eyes off of Nessa.

I shouldn't find her display so attractive, especially when there's blood all over the fucking walls and floor, bullet casings decorating the space and dozens of men that hate me glaring in my direction. But I pay them no mind as I walk to Nessa and wrap my arm around her waist. I feel the press of her gun in the waistband of her jeans at the bottom of her back and I wrap my fingers around it before pulling it free.

I push my lips against Nessa's cheek softly, pecking her lightly before turning back to face the rest of the men on trial.

My eyes rove over their bloodied and bruised faces, but none of them stand out to me. It doesn't take me long to notice that my father's absent from the line up either.

"Where is he?" I ask, my voice the only one to be heard in the deafening silence now occupying a space that could have been mistaken for a battlefield only moments ago.

I turn on my heel, searching for the only man I know will give me a straight answer. My shoulders tighten with unease as Thomas assesses me. The gun sits heavy in my hand as it rests against my thigh. My hair is a mess of knots and ragged curls and I wouldn't be surprised if there are streaks of blood marking my skin.

I feel spent. Like I've given all of my energy to just surviving today.

"Bring him in," Thomas orders and I keep my focus on him

until a guy the size of a fucking mountain drags Seamus to a halt in front of me.

He grunts with discomfort as the enforcer shoves him to his knees. I grin ruefully as the guy's fingers dig into my father's bullet wound and I hear the sharp inhale Seamus has to take to stop himself from screaming.

Thomas calls his man back, and I lift my arm, aiming the gun steady at my father's head. I feel Nessa's eyes on me, and as much as I crave the feel of her comforting touch right now, I know I have to do this alone.

I have to prove myself. Not only to Thomas and the rest of the Cavanaugh clan, but to myself too.

Prove that I can be free of his tyranny.

Prove that I can be the one to put an end to it all.

"Any last words, Da?" I ask, my tone laced with disgust as I move forward to point the barrel of the gun against his head.

"You'll fucking pay for this, you useless fucking cunt. I should have killed you years ago when your mother died. You didn't deserve to live after taking her from me. It should have been you in that casket, not her!" he seethes.

I feel hot spit hit my face but I don't bother to wipe it off. It's not the first time he's said those words to me, and it's certainly not the first time he's dared to disrespect me by spitting on me. But it will be the last.

Taking a deep breath, I force myself to look him in the eye.

"Seamus Branigan, you are hereby sentenced to die, execution style."

I widen my stance and pull the trigger.

The force of the gun ricochets through me but I stand firm in my place and don't bother to close my eyes at the feel of the blood spraying my face.

I watch with complete satisfaction as Seamus tilts back, his head smacking harshly off the floor. Blood pools beneath him and I watch his chest intently, waiting for a breath. Once I'm certain that he's dead, I lift my gaze to meet Thomas'.

We stare at each other for a long moment. When he nods his approval at me I drop the gun and walk away.

My father is dead, and I'm finally free.

36

Nessa

We don't hang around the warehouse. Thomas will take care of the mess, and though he made us promise to return to the manor and meet him there, we've taken a detour.

There's too much between us that needs said. Too much to leave it wait.

The Church is empty. Sebastian waits outside, watching Siobhán and I disappear down the centre aisle before he pulls the door shut. There's a heavy weight in the air, the death of her father clouding around her like a storm brewing.

The bang of the heavy front door falling back into place echoes around the high ceiling.

Siobhán pauses in front of the altar, staring up at the larger than life statue of Jesus on the cross. We never got round to taking it down, and it's a little worse for wear now. His feet are spattered with blood stains and the paint is chipping from his face.

Siobhán stares at the closed eyes, the peace across the martyr's face and tips her head back and laughs.

I barely feel the pain in my arm or neck, the warmth of my own blood on my skin, as her laugh dances through the old church like a hymn.

Siobhán laughs until she's shaking and the sound turns wet, the stone beneath her feet shiny with tears. There's nothing to say, nothing that will make any of this okay, so I stand there and watch her as the bleeding on my neck and arm calms down.

It's really only a graze, and it might hurt like a fucking bitch, but it won't kill me. I'll get Sebastian to stitch it up when we get home. The nick on my neck is shallow enough to be even less of a concern.

Siobhán turns, her cheeks wet but smiling. She stretches her arms wide and tips her head back.

"I don't think God can hear me," she says, voice quiet. "But for the first time, I mean it when I say *thank God.*"

I move toward her, bringing her close to me and pressing my forehead to hers. "I'm so fucking proud of you."

"I'm still mad at you," she tells me, but her gaze is fixed to the bloody tear on my sleeve.

I scoff, and bend to press my lips to her. She tastes like salt and freedom.

"I still want an apology," she says against my lips.

"From who? Your father, God or me?"

She inhales deeply. "All of you. But one's dead and one's a fairytale so I guess I'll settle for you." She pulls away and pins me with a stare. "Get on your knees and repent for your sins. Pray for my forgiveness."

At the abandoned altar that hasn't seen religion in years, I sink to my knees before my God.

"Forgive me, Goddess, for I have sinned," I whisper, the

stone cold beneath my knees. My arm aches and I hold on to the pain, hold on to the guilt and the hurt and I mean it when I pray to her. I mean it when I lean forward and press my head to her bloody shoe.

"Confess," she says, and I swear in that moment, silhouetted by the cross and the moonlight filtering through the stained glass, she is the nearest thing to an angel I've ever seen.

"I betrayed you," I start, kneeling back on my heels so I can look in her face before pressing my cheek to her thigh and leaning against her. "More than when I gave away your whereabouts to your father. I betrayed you every time I acted like all I wanted from you was your mouth and cunt. I betrayed you every time I pushed you away. I betrayed you every time I told myself I didn't want you, couldn't have you."

Siobhán looks down at me, face unreadable. There's a predatory gaze in her eyes that reminds me of when she fucked me with my own knife. This game we have, the balance we're constantly fighting to keep, only makes me want her more. Most of the time, she lets me dominate her, take what I need.

But sometimes, she's just as hungry for a willing meal.

She reaches down to me silently, expression serene, and hooks her thumb over my bottom lip. With a harsh movement, she forces my mouth open, her grip on my chin keeping me from fighting back.

Not that I would. I'll apologise however she wants, even if it means she rips the words straight from my tongue.

"Drink," she says, sticking her tongue out, spit pooling on the tip. I mimic her, sticking my own tongue out and gasp as her spit drops from her mouth to mine. I swallow it like its ceremonial wine.

She steps away, up onto the altar itself, pausing to shuck off her clothes and throwing the bloody garments unceremoniously to the floor. I stay there, stuck to the floor, unable to do anything but wait for her to let me apologise again.

She hops up onto the raised, stone platform that was once laid out for Eucharist, and spreads her legs.

"Crawl to me like the desperate little sinner you are," Siobhán says, voice strong and tinged with anger now. My arm protests as I obey with gritted teeth, the pressure on my injured limb causing more blood to gush from the bullet graze. I leave a trail of blood on the steps, and by the time I'm kneeling between her parted thighs, my hand is crimson with it.

"Eat," she tells me, like a priest demanding me to accept the body of Christ.

I have never felt inclined to believe in a god, but there on my knees for this girl, her taste on my tongue as I lap at her, I know this is sacred.

"I know that I am a sinner, and I ask for your forgiveness," I pray as I press myself closer, my tongue dipping inside of her. I've heard enough of the hushed, fearful redemption prayer from people who knew their time left was short. They only ever repent when hell is within reach. I guess, in that way, I am no better than them. Surviving this all just to be left alone, to be shunned by the girl I've given too much of myself to, would be a fate far worse than eternal damnation. "I trust and follow you as my saviour."

It doesn't matter if she believes me or not, it's true. She has irrevocably changed me and though some part of me still squirms in discomfort at the fact, there's another, more self aware part of my brain, that is grateful.

"That's it, little sinner, clean up all the messes you made,"

Siobhán coos at me, pushing my face against her cunt. Her soft thighs, the wet centre of her, the way her fingers scratch at the edge of the stone altar - it's all that matters.

She is all that matters.

"I'm sorry, darlin'," I murmur as I run my tongue gently over her clit, earning myself another push at the back of my head. Taking the hint, I grab her thigh with my good hand, pushing her legs wider, and suck her clit into my mouth.

She shatters, and between lapping at her, I apologise again and again, her scream and my confessions filling the church, a sermon to the people we were, to the people we're becoming.

"Come here, Ness," Siobhán says when she catches her breath, snapping her legs closed and standing. "Let me anoint you. Let me wash you of your trespasses."

I get to my feet and she presses her palm flat between my breasts, shoving me backwards until my thighs hit the altar. She keeps pushing until I'm lying down on the cold stone, and I jolt a little at the harsh press of the stone against the graze on my arm. My knees are bent over the edge of the raised platform, my feet dangling a few centimetres off the ground. Siobhán steps between my knees and forces me to lift my hips so she can yank my underwear and trousers down.

She doesn't waste a single second once I'm bared to her, thrusting two fingers inside me. I'm soaked, and with the taste of her still on my tongue and the unforgiving, brutal way she fucks me with her fingers, I'm on the edge almost immediately.

"Give me what I'm owed," she demands of me, rubbing my g spot relentlessly with every thrust of her fingers. The pleasure is too much, tightening and burning inside me until I can't take it anymore.

I come so hard I see stars. Half alive and still pulsing with pleasure, I almost don't notice Siobhán moving.

She leans over me, raising the fingers that were just inside me to my face. Slowly, deliberately, she swipes warm wetness over my lips, using my own cum in place of oil to anoint me.

My heart beats so fast I'm slightly concerned for my own health.

"You're forgiven, Nessa Tobin."

37

Nessa

"Do you think you could scream any louder?" Sebastian says dryly as Siobhán and I exit Church.

Siobhán raises an eyebrow at him. "Nessa had a lot of confessions to work through."

He snorts and shakes his head fondly at her and my chest tightens. He's a twat sometimes, but I'd be fucked without him. The fact that he and Siobhán get on so well makes me feel far sappier than I ever want them to know.

"I'm sure she did," he says with a wink. "C'mon, I'll drive."

Pins and needles are devouring my arm now, and I frown down at the limb. I'm covered in blood, the taste of both Siobhán and I on my lips, and a lightness in my chest as we slide into the back seat of Sebastian's car.

He gets behind the wheel and revs the engine, careening us out of the car park and onto the main road that leads out of the city.

"Don't bleed out on my expensive leather," he grumbles as we pass the city limits and the grey landscape shifts to shades of fading green. The trees are shedding their leaves in earnest now.

"Oops," I deadpan, making a mental note to hire someone to clean the car professionally. It's probably the least I can do considering he's just guarded the door so I could fuck my girl.

"What's going to happen when we get back?" Siobhán pipes up, though she doesn't sound scared.

"We'll be put under investigation," I say, sighing and pinching the bridge of my nose.

"You've got a good pain tolerance, right, sunshine?" Sebastian asks cheerily from the front seat, looking over his shoulder to grin at us.

In answer Siobhán just sighs. "Drive faster. Let's get this shit over with." Both of us raise a brow at her response, but she's stretching out across the seats, resting her head in my lap and yawning.

I wish I could tell her the worst of it is over now. But as much as I want to believe that, I don't know. I don't know what we're walking into. I don't know what Thomas is going to do to me, especially once I ask him about his mystery child.

So instead, I stroke my hand through Siobhán's tangled mess of hair and let her rest on my lap.

The ride is over far too soon. The manor looms before us, and though Sebastian helps me out of the car, I can't hide the way I wince as my body complains at me for moving. My muscles ache and if the gash on my arm keeps pulsing with pain, I might just cut the damn thing off entirely.

Siobhán stomps up the drive, glaring daggers at the front door. I half expect the thing to burst into flames under the heat of her stare.

"Christ, was she always this angry?" Sebastian murmurs to

me and I smirk.

"Yeah," I say, not taking my eyes off her, "but that's why I love her."

Wisely, he doesn't comment on what I've just let slip, instead he nudges my shoulder slightly as we drag our feet up the steps. I inhale deeply and reach for the handle, only to have the door swing open. I fall forward a few steps before catching myself on the door frame.

"Inside. All three of you. You know where to go," Thomas snaps, and the cold fire in his voice makes my spine snap straight.

I do know where to go. But that doesn't mean the walk there is easy. Siobhán follows closely as Sebastian and I lead the way down to the basement, where we've kept her these past few weeks. Thomas' heavy footsteps are like thunder down the old steps and when Sebastian reaches for the door beside Siobhán's room, it opens without resistance.

Fuck. Fucking fuck *fuck*.

My whole body runs cold as we step inside, but I know there's no other choice. There's nowhere to run and if we tried, we'd be dead before we even took three steps.

Thomas is the most dangerous man I've ever met but until now, I've never feared his violence. It has only been used to protect me, never against me.

He turns to me, and suddenly I'm a kid again, shaking on the street, blood covering my face, chest and hand, and shattered glass at my feet.

There's nothing but disappointment in his face and it hurts worse than the stupid wound on my arm.

"Stitch her up, Anji," Thomas instructs, looking behind me. It's only then I register that we're not alone in here, and that

Sebastian and Siobhán are already being ushered into separate rooms. My girl catches my eye as she brushes past me, Aoife's hand on her arm.

Aoife is one of the other high ranking female enforcers under Thomas' rule, handling ninety percent of our weapon trade and stock, and there's sympathy in her brown eyes as she pulls Siobhán away from me.

"Come on, Nessa," Anji coaxes, and I sigh in defeat. I let myself walk the few steps to the little table that's been set up and collapse into the old wooden chair. It creaks under me like it too is about to give out.

Anji plucks a needle from the small medical kit on the tabletop and I busy myself with analysing the room I've seen a thousand times to avoid looking at the sharp tip of it.

It's barely worth looking at at all. Stone walls like Siobhán's glorified cell, and a generous blood stain beneath the table. If we can help it, we keep the tortures to beneath Sinners, preferring not to have to bring the people we hurt to our home. But sometimes, like now, it can't be helped. These rooms are often left empty, making it a useless distraction.

I wince when Anji cuts my sleeve, peeling it from my skin, and rubs at the wound with an alcohol wipe. All three of us are silent as the needle sinks into my flesh and the thread pulls the edges of the wound together. His stitches aren't as neat as Sebastian's, but Anji's as used to this as the rest of us, and it's over fast.

Only once Anji's packed up the first aid kit and is leaving, does Thomas speak.

"I treated you like a daughter. As much a child of mine as Oisín is. And after everything I've done for you, this is how you repay me?" he says, far too calm now.

I tip my chin up, meeting his icy blue stare. "You cut me out, Thomas. I've been nothing but trustworthy for eleven years. Eleven years, I've given you all I had. And you *cut me out!* Like it meant nothing, like *I* meant nothing-"

"I did nothing of the sort!" he roars, and the sudden change in his tone sends me reeling. "Do not talk of things you know nothing about."

I seethe, my own anger rising to meet his. "Tell me why then. Tell me why you stuck me with babysitting duty and hid all the rest from me. Why you wouldn't let me help with the fucking *war* Siobhán started!"

Thomas' fists clench but he makes no move to hurt me. "Everything I have done has been to protect this family. To protect my children."

That fucking word again.

Something stirs inside me though as I remember the file that Seamus sent me.

"Children. As in two?" I question him and he hisses a breath.

"That fucking prick, even in death he's meddling in my business," Thomas mutters as he curses Seamus Branigan's name and my heart thunders inside my chest.

I arch a brow at Thomas as I wait for him to go on.

"Before I explain myself, I need you to know that I was trying to protect you," he says, his voice gruff as he rubs his hand down his face.

"From *what?* The Branigans? Because-"

"From yourself, Nessa."

"I don't understand." Confusion and anger make my stomach roll. The admission hurts more than the stitches and I hate the way my voice cracks. I am so tired. And so *sore* in every way a body can ache.

Thomas sighs and for a second, I swear I see the same exhaustion, the same ache, in him. "Do you remember how I found you?"

I nod. It's not like I could forget the night, the boy, the blood, then the body. No matter how much I'd like to erase it, the memory refuses to unstick itself from my mind.

"It wasn't the first time I'd met you."

I blink at Thomas, confused as I try to wrack my brain for another encounter with him prior to the incident with the boy.

"When?" I ask, my palms sweating as I force myself to sit still.

"The day you were born, Nessie," Thomas coos with tears in his eyes. and I swear I black out.

Stars dance in my vision and I sway in the chair as I struggle to breath. There's no fucking way Thomas knew me when I was a babe, no fucking way. Because if he knew me then, that means he knew my mother.

"How?"

"Fiona, your mother, was my wife." His voice is thick with emotion, but I can't focus on that right now.

All I can think about is the fact that my mother, the person who left me for dead on the streets, was Thomas Cavanaugh's wife.

Shaking my head, I try to clear the hundreds of thoughts racing through my mind.

I can't make sense of it all.

I knew he'd had Oisín when he was young, and that he'd had a wife at some stage. That wasn't a secret. What was though, is why she was nowhere to be found.

I'd heard the stories and the gossip about how his wife had

left him but there had never been any mention of a second child. And nobody had ever dared to speak his wife's name either, not even Oisín, who'd once confessed to me he didn't remember her at all.

"That's not possible," I murmur, shaking my head as I desperately try to piece it all together.

"We'd been together a few months before she fell pregnant. As soon as I learned she was pregnant with Oisín, I asked her to marry me. I was young and naive, but I wanted to do right by her. She said yes, so we got married," Thomas huffs and I watch him as he shifts from one foot to the other, as though he's uncomfortable telling me all this.

"Go on," I croak, needing to hear the answers no matter how much I might hate them.

"A year after we had Oisín, she was pregnant with you-"

I stop Thomas, raising my hand in the air. I can't breathe.

"Are you telling me that I'm your daughter?" I hiss, standing up from the chair.

It's not fucking possible.

My mother was a drug addict. She was incapable of caring for herself, never mind a child. She was selfish, harsh, and unloving. There's no way Thomas would have been with someone like her. Someone as cold, as– Bile climbs my throat and I fall to my hands and knees before vomiting on the concrete floor.

Thomas rushes to my side, reaching for my hair to hold it back but I swat him away. I can't handle his touch right now. Not after all I've learned.

My stomach lurches again as I'm assaulted with memories of my childhood.

The nights I spent hungry and frozen, crying out for my

mother as I watched her *sleep* on the ground beside me.

The time I spent in foster homes, bullied, beaten and broken by the older kids and the adults because I dared to exist.

The horrors I faced as I went through puberty.

My time on the streets.

The boy.

My stomach empties again and tears stream down my face.

How the fuck did this happen?

"I tried to find you, you know, when she left. She just took off one night and dragged you with her. She left Oisín behind. I think it's because she thought if she took him, the entire Cavanaugh clan would be after her for stealing the heir."

"So she stole the child nobody ever gave a shit about instead," I snap, my throat burning from expelling the contents of my stomach.

"*I* gave a shit about you. I fucking searched for you for years, but I couldn't track her no matter how much money I threw around, or how many hours I spent crawling the streets. Not until that night. I didn't know it was you at first, but when you finally opened up to me about your childhood, I was able to trace Fiona's history. The more I learnt, the clearer it became that you're my child."

"Why didn't you tell me?" I ask, my voice cracking as I feel my heart shatter inside my chest. I look at Thomas, and I can't stop the fresh wave of tears that slip down my cheeks as I find him crumpled against the wall. He looks completely defeated.

"I couldn't. Not after everything you'd been through. I couldn't admit to myself that I wasn't able to protect my little girl from all that pain and suffering, and I couldn't risk you hating me and leaving. Not when you needed me." Thomas' voice breaks as he admits it all. "I couldn't lose you again,

Nessie. It nearly killed me the first time."

I take a deep breath, and try to collect myself, because he's right.

If he'd told me then that he was my father, I'd never have stayed. There's not a chance in hell I'd have heard him out, or shit, even allowed him to explain his side of the story.

I was too fragile, too angry, and too broken to hear any of it.

"Is that everything?" I ask, unable to take any more lies.

Dragging myself upright, I shift until my back is against the wall.

"No," Thomas murmurs, and I curse him beneath my breath. Of course it isn't. It's not bad enough that he's spent the last eleven years lying to me, of course there has to be more.

"What is it then," I snap, done with this entire fucking day.

"Do you know who the boy that attacked you was?" Thomas asks.

I shake my head. The boy is faceless now. Just another greedy pair of hands thinking he could take and take and take because nobody would mourn the empty shell he left behind.

"I sent Oisín away on the day of his wedding, to Italy, for a reason. To patch up relationships with the DeSantis."

I frown. "What do they have to do with the…boy?" We've had dealings with the Italians before, and as far as I was aware, Thomas and Renato DeSantis were on good terms.

"Because the *boy* was Renato's nephew."

Fuck.

38

Nessa

"Hold still you fucking cunt," the boy hisses as he scrambles to pin my wrists in his huge hands. His breath reeks of alcohol and I struggle to understand the words beneath his thick accent. My stomach roils as I feel the press of him between my thighs. He uses his knees to pry my legs apart and I feel my hips groan in agony from being stretched too far. The buckle of his belt digs into my pelvic bone and I clench my teeth together, refusing to give him the satisfaction of hearing my cries. At least he hasn't managed to rip my jeans off yet.

"Fuck you," I grunt as I desperately try to buck him off me. Of all the nights to have to fight off a raging lunatic, it had to be tonight.

I haven't eaten in two fucking days. I swear my stomach is close to hitting my back at this stage, and black dots have been dancing in my vision all evening. It's late enough that I'd figured it would be safe to troll the bins of the restaurants on this street, but I should have known better.

I should have known that this side of Killrover is never fucking safe for a girl like me. Too many drunken arseholes, too much risk.

I press my heels into the wet cobblestones once more, my shoes sliding on the slippery surface, and try to lift my hips enough to break free. But it's useless. He's too heavy to move.

Tears gather in my eyes but I blink them away. I refuse to let a single drop fall. I refuse to break.

This isn't my first time dealing with a man who thinks he's entitled to my body, and given the fact that I'm currently sleeping behind a bush in the public park on the other side of town, I doubt it'll be the last.

"Get off me!" My voice cracks as I roar at the boy above me.

He rears back his fist and punches me right on the temple. Spots darken my vision and I have to force myself to stay awake. Pain blooms along the side of my head and I want to be sick.

Holy fuck, that's going to bruise for sure.

My tongue feels heavy in my mouth as I try to find my words. The ground beneath me feels far more comfortable than it has any right to and I know then that I'm in deep shit as my eyes begin to roll back into my head.

Fuck!

I close my eyes as I try to regain control of myself but the next time I open them I find that my ankles are trapped by my jeans.

No. This can't be happening.

I haven't escaped from a foster home where perverse boys tried to watch me shower and the foster dad tried to rape me just to end up on my back, about to be used by another tiny dicked bastard.

The boy relaxes his hold on my hands and I work to take measured breaths so that he doesn't realise I'm conscious again.

I hear the tell tale sign of him rising to his feet, followed by the jingle of his buckle opening and I feel like I might be sick.

The only thing keeping me from losing the bile climbing my throat is the knowledge that my cotton underwear is still in place.

I listen carefully and bite the inside of my cheek when he sways on his feet, too drunk to control his body. He lands against the bottle bin behind him and it wheels away, no brakes to keep it in place. I peek at him from beneath my lashes and it takes every ounce of self control to not move when he turns to kick the metal bin housing what was meant to be my dinner for the night.

As he faces the opposite end of the alley, watching the bin roll downhill all the while screaming at it, I sneak my hands up beneath the bin behind me. My fingers scream at me for moving them and I know then for sure that he's broken at least two of them while scrambling to subdue me.

Bastard.

Ignoring the pain I continue to inch them across the wet ground until I feel the sting of something sharp stabbing my the tips of my fingers.

Praying like hell that it isn't an addict's old needle, I grunt as I flex my fingers around the sharp edges. It's much bigger than I'd anticipated and it digs into my palm, but I bite my tongue so as not to make another sound.

Ever so slowly I pull my hand back, hiding what feels like a shard of glass beneath my fingers. I keep my eyes on my attacker the entire time, terrified that he'll return his attention to me before I'm ready to defend myself.

He rakes his fingers through his dark hair and his broad shoulders rise and fall rapidly with each breath he takes.

I slowly drag my legs upward as a trembling hand reaches down to grab the waistband of my jeans. The heels of my shoes are tucked up as close as possible to my ass so that I don't have to shift my upper body too much, but the position leaves me completely vulnerable.

My fingers fumble over the edge of my jeans and I feel myself holding my breath.

If I can just get them up, I might stand a chance of running.

Just as soon as I begin to slowly shift the material back up my legs, the boy comes rushing back.

I scream as the back of my skull reverberates of the cobblestones beneath me, his handprint smarting on my face. The dickhead smiles as he leans forward, his thick fingers wrapping around my throat.

"Stupida puttana del cazzo," the boy grumbles and it takes me a second to recognise the language as Italian. I haven't a fucking clue what he's just said, but I doubt it was anything too kind.

Air leaves my body as he tightens his hold on my neck. Blood drips from my fingers as I hold the glass shard tighter, and I struggle against his wandering hands.

Within seconds he's ripped my underwear from my body, the thin material shredded to shit is clutched in his hand, and I see red.

Raising my hand with the sharp shard in it I put as much force as I can into aiming for his shoulders, his chest, and anywhere else I can reach in my pinned position.

I gasp for air as his body collapses on top of mine, his fingers falling limp from my throat, but I don't stop.

Instead, I roll us until I'm perched beside him and continue to pierce him with the broken glass.

I black out as I lose control of myself as I stab him over and over. His blood coats my body but I pay it no mind as I desperately grasp for control over the situation.

When I return to reality, I feel hollowed out inside. Collapsing back onto the ground beside the body of the boy I take heaving breaths. My body shakes as I'm flooded with more adrenaline and I can't stop the screams leaving my throat.

How the fuck did this happen? How did my life come to this?

Anger and fear course through my veins and I shiver uncontrollably as I hug the glass to my chest. I fix my eyes on the shine of the street light against the brick wall and try to tell myself that I'm okay. I survived. I just need to get my shit together enough to get out of here and pray that there's no security cameras on this alley.

I zone out as I force air into my lungs and try to find the strength to move. A shadow crosses the light and I start, terrified that somebody's found me. Found him.

I lift my head and my eyes dart around the alley, searching for the person creating the shadow. It doesn't take me long to find him, and I shrink into myself as he takes measured steps towards me. His hands are raised, as though to show me he's unarmed, but it does little to staunch my fear.

As he steps into the light, I aim the shard of glass now coated in the boy's blood at the strange man. I barely recognise myself as I bare my teeth in his direction. I feel fucking feral.

"It's okay little miss, I'm going to help you," the stranger says. I stare as he bends his knees to reach my eye level. His pale blue eyes don't dip below my face, not once.

My eyes track every move he makes, as he pulls a pack of cigarettes from his breast pocket, unsure of how to respond. After everything that's just happened the last thing I want to do is make the mistake of trusting a stranger.

"Name's Thomas Cavanaugh," the man introduces and somewhere in the back of my mind I recognise the name.

I say nothing. Instead I inch myself further away from him, pressing my back to the giant bin behind me. I continue to aim the glass in his direction but he doesn't seem bothered by the sight of it, or the body at our feet.

He takes a step forward, crowding me now. I press myself flat to the cool metal of the bin, I can't help the pained whimper that escapes me when my head connects with it.

A ringing starts in my ear and I feel my stomach contract once more. Unable to stop myself this time, I turn my head to the side and vomit. Bile burns my throat and my nose as I empty what little was in my stomach.

"Christ. Ya probably have a concussion. We need to get you seen by a doc," Thomas hisses.

He crouches down beside me, gently gripping my chin to wipe the vomit from the edge of my lips.

I groan as pain shoots through me once more and I wince as my legs kick out.

It isn't until I look down at them once more that I remember my jeans are still wrapped around my ankles.

I pick up the shard of glass I'd dropped while I was busy getting sick and aim it at Thomas once more.

"Turn around and take three steps back. I'm not afraid of using this thing," I command, as I reach for my jeans.

A sly grin lifts Thomas' scarred lips but he does as I ask.

Once I've dragged the material up my legs, I huff a breath and force myself to stand up.

Peering over his shoulder, he checks that I'm decent before nodding at me. As I stand there in my sopping clothes, blood caking my skin and a murder weapon in my hands it hits me that this is Thomas fucking Cavanaugh, head of the Cavanaugh clan.

"You're not going to take me back to wherever the fuck it is you lot do your business and kill me for this are ya?" I ask. I'm grateful that my voice comes out stronger than I feel.

"Why the fuck would I do that?" he chuckles, taking a pull from his cigarette.

"I dunno, I'm not exactly up to date on the latest rules for this town, but I doubt girls like me get to live after doing the shit I've

done tonight. Granted he was a rapist piece of shit and he deserved it, but still," I shrug as I look down at the ground.

"I figured you had a good reason for it. Never known a kid to go round murdering lads for the craic," he huffs before spitting in the direction of the boy's body. I shift on my feet, still unsure as to whether I can trust him or not.

Sensing my unease he takes a knife from his pocket and extends his arm towards me, offering it freely. I take it from him. It feels good in my hand, the handle nicely weighted and perfectly balanced against the blade.

"C'mon. We best make a move on before the Guardí come sniffing 'round this side of town, and I could do with a fucking drink. Leave the glass, I'll have a crew clean up this mess and we'll get you fed and seen by a doc."

Deciding that going with Thomas Cavanaugh can't be any worse than the shit show I've faced tonight, I lift my head, square my shoulders and follow him out the alley.

My world tips on its axis as I recall the night I met Thomas. There's no fucking way that boy was a DeSantis. He was just an Italian kid who thought he had a right to what wasn't his.

"Are you sure?" I ask, my teeth clenched as my heart gallops inside of my chest.

Thomas looks at me with pity in his eyes but it only fuels my anger. Of all the fucking pricks to stick their hands where it didn't belong it just had to be Renato's nephew. And of all the men to find me afterwards it just had to be my *father*.

"He went on a night out with a couple of his cousins. It was his first time in Killrover, and he wasn't used to drinking at the rate that we Irish do," he chuckles dryly. "At some stage during the bar hop, he got separated from the lot of them. They figured he'd found a girl and gone home with her, thought nothing of it and continued on their way to the next pub."

Me. He'd found me. In an alley, surfing through the bins from a restaurant hoping to find some food that wasn't covered in grime, mould or bugs so that I could eat without it making me sick.

I cringe as I feel my stomach pang with phantom hunger pains, but I ignore it otherwise. Nothing's going to ever ease that pain, not even the rogue protein bars I stuff in my pockets out of habit, and I hope it's one I never have to feel for real again.

"I was walking across Maryfield Street, on my way back from a meeting, and I heard a scream. At first, I thought nothing of it. It's not uncommon to hear shouts and roars being let out on a Saturday night. But then I heard it again, and again. It was clear it was a kid screaming. I might be an asshole, but I'm not a complete wanker." Thomas sighs as he rests against the brick wall behind him.

"That's how you found me," I say, shaking my head as it all suddenly makes sense. "I'd gathered that someone might have heard me that night, but given the state of Killrover at the time it wasn't likely that anyone would pay any mind to my cries," I murmur, my eyes glazing over as the memory assaults me again.

My stomach roils as I smell the bitter scent of DeSantis cologne and beer stinging my nose as he'd pinned me to the ground beneath him.

"By the time I made it down there, Daniel DeSantis was dead, and you were covered in his blood. It was obvious from the state of ya what had happened. I don't think you'd even noticed me at first. It took a while for you to come back from wherever your mind took you during the fight.

Jesus fuck this is all such a mess.

"I took you in that night because I knew that once the DeSantis found him, you'd be slaughtered for what you'd done. And you had fight in you. Obviously at the time I didn't know…" he clears his throat before continuing. "I didn't know that you were my daughter then. But after I found out, I did everything I could to keep you safe. I trained you, protected you, and gave you everything I had, hoping it would be enough. All that time spent loving you from a distance, never able to tell you who I really was scared that you'd turn your back on me, and still you did it anyway," Thomas hisses the last few words and I have to stop myself from flinching.

"I didn't ask for any of this Thomas," I tell him. Shame coats my skin, thick and heavy as I force myself to swallow past the lump in my throat.

When I'd stepped in here earlier I'd expected the same brand of violence I'd learned to inflict on so many. Not a torturous trip down memory lane and a whole new family history. I hadn't expected to have my emotions used against me.

"So, what happens now?" I ask, my voice void of any emotion. I'm too tired to think, too tired to care anymore.

"I don't know Nessa. I don't know what to do with you. How am I supposed to trust you again?" Thomas asks.

I can't stop the rough laugh that escapes me.

"How the fuck am I supposed to trust you either, Thomas? Eleven years you've been lying to me," I hiss, unable to get the words past my tightened throat.

Tears sting my eyes again and I hate myself for them. I hate myself for the mess I've created. The mess this all became.

I haven't cried since that night eleven years ago, but I can't seem to stop the tears streaking down my face now. I hadn't allowed myself to feel this vulnerable and I'd promised myself I never would again.

I thought I was protecting him, protecting the family he's given me, but the only thing I've done is destroy it all under the guise of loyalty only to discover that he's done the same to me.

We've done nothing but break every vow we've ever made to each other.

Sniffling past my clogged sinuses, I work to get a hold of myself. I have to fix this- well, as much of it as I can. There's no changing any of the family stuff, but the rest I can do something about.

My mind races as I try to figure out what to do, until I finally have the answer that will suit us both.

"You need the war to end right? Now that Seamus is dead the Branigans are sure to be out for blood now more than ever. What if I said I could make that happen?" I huff, my throat tight.

"Nessa, there's no fucking way-"

"Just fucking listen to me," I snap, done with all of it. I need to get out of here, to focus on something, anything else. I can't let myself think about the reality of my situation.

Thomas narrows his eyes on me, but he nods one.

"I think I can fix that at least," I say, my eyes squeezing shut as my voice trails off.

"Alright," Thomas sighs and I echo it with a sigh of my own. "What are you thinking Nessie?" he huffs, reaching into his breast pocket to grab his cigarettes.

He offers me one, and I take it. Pushing down on the lighter, I watch him through the flame as I voice the one thing I know we can do.

"A wedding."

"That won't work," he says while shaking his head and exhaling the smoke.

"Oh it bloody well will. I'll marry Siobhán, and then the war will end."

Rising from the floor I don't wait to hear his response.

I grab the handle, ready to storm out of here but before I can, Thomas has his fingers wrapped around my wrist.

"Nessie, just know that I never stopped loving you," Thomas croaks, almost as if he's pleading for my forgiveness.

"You can't just drop the fucking bombshell that you're my *father* and expect this to be a big family reunion!" I hiss, unable to hide the venom in my voice.

Before I can say any more though, the door swings open and Oisín steps in.

Fucking wonderful.

39

Siobhán

I startle from my position against the wall as Oisín comes barrelling down the hall. His steps stutter as he rounds the corner and comes face to face with me sitting on the floor outside the room Nessa and Thomas have been holed up in.

Ruffling his hair, he takes a deep breath as he looks down at me. I've never felt so awkward in my life as I sit outside the room the woman I love is being tortured in, with my ex-fiancé watching me like a hawk.

Neither one of us say anything for a few moments, unsure of where to start. I open my mouth to at least say hi, but before I can choke the syllable out he's clearing his throat.

"How long have they been in there?" he grunts, his eyes manically searching the hall. It's been a few weeks since I've seen him, but he looks completely different now.

He no longer seems to look at me with utter hatred, instead, it's almost as though he watches me with blatant curiosity.

"A few hours now," I reply, as I drag my eyes down his body, looking for any other changes.

My heart gallops inside my chest as he curses up a storm and reaches for the door. I'm not sure what all he knows, or hell when he even got back from wherever the fuck it is Thomas has been hiding him, but I worry that he won't react kindly to Nessa's betrayal.

As he twists the handle on the door, I catch myself rushing upright to grab his arm.

No matter how strained or awkward things are between Oisín and I, I can't allow him to partake in Nessa's torture too.

He looks down at the point where my fingers rest on his forearm, as though he's affronted by my touch but I pay it no mind. I don't have time to waste on being offended by my ex-fiance's response to my nearness.

"Oisín, look I know I have no right, but I'm asking you to forgive her. I don't know how much you know, but I do know that Nessa loves you and that she regrets ever betraying Thomas," I tell him, hoping like hell that it's enough to give him pause.

"What the fuck as she done now?" he huffs, confusion lining his face.

"I'll let her be the one to tell you that, but just know that she's sorry," I murmur as I release my hand from his arm.

Without hesitation he opens the door and pushes past the threshold.

He doesn't bother to close it in his wake, but I don't dare to follow him inside. As much as I'm dying to see Nessa, to hold her and kiss her, I won't be another pawn in Thomas' game with her.

"-never stopped loving you," Thomas is saying, voice pleading.

"You can't just drop the fucking bombshell that you're my

father and expect this to be a big family reunion!" Nessa shouts back, but there's only hurt, no heat, in her words.

Oisín freezes in the doorway. I nearly run straight into him, barely catching myself.

"What the *fuck?*" he breathes, mouth hanging open as he stares at his father.

All I can do is blink between the three of them, the shock radiating the room seeping into me, too. Confusion and surprise and anger flit through me so fast I can barely make sense of what I'm feeling.

I reach for Nessa instinctively, shoving past Oisín until I can wrap my arms around her waist. She lets me, but doesn't return the embrace as she stands there, staring at Oisín.

"You're my brother," she says, the words clipped and short. "Apparently."

"Jesus fuck - Da, you're not serious?" Oisín starts, wide eyed.

Thomas sighs and looks between the two of them. "It's the truth, son. I'm sorry-"

Nessa cuts him off with a bitter laugh. "Yes, we're all *very* sorry today, aren't we?" she snaps, and Oisín turns to her.

"Why the fuck are you even in here?" he asks, gesturing to the tight space around us.

Nessa grits her teeth and grabs my hand tightly as she runs through the quick version of the shit show that's gone down. Frustration laces every word she speaks.

"Jesus, Mary and Joseph you've gone and fucked it right up for yourself haven't ya?" he tells her, anger sneaking into his tone. He laughs a little, pinching the bridge of his nose as though staving off a headache.

I don't know him well enough to know whether the sound

is a blessing or a curse, but when I hear Nessa readily agree with him I pray it's the former.

I keep my hand tight in Nessa's as Thomas interrupts to go over the plan with Oisín. I see the way all three of them are analysing each other as if they've never seen one another before. Oisín and Thomas share a lot of similarities, but I'd have never guessed Nessa was related to them. Her hair is blonde in comparison to their dark brown, her eyes green to their blue. But as I stare between them, I see the way her lips are shaped like I can imagine Thomas' were before the scar. How Oisín's eyes have a green ring around the pupil before they fade to blue. I zone out, lost in my analysis of them all, as they talk about Nessa's plan to return me, unable to stomach hearing it again.

I only zone back in when I hear Sebastian's voice.

"Oisín." Sebastian stands in the doorway, his eyes wide and his voice strained.

Oisín turns to him, opening his mouth as if to speak, before thinking better of it and turning away. I watch the hurt decimate Sebastian the second before he gets it under control and puts on his signature smirk.

My heart aches so badly. I don't know how to fix anything between the four of them. I don't even know *why* Sebastian looked like someone had gutted him, but fuck, I'm sick of the people I love being hurt.

Unable to stand the tense silence, I cross to Sebastian and pull him in for a hug.

"You're okay," I breathe, taking in the fresh citrus scent of his clothing. It's tarnished by the tang of copper from the blood coating his clothes, but I don't care. I pull him closer to me, too relieved to give a shit. I'd been worried the entire time he was being *investigated*.

"I'm alright sunshine," he agrees, exhaustion plaguing his words.

As I pull back to get a better look at him, I notice a shiner darkening his eye and a small cut on his cheekbone that wasn't there before, but otherwise he seems relatively unharmed.

"It's nothin' sunshine," he assures me. "I just pissed Anji off a little more than I probably should have before he set me free."

I nod my head once before tucking myself into his side, listening in on the conversation resuming in front of us.

"Italy then, huh??" Nessa huffs, the fight leaving her body. There's still a deep pain in her green eyes, but she's obviously missed her…friend. Brother. Fuck this is a nightmare.

"Yeah, Italy. Da sent me over there to deal with the DeSantis. Ended up married to the mafia princess too," Oisín laughs it off but I swear Sebastian tenses beside me.

I lift my head to look at him, and it doesn't take me long to recognise the hurt and sadness returning to his pretty boy features. I can guess why, but I don't bother asking. Not when he's this upset.

I clutch his hand in mine, hoping I can offer him even the smallest comfort, and forget the rest of the conversation happening inside the room as I wait for Nessa to be set free.

I look to Nessa, checking to see that she's alright. There are no obvious bruises or signs of torture marking her, but there's a complete and total exhaustion seeping into her skin.

I can't imagine the toll the conversation with Thomas has had on her. I want to wrap her up in my arms and hold her tight. To promise her that everything will be okay. To make her forget the pain.

Soon enough the conversation comes to an end, and I'm

dragged away from Sebastian's side. Nessa wraps her arms around me, and I feel my body relax, like a weight has been lifted from my shoulders.

"It's okay Ness," I whisper into her hair, uncaring that we're both bloody, filthy and sweaty. Uncaring of anything except the fact that we made it out and none of us are dead.

Sebastian joins in the hug without invitation, wrapping his big arms around the both of us right there in front of Thomas Cavanaugh and I have to smother my laugh.

After everything we've been through, I'm glad that some things, at least, haven't changed.

Oisín stands at the side of it all, watching us with curiosity in his eyes. "How cute," he teases Nessa, and Sebastian and I let go. It's odd, looking my ex-fiancé in the face now, knowing what I do about him and Nessa, and feeling absolutely nothing aside from curiosity. I no longer feel the burning hatred or fear I once did, and it's almost cathartic to realise that.

I don't know the man, but I am at least a little happy he wasn't killed. Especially for Nessa's sake.

"You have so much fucking explaining to do, asshole," Sebastian starts, stepping toward Oisín, who just tips his head up to stare Seb down. I notice the way Sebastian's hands flex like he's holding himself back, the way they're standing nearly chest to chest and my suspicions rises again.

Before I can say anything, Nessa's sighing beside me and threading her fingers through mine. Her arm has been stitched, and I'm pleased to see that no new blood stains her skin.

Thomas catches Sebastian by the shoulder, pulling him back from Oisín before giving us all a sharp look.

"Bloody children the lot of yis," he huffs, and I have to

swallow my laugh at the irony of it all. "Go get yourselves cleaned up," Thomas orders us, waving his hand through the air.

Aoife appears at his side, and he mumbles something about needing a drink while she laughs. For the most part, all she did was chat to me about how tired she was for our 'interrogation'. Apparently, murdering the man of the enemy gang was enough to get me in their good books. I did assure her that I have no desire to take over the Branigan name, and she smiled a little sympathetically at me and told me I didn't seem the type to run a gang.

I wasn't entirely sure it was a compliment, but I chose to take it as one.

"C'mon," Nessa says, nudging me forward with her good shoulder. "I want to wash that bastard's blood off us both and watch it swirl down the drain. Let's erase him altogether."

I kiss her, not giving a single shit that the others are watching, because fuck does that sound like the best thing ever.

I can't rip Seamus from my bloodstream, but I can rip him from my future.

"Bath's ready, darlin'."

Nessa's bathroom is warm, the air a little clammy, from the heat of the water. Steam rises from the surface, breaking through patches of thick bubbles. The tub is large, though not quite big enough for both of us to stretch out. She gets in first, stripping quickly and practically diving into the water.

I'm sure she shouldn't be getting her stitches wet but she doesn't seem to care. I follow her more slowly, peeling away the sweaty, disgusting clothes from my equally sweaty and disgusting skin. I didn't think I was cold, but as the water meets my feet, I realise that I'm shaking.

"Adrenaline drop," Nessa murmurs as I sink in fully, knees pressing against her legs as I try to fold myself into a comfortable position. "Come here, angel."

I want to cry at that word. I'm far from an angel. I'll never be able to dress in white again.

I accept her embrace eagerly, positioning myself between her legs as she pulls my back to her chest. We're both too tired to fuck around, but the feeling of her bare skin against mine is nothing short of luxury.

"So," I begin as she traces slow, soft lines up my arm with her fingertips. "What happens next?"

She chuckles, and I can feel her shaking her head behind me. "I don't know how negotiations are going to go now that Seamus is gone but…"

She trails off as if unsure of what she's about to say. I wait, as patient as I can be, and let her hand wander as she thinks.

Finally, she breaks her silence. "A marriage may still be the easiest, fastest way of calling a cease fire between us," she says carefully. "I'm assuming a Branigan will take over from your da?"

I nod. "Patrick. My cousin, my da's brother's son. I don't see what he's got to do with marriage though," I huff. The relationship between Patrick's family and mine had been a point of contention for as long as I remember with my uncle Declan, hating Seamus for how he treated me. I was forbidden from seeing my uncle or my cousin, but the few times I'd managed to speak and spend time with Patrick growing up were some of the best times I had. We grew distant though after Declan died. Patrick couldn't stand to be around Seamus after his da had been sent unarmed to a trap. He couldn't face Seamus, knowing that my da had orchestrated Declan's death.

But he'd helped me when I needed it most though, and I know that he's a far better fit than I will ever be. I don't want to rule a fucking gang. I just want peace.

"The marriage has nothing to do with him, darlin'. But I'm assuming that once you're married you're not exactly going to want to take over the Branigan gang," she hums.

I go still. She can't be serious. "I'm not fucking marrying Oisín. He's married to some Italian girl anyway, now. Seriously, Ness, what the fuck-"

"Not Oisín," she laughs, banding her hands around my waist and leaning her head on my shoulder as she chuckles. "Well, since Thomas is my da, and I'm technically a Cavanaugh by blood, I'd do."

"You want to marry me?"

Nessa kisses my damp skin. "I did swear an oath to you in a church already. What's another vow?"

It's the most romantic thing I've ever heard.

I turn just enough to be able to kiss her, my tongue sliding against hers. It's a soft and slow and sweet kiss and my heart aches with it.

"I love you, Nessa Tobin," I whisper against her mouth, not giving a shit if it's too soon. I need her to know. I couldn't stop the words if I tried.

"I love you too, darlin'," she answers quickly, kissing me again before we pull away.

I feel as light as the bubbles floating on the water. Like nothing hurts now, because someone loves me. *Nessa* loves me.

Despite everything, I can't help but think I must be the luckiest fucking person on the planet.

"I'm all out of parents to give me away," I say as I resettle, and Nessa grabs a wash cloth, beginning to wash me gently as I speak.

"I never had any," she states simply. Then, with a short, humourless laugh, "Until today, I suppose".

Curiosity is killing me, but she's never really spoken about her past, and I don't want to push her. She must sense it, because she just sighs and starts up again, still washing the blood and dirt from me.

"When I was eight, my mother left me on the street. I never knew her sober, and the drugs took her from me before I even really had her. I was scrappy though, even then, and it took a good few months for the social workers to catch me."

I go to speak, but she shushes me and encourages me to scoot down so she can dunk my hair in the water.

"I'll spare you the details, but eight or so years in foster care damaged me worse than the streets ever did. I got sick of it at sixteen and ran. But I didn't have a real plan– I was just a desperate kid tired of being treated like I didn't matter. I managed a couple weeks, nicking cash from people's pockets and scavenging for food. It was fine. Until the boy found me." She pauses to work cherry scented shampoo into my locks, and I can't tell if the way she runs her fingers through the tangles is soothing her or me more.

"He was drunk and stupid and I was a girl. He had my pants down and his belt undone before I stabbed him with shattered glass. He was the first person I ever killed, and even then, I didn't regret it. Still don't."

"How did Thomas find you?"

"Like that. Bloody and exposed and scared as fuck. He knew what I'd done. Took me in and cleaned me up and gave me somewhere safe to heal. He trained me, and I just...didn't leave. Now, I know that it was his own guilt for not finding me sooner eating away at him but back then...I just thought I owed him. For saving me."

I nod, my heart hurting for the scared girl she'd been, for the chances she never had.

"Never thought I'd be thanking Thomas Cavanaugh for something but fuck am I glad he found you," I say, leaning into her touch.

She snorts. "Me, too. He's an arsehole, but me, too."

Nessa tells me, as she rinses my hair and massages conditioner through it, about the Di Santis, and the shit show she set in motion by murdering the man who tried to rape her.

It's a problem for another day, I decide. Thomas clearly is already fixing it, judging by Oisín's new marriage.

Guess we're both ending up married after all. Though, I'm far happier about this wedding. I hope he is, too.

"Tell me about your Mam," Nessa asks.

"I can't," I admit, pain lancing through my chest. "I never knew her. She died in childbirth. Too many complications. She never even got to hold me." My voice breaks a little on the last word and though I've had my entire life to come to terms with it, it still hurts like a fresh wound.

Nessa holds me tight. "I'm sorry, darlin'. For the record, I think she'd be proud as fuck of you."

I wipe at the tear on my cheek and nod. "I hope so."

"For the record," Nessa repeats, grabbing my chin and making me turn my head to look her in the eye. "I'm proud as fuck of you, too."

A minute passes, with Nessa running soapy hands over me, and me glaring at the way the stitches are pulling as she does. I can sense the question rising before she says anything.

"Darlin'…who's Conor?"

I stiffen. "What?"

"I heard Seamus mention him. When I was…indisposed. I've never heard you speak about him." Her voice is soft, open, completely lacking judgement but still, I'm tense as fuck.

"He was my bodyguard," I start. She's just admitted her whole traumatic past to me, the least I can do is open up about mine too. But even now, three years later, the thought of the whole ordeal makes tears prick at my eyes. "And then he was more. We were never *dating* or in a relationship as per but we were…more than friends. More than professional."

She nods, understanding. "Close, then."

"Yeah," I whisper. "We were close. He was only the second person I'd ever been with - the first was a random girl in the bathroom of a pub." Nessa snorts and I can't help laughing at myself. "We messed around for months. I liked him. He made me feel safe and happy and when I was with Conor, there was no expectation put on me. He kept me safe." I pause to sigh, chewing on the inside of my lip. "And then my da found out."

Nessa inhales sharply as if she knows where this is going. Her arms tighten around me and I take the comfort, leaning back against her warm body.

"He strung Conor up in the basement of our house," I say slowly, feeling residual dread rise in me as I tell the story. "And made me sit and watch as he tortured him. It lasted for hours."

"Jesus," Nessa murmurs, kissing my shoulder.

I close my eyes against the weight of the past. "Afterward, he made me scrub my lover's blood from the floor with nothing but water and a toothbrush." I focus on breathing slowly, trying not to let the horror control me. "The lesson was clear. No friends. No relationships. Nobody. Seamus wanted me alone, under his control, and silent. And I was. For years after, until the wedding."

Nessa's silent for a minute as she takes in my admission. "You're the strongest person I've ever met, Siobhán."

All I can do is offer her a shaky smile and honesty. "Likewise, Ness."

I almost miss the phone call because I'm listening to Sebastian shouting. His room is two doors down from Nessa's and though we can't hear exactly what's being said, the anger is palpable.

As it is, Nessa answers the phone on the last ring and frowns before she hands it over to me. I take it from her like it's a live bomb, swallowing as I put it up to my ear.

I still expect to hear Seamus' voice, chastising me, asking me where the fuck I am and why I'm not at home.

Instead, it's my cousin's voice that greets me.

"Shiv?" he asks, as if wondering whether Nessa's hung up on him.

"Patrick?"

"Oh thank fuck," he sighs, relief evident in his voice. "We heard everything. I wish I'd been there. Uncle Seamus really dead?"

I scoff, throwing myself back on Nessa's bed, wet hair sticking to my skin. I'm still wrapped in a towel fresh from the bath, and Nessa's rummaging through her closet while listening in.

"Yeah, Patrick, he's really dead," I drawl, laughing a little.

"Made sure of that."

"Knew you were more vicious than you got credit for," he teases, but there's a tension I can feel even through the phone. "So, look, you're the heir-"

"I rescind any claim to the gang," I tell him in a rush, meaning it. "You should have it. You've got this shit in your blood more than I do."

"Shivvy, are you sure?"

"So fucking sure. I only ever wanted out, Patrick. And I did. I'm out. I don't want back in."

"You're leaving?" he asks, disappointment in his words.

"Nah," I tease, sitting back up just to watch Nessa's reaction when I say, "In fact, I think we should kick off your coronation with a good old peace treaty."

40

Siobhán

Sebastian and Oisín are nowhere to be found, so Nessa and I trudge to Thomas' door alone.

After the call with Patrick last night, we passed out for nearly twelve hours. I woke with my limbs tangled in Nessa's, her body warm against mine, her cherry scent in my nose feeling so happy I scared myself.

As much as I want to ignore the entire world and spend the day in bed, sleeping and kissing and being absolutely disgustingly in love, the real world just won't leave me the fuck alone.

"He's not in there," a feminine voice shouts up as we near his office door. I stop, frowning as I look around. Aoife stands at the end of the hall, smiling at us.

Nessa raises a brow. "We need to talk to him."

She nods, her curly hair falling across her face. "Library. He sent me down for whiskey." She rolls her eyes as she says it, before continuing to the staircase on her mission.

I don't bother hiding my excitement at being in the library again and Nessa's either too distracted or in too good of a mood to give me shit for it.

"Thomas?" Nessa calls out, and an answering grunt comes from the fireplace.

As much as I want to stop and run my hand over all the books, to breathe in the perfect scent of pages and wood, I don't. I walk beside Nessa towards Thomas with my head held high, nerves rattling inside me.

"Ah, if it isn't the head of the Branigan gang," he greets with a raise of his nearly empty glass. He doesn't sound drunk, which is promising.

"I'm not taking over," I tell him. "My cousin will be."

He narrows his eyes at me but nods once, as if he isn't surprised by this at all. "Patrick Branigan?"

I'm not shocked that he knows exactly who I mean. "The very same," I tell him.

I can practically hear him thinking. "Christ," is all he says, leaning back in his chair and staring into the fire.

Nessa steps forward. "We wanted to talk to you about the truce."

He turns back to us immediately. "She's not the head," he says, gesturing to me. "And there is no truce. Not since the wedding blew up."

"You got another alliance out of your son, though. Why not your daughter, too?" I say a little unkindly and he bristles. Beside me, Nessa chokes on her breath. Cursing myself for that comment, I try to smooth it over. "What Nessa's saying is, the agreement could still go ahead."

Thomas cocks his head to the side, eyes flicking between me and Nessa. I see the second he figures it out.

"Patrick is willing to meet you," Nessa adds, crossing her arms over her chest. "Neutral ground, tonight at eight. At

Libby's."

The man just sighs heavily, then pushes to his feet. "Find my…" he stops, swallowing thickly and looking away from Nessa. "Your brother. And Sebastian. Tell Patrick we'll be there."

Aoife appears with his whiskey, but he pushes past her and out of the library, leaving her frowning in his wake. I only feel relief, that our idea hasn't been shot down immediately, that he's willing to consider an end to the feud even after all that's happened these past weeks.

Now I just need Patrick to behave.

Libby's, as it turns out, is a tiny little diner in the heart of Killrover. True to what Patrick and Nessa had claimed about it being neutral ground, it straddles the territories - at the corner of two streets, one belonging to the Branigans, the other to the Cavanaughs.

Nessa, Sebastian, Oisín, Thomas and I step through the doors and are immediately hit by a wave of warmth. The stark contrast from the chill outside and the heat of the diner makes sweat break out on my forehead. Immediately, I shuck off my jacket and look around for Patrick.

I know this meeting is important as hell, but more than that, I just want to see my cousin. The only real family I have left.

Booths line the large windows facing out onto the street, and five or so more tables are set up between them and the counter. Display cases full of cakes and pies line the counter area, a till and large coffee machine taking up the rest of the space. On the right, there's a swinging door marked *kitchen* in messy permanent marker, and on the opposite wall, to our left, are the toilets.

The chequered tile is slightly sticky under my feet, and the lights are so bright I have to blink a few times as my eyes adjust to it. The walls are painted pink, and there's a few…interesting art pieces hung on the walls. One, a woman with a cherry in her mouth, her tongue sticking out obscenely and saliva dripping from her lip. The smell of coffee and sugar is thick in the warm air, and my stomach rumbles.

I don't know who the fuck Libby is but I know I want to meet her.

Patrick is stretched across the vinyl in the furthest booth, a grin lighting up his face when he sees me. His dark copper hair is braided back from his face, and he's gotten more tattoos since I saw him last, nearly rivalling Sebastian for how much skin is covered. He stands, opening his arms wide for me and I only hesitate for a second before breaking away from the group and running into his embrace.

He smells like smoke and his arms wrap around me so tight it hurts but I don't care. He kisses the top of my head in a brotherly gesture that makes me want to cry, cursing a little when my hair gets caught in his lip ring.

I laugh as he extracts himself, looking up at my cousin. "I'm so glad you're not dead," I tell him, smiling wide.

He laughs, the sound gruff and rubs his hand over his short beard. "Me, too, Shivvy. You gonna introduce me or what?"

I roll my eyes but step back, gesturing to Thomas. "Patrick, meet Thomas Cavanaugh. I'm sure he doesn't need an introduction."

Thomas offers him no more than a raised brow, but Patrick doesn't give a shit. He steps forward, hand out and says, "Let's start this on the right foot, eh?"

I watch as Thomas grunts and takes Patrick's hand, shaking it tightly. The men at Patrick's back nod a little at us and I don't recognise any of them.

"What happened to Da's men?" I ask Patrick as we sit down, Sebastian, Oisín and Patrick's men standing guard at the edge of the booth. Nessa and Thomas sit across from us, Nessa's foot against mine.

"Told 'em they could pledge allegiance to me and be punished for their involvement in your father's shit, or they could get in the grave," he says simply, grinning still. "Most of 'em told me to get fucked so we dealt with 'em like the traitors they were."

It shouldn't make me happy, but it does. I fucking hated those men.

"Thanks, Patrick," I murmur and Nessa's leg rubs against mine. I smile at the contact and though the air is tense with the history of the families, hope rises inside me until I'm so light I swear I could float.

"Right then," Patrick says when Thomas stays silent and continues to glare at everyone. "Let's get this treaty sorted, shall we? I have a whole gang to renovate ya know."

I snort, and even Thomas' lips tug up in a small smirk.

"Fine."

"Alright, wedding round two," Patrick begins and I don't even bother hiding my laugh at the horror on Thomas' face at Patrick's casual attitude. "Same rules as the botched one, I assume. Shivvy marries Nessa and the feud ends. One of mine and one of yours, joined forever in *holy matrimony*. A lovely, giant metaphor for two families becoming one." Dramatically, Patrick holds his hand over his heart as he leans forward. Sebastian snorts and I try my best to pretend that I'm not choking on my own laughter.

Across from me, Nessa has her head in her hands, groaning.

Before Thomas can even attempt to answer Patrick's rambling, an older lady approaches us, batting Sebastian out of her way with the back of her order pad.

"Ah, Libby," Thomas greets, clearly grateful that she's saved him from answering Patrick.

"You know the rules, Tom," she snaps at him, though the nickname makes my eyes go wide. "Order up or take your little lackeys and meet on another street corner."

Nessa grins, and I decide I was absolutely right in my love for this woman. She's short, with curly grey hair tied up in a tight bun, both laugh and frown lines etched into her brown skin.

Hurriedly, we order coffees and Patrick orders pie, and Libby nods happily to herself as she shuffles away to get our drinks started.

It takes two rounds of coffee for Patrick and Thomas to agree on terms, mostly because Patrick keeps getting ideas for the damn wedding.

"I don't give a shit whether the flowers are roses or lilies," I tell him, resisting the urge to smack my head off the table.

"It's your *wedding*, Shiv, ya need to think about it!" he argues, and I groan.

"I've already had a fucking wedding, Patrick," I remind him, as Nessa shoots a death glare at Oisín for having the audacity to be my groom before her. "I don't give a single shit. Please just agree on the damn treaty so we can go home. I need to sleep for about two weeks after this."

Thomas nods in agreement, every bit as exhausted as me. "I think we're agreed. Upon the marriage of Nessa Tobin and Siobhán Branigan, the Cavanaughs and Branigans will no longer be at war. A peace treaty, if you will."

A collective sigh comes from all of us, and I sink back into the booth, relief coursing through me. The idea of being married as a pawn should rile me up but I find I don't give a shit. I don't want more people dead. I want peace for myself, and I don't want to leave Nessa's side.

This will be my last contribution to the life I was born into. A better start to Patrick's rule. It feels right, a full circle, a finality that comforts me more than the thought of my future ever has.

"One week," Thomas repeats, and we all nod. One week, and this will all be over.

And my life will finally begin.

41

Siobhán

My wedding dress is beautiful. The perfect shade of crimson, like fresh blood. It's long, stopping just short of the floor, allowing my silver heels to be seen.

My hair is loose, flowing in soft curls down my back, a floral headpiece woven into the strands at the top. A sweep of black winged liner highlights my eyes, and my lips are a matching shade of red.

I look powerful. I *feel* powerful.

"Ready, Shiv?" Patrick appears in the doorway, in a black suit but no tie. His hair is loose like mine, and nearly as long. His blue eyes meet mine in a look softer than my father ever gave me.

"You don't have a boutonnière." I frown. My father didn't wear one either, and for some reason the lack of floral adornment pisses me off. I don't want to picture Patrick as my father, the man who tried to give me away weeks ago.

He frowns down at his shirt. "I forgot. Florist had a hard enough time finding the right colour of wild roses for your bouquet."

In the end, I'd let him help considering he cared far more about the details than I did.

I smile at him, grabbing my bouquet. It's a beautiful mix of pink and white wild roses, and I must admit that I love it. I'm in my old room at my father's, now Patrick's house, and I know this is the last time I'll step inside it. My things have already been moved into the manor, and the room is bare save the vanity and the memories that are built into the brickwork.

"I see ya skipped the pretence of innocence this time," he comments with a grin as he takes in my dress. I grin back at him, plucking a single white flower from my bouquet and reaching up, tucking it into his hair as a mock boutonnière.

"Now we match," I tell him with satisfaction. "Red just suits me more, don't you think?"

"You look beautiful, cousin," he says with a sincerity I rarely see from him. In the week since the meeting, we've spoken nearly every day, finding the familial connection we were denied for years.

Patrick understands the guilt I carry on my shoulders, and though he carries his differently, it's just as heavy for him. I want nothing to do with my father's legacy, but I refuse to let Patrick bear the weight of it alone.

"Nessa's waiting," he tells me with a wink and excitement and nervousness mingles in my stomach. "The car, too."

I have to remind myself to breathe as he takes my arm to help me descend the stairs in my heels. My father's ring adorns his pinky finger now, and I can't help but feel like it suits him far better than it ever did Seamus. If anyone should proudly display the Branigan crest, it's Patrick. When we reach the front door of the house I grew up in, I sigh and turn to my cousin.

"What are you gonna do with this place?"

Patrick scratches his beard. "I'm renovating it. It'll be unrecognisable in a month."

Relief sweeps through me, tinged at the edges with a grief I can't name. "Good," I say firmly.

We walk out to the waiting car, and when we pull away from the house, I don't look back.

Blessed Hearts looms above us, stained glass glittering in the pale winter light. The air is bitter with the cold, and clouds gather heavenward. I shiver slightly and Patrick pats the hand I have resting in the crook of his elbow.

"Ready?"

We stand at the doors, anticipation burning through me, and when I answer, I mean it with my whole racing heart. "Ready."

The doors swing open and the wedding march greets me.

Unlike last time, the pews are mercifully empty and I don't struggle to walk in a dress made from a stupid amount of fabric. Patrick walks me down the long aisle toward Nessa and the second my eyes find her, I forget how to inhale properly.

Her blonde hair is tied up, a few strands framing her face. Her lips are glossy and dark black eyeshadow frames her emerald eyes. And her dress...*fuck*.

The long, black material reaches the floor, pooling slightly at her feet. It has a high neckline, tied around her neck like a choker, with a long ribbon stretching down the open back. Her right leg is completely exposed with a slit that reaches her thigh, exposing a dagger holster in place of a garter.

I nearly die right there. Patrick has to remind me to keep walking, a sharp tug on my arm making my feet move faster, desperate to reach her.

Sebastian, Thomas and Oisín stand at her back, and Sebastian grins at me as I approach, giving me an enthusiastic thumbs up.

"Who gives this bride away?" Father Donnelly asks, and I have to resist the ridiculous urge to laugh. How, in the space of a month, have I been here twice?

This time though, I don't have a gun hidden under my dress or the urge to scream rising in my throat. No, all I feel is a sense of rightness. Like this was where I was meant to be all along.

"I do," Patrick says proudly, squeezing my arm before standing behind me as I take my place before Nessa.

I can't help it. I wrap my arms around her and kiss her, despite hearing Father Donnelly tut his disapproval. Fuck him.

"I love you, Ness," I whisper against her glossy mouth before I pull away and hand Patrick my bouquet, finding my place again. She grins at me, eyes heated as they rake over me.

Donnelly eyes me. "Let's try this again shall we?" he asks, lips pursed. "Siobhán Branigan and Nessa Tobin, have you come here to enter into marriage without coercion, freely and wholeheartedly?"

"Say yes this time," Sebastian hisses in a stage whisper.

Nessa raises her brow in expectation and I laugh as I say, "Yes."

A grin breaks out on her face as she echoes my answer, reaching to take my hand.

"Excellent," Father Donnelly says, relief clear in his voice.

"In that case, are you prepared, as you follow the path of marriage, to love and honour each other for as long as you both shall live?"

"I am," we both utter at the same time, not looking away from each other for even a second. Nothing exists in this moment except Nessa and the annoying but necessary priest.

"Since it is your intention to enter into the covenant of Holy Matrimony, join your right hands and declare your consent before God and his Church."

We obey, our fingers twining together tightly. I swear she must be able to feel how hard my heart is beating as she sweeps her thumb over the pulse at my wrist.

"Siobhán Branigan, do you take Nessa Tobin to be your wife? Do you promise to be faithful to her in good times and in bad, in sickness and in health, to love her and to honour her all the days of your life?"

My breath shudders in my chest as I blink back tears rapidly, joy overflowing as I say, "I do."

"Nessa Tobin, do you take Siobhán Branigan to be your wife? Do you promise to be faithful to her in good times and in bad, in sickness and in health, to love her and to honour her all the days of your life?"

Nessa's eyes don't leave mine as she smiles softly at me, the most beautiful thing I've ever seen in my damned life. "I do."

Father Donnelly nods. "What God joins together, let no one pull asunder."

I know, by the glint in her eye, that we're both thinking of the only god we've ever felt. Of the altar, and her blood and the way Church felt full of something so much bigger than us that night.

"Who has the rings?" the Father asks and Sebastian swears

as he fumbles for the rings in his pocket. I catch the way the priest's jaw ticks and bite my tongue to smother my laughter. I don't like the bastard, but he's crooked as fuck and so he's the best choice for a marriage meant to unite two gangs.

The priest blesses the rings but I hear nothing he says. My world begins and ends with the woman in front of me, and when I take Nessa's ring in the palm of my hand, the jewellery warm from Sebastian's pocket, I can't stop the happy tear that spills over.

I hold Nessa's hand in mine as the words that will seal our marriage spill from my lips. "Nessa, receive this ring as a sign of my love and fidelity. In the name of the Father, and of the Son, and of the Holy Spirit."

I slip the simple silver ring onto her finger, and she squeezes my hand as she repeats the words.

"Siobhán, receive this ring as a sign of my love and fidelity. In the name of the Father, and of the Son, and of the Holy Spirit."

She slides the ring onto my finger and I don't bother waiting for the priest to tell us we can kiss. I jump into her arms, pressing my lips to hers, smiling so hard that our teeth clatter together.

Sebastian whoops, and Patrick joins in until we're surrounded by them cheering. Nessa's hands are tight on my waist as she holds me to her.

"My wife," she whispers, pressing her mouth to my neck and kissing my pulse. Those words make me weak at the knees and I moan slightly against her ear.

She chuckles, and pulls away to grin at me. We're the same height with me in heels, and I like the advantage it gives me as I steal another kiss.

"Come on," she says, tugging on my hand. "We have somewhere to be."

I frown at her. "That eager to leave the church? Scared you'll spontaneously combust?"

She tuts at me, and I'm sure that if we were alone she'd punish me for the remark.

"Bags are in the car!" Sebastian shouts after us as she drags me back down the aisle. I hear Patrick whoop at our backs, but I give in, running after my wife and into the car idling at the curb.

42

Nessa

"Did you think I wouldn't give my wife a honeymoon?" I ask her, narrowing my eyes at Siobhán's shocked expression.

"I didn't think…with everything going on…" she trails off, shrugging. Excitement makes her giddy, and she bounces as we exit the plane. I know she means the war, the treaty and the mess left to clean up, but also the revelation that my father has been in my life for eleven years, that one of my best friends is actually my brother. My head is still a mess, and I spend too much time trying not to think about it all. In truth, I need this trip as much as she does.

We're still in our dresses, though I had to leave my dagger with Thomas at the church, as we step off the plane. It's bright, early morning, and at least ten degrees warmer than the weather in Ireland.

"I heard you wanted to see France," I tell her with a smile, watching her eyes water as she breathes in deeply.

"I can't fucking believe Sebastian told you," she laughs, bottom lip wobbling a bit. I grab her, holding her close to me because I can't bear to not touch her, even if they're happy tears.

I haven't felt happiness like this in…well, maybe ever. The undiluted joy on her face as she takes in her first view of the country is almost enough to make me tear up too. Instead, I drag her down the steps and into the airport to grab our luggage.

The entire time, she bounces like an excited puppy, trying to pronounce the French on all the signs and reeling off all the food she wants to try.

I never want her to stop talking. The pure excitement that drips from her every word is enough to sustain me completely, I'm sure of it. I need nothing but her.

I find our taxi easily enough and listen to my wife talk the entire way to the villa.

"It's beautiful," Siobhán breathes as I lug our suitcases up the short driveway. The villa is on the outskirts of a small town in the south of France, so close to the beach we can hear the waves.

Two stories of old, brown stone and bright white shutters that look like they've just been freshly painted. Two little potted trees frame the front door and Siobhán is bouncing from foot to foot in front of it eagerly before I can catch up.

I can't help but laugh a little at her eagerness, it's infectious, but all I can think about is tearing her dress off and tasting my wife. Sebastian helped me pack our bags last night, and she has an entire new wardrobe in hers that's far heavier than I anticipated. I drop the bags at her feet, kissing her quickly, before locating the key box and punching in the numbers the hosts had emailed over when I booked the place.

I swing the door open and shove the bags inside, locking it behind us quickly. I don't give Siobhán a second to explore, swinging her into my arms and ignoring her shout of surprise as I carry her upstairs and into the master bedroom.

"Explore tomorrow," I tell her as I kick open the door and drop her onto the bed, crawling over her and kissing her neck.

She sighs against me, wrapping her legs around my waist. "Promise you'll take me to get proper croissants in the morning," she says in a teasing tone, like she's not as desperate for this as I am. But she's shifting under me, trying to grind against my thigh as I press myself between her legs, her dress rucking up and exposing the garter tied around her thigh.

"I'll buy you whatever the fuck you want," I promise her, eyes glued to the piece of lacy fabric. "As long as you tell me I can take that off with my teeth."

She giggles and the sound makes my heart pick up pace. Fuck, does she have to be so perfect?

"That's the point," she teases, wiggling her ass a little.

"How did I get so fucking lucky?" I murmur as I grab the material of her dress and shove it up, exposing the lacy red thong she has on. I swear, heat pooling in my core, and she grins.

"I never thought being kidnapped would be the best thing to happen to me," she laughs as she reaches for the clasp at the halter neck of my dress. "But fuck am I glad you found me, Ness."

"Let me show you how glad I am," I say, letting her undo my dress. I sit back so I can shed the fabric altogether, leaving me in just my black bra, underwear, and now empty thigh holster.

I go to undo the holster, but Siobhán grabs my hand. "Leave it on."

"Fuck me," I say, my fingers in her hair and my mouth on hers before she can say any more. I need her, so badly I'm burning with it.

I kiss my way down her neck, reaching behind her and finding the zip of her dress. I peel the soft fabric away, dragging it down her legs before throwing it to the floor with my own.

She shivers as my eyes rake over every perfect inch of her. I nip at her collarbone, the swell of her breast, her peaked nipple through the thin lace. She gasps and squirms, her hands in my hair, urging me closer.

"Perfect," I murmur against her soft stomach, moving down her body and licking the junction of her leg and her hip. I allow myself a single taste of her through the barely there fabric of her underwear, pressing a kiss to her clit, before finding the fabric of her garter.

She moans and fights to keep still as I take it between my teeth, scraping the sensitive skin of her inner thigh in the process. Slowly, I drag the garter down her leg, until it too joins the dresses on the floor.

"I need you," she whines, cheeks flushed and eyes wide.

"I know, darlin'," I soothe, stroking my hands up her legs, savouring every shudder she makes. I cup her pussy with my left hand, smiling at the ring sitting on my finger.

"Please, Ness," she begs, trying to grind against my palm. "Don't tease me. Not now. I need my wife to fuck me."

Those words are the death of me. In an instant, I'm dragging the crotch of her underwear to the side, not bothering to take the time to take it off fully, and swiping my fingers over the wetness waiting for me.

"This cunt is mine," I tell her as I slip two fingers into her heat. "Forever, Siobhán."

She nods frantically as I curl my fingers, finding the sensitive patch of nerves. "Forever," she pants, head pressed into the pillow as her hips move with me.

I fuck her hard and fast, watching the way she responds so well to me, how she clenches desperately around my fingers, how her eyes flutter shut and the pleading whines escape her throat.

I kiss her hard when she comes, swallowing every moan. They're mine, she's mine, every inch of her, every sound she makes, every orgasm she has.

Mine.

Satisfaction floods me, a deep rooted happiness that I always thought was a myth. Surely, nobody could love so deeply they felt it in their bones.

But I understand now, as I stare down at my wife panting and smiling at me. I love her so completely it fills every fucking inch of me.

"Come here," she gasps, her hands finding my own thighs and tugging me harshly. "Sit. Face."

I snort a laugh, but shimmy out of my wet underwear, leaving the holster, and straddle her chest. She frowns dramatically up at me.

"I said, *sit*, Nessa," she demands, fingers digging into my thighs as she tries to tug me on top of her.

I only have so much self control, and she's snapped it between her teeth. I frame her face with my thighs and let her tug me down so my cunt is above her mouth. I reach forward, grabbing the wooden headboard to support myself as she licks her way from my cunt to my clit.

"God," I groan as she presses her tongue into me, moaning against me like she's getting just as much pleasure from this as I am.

She fucks me with her tongue, sucks on my clit, ruins me until I'm coming on her face, shuddering and holding myself up on the headboard.

Spent, I collapse beside her in bed, kissing her and tasting myself on her tongue. She curls against me happily, her head on my chest and her arms around my waist.

She yawns, and I wrap the duvet around us tightly.

"Sleep, darlin'," I tell her, kissing her head as she sighs happily. "We'll buy croissants in the morning and eat them on the beach."

She mumbles a *yes please* before she's asleep, breathing heavily. I lie there, awake and listening to her breathe, analysing the happiness that's taken over me completely.

With my wife in my arms, I let myself sink into the soft darkness of sleep, knowing that nothing I can dream will be as sweet as my reality.

For the first time in over ten years, the nightmares don't find me.

Epilogue

Oisín

I sip at the whiskey on the rocks sitting in my hand as I sit across from my father. It's been weeks since we've sat and talked, but given the mess the girls created while I was gone, I can't blame him for not taking the time to see me properly any sooner.

I look at him as he bounces back in his chair, a matching glass in his hand and a cigarette burning away in his mouth.

He looks completely worn out, as though the last month has taken a piece of him. Cut something vital from his soul.

"Christ above, say what it is you want to say, Ois," he grumbles and I can't stop the smile that etches across my face.

"Nothin' at all Da, just taking a look at ya is all. You seem tired," I comment and he peeks an eye open to glare at me. The side of his lip with the scar twitches as he struggles to hide his grin. We look alike, the same slightly crooked nose - though his is worse than mine given how many time it's been broken - and my eyes have more green than his. A trace of my mother, I suppose, considering the colour of Nessa's, too. My sister.

I'm not sure I'll ever get used to that.

"There it is, you prick," he laughs and I join him.

Our laughter dies fast. The last month has been hell.

The second the arranged wedding fell apart, I was on a plane to Italy. Far away from the war and the Branigans. It didn't matter how much it hurt to leave, it had to be done. I understood that.

But when I came home, married to Serafina DeSantis, I knew I'd be walking into a new line of fire with Sebastian. That hurts more than I'm willing to let myself think about. I take another long drink of liquor, letting it burn away the ache.

Despite the shit show I've just come out of, I'm grateful to be able to spend time with my father. Grateful we all survived.

Anger twists my gut as I think about Nessa's betrayal. Because of her we could have lost him. I love that girl but fuck me sometimes I just want to smack her upside the head and knock some sense into her.

"Hey, none of that, son. I know that look, and I think we can both agree that Nessa's been put through the ringer enough," my father commands, and I grunt before nodding my head.

"I know. I just can't help thinking about how wrong it could have all gone. For all I know, I could have been coming home for your fucking funeral and not to word of Seamus' death," I growl. I'd hated Seamus Branigan my entire life, but after hearing about his treatment of Siobhán I wish I could have strangled him myself.

I don't particularly care for the girl, but no parent should ever treat their own flesh and blood so horrifically. An unpleasant, heavy feeling sinks in my stomach as I realise my own father *has* treated his flesh and blood so terribly. Thinking of Nessa alone in the system, then on the streets, with nobody to fight for her, makes me sick.

I push those feelings down, too.

"Well, I'm still alive and kickin' and you won't be getting rid of me anytime soon. Now, tell me where we're at with the DeSantis."

I swirl the remainder of my whiskey in the glass before knocking it back and draining it.

"The Russos are pressing them hard. They've got good trade going with the guns and the drugs, but the Russos are pushing to set up skin markets across the country. It's bad Da, they're gonna need us," I tell him as I reach for the decanter on the desk. I fill my glass to the brim. If I've to discuss the horrors I've witnessed these past few weeks then I'm going to need to be a lot less sober than I am now.

"Talk to Nessa when she gets back from her honeymoon. You're going to need her. Sebastian too," Da sighs, pinning me with a look as he leans back in the chair again.

My heart twists at the thought of Sebastian. Turns out, no amount of whisky will drown that out.

You had no right to marry her without speaking to me first!

He'd been fuming after finding out that day. And in truth, I can't blame him.

He's right.

But I had no choice. Not when it came to building alliances we desperately needed during the war. And especially not when it meant saving Nessa's arse from their revenge plan.

Realising that I haven't responded to my da's order, I nod my head.

Rapping my knuckles on the desk once, I stand up and say goodnight to my father before heading towards the door.

If I've any chance of getting ahead of this mess, then I need to find Sebastian.

I just hope he can forgive me before it's too late.

Pronunciation Guide

Names:

Siobhán: ***Shiv-awn***
Oisín: ***Ush-een***
Seamus: ***Shea-mus***
Aoife: ***Ee-fa***

Translations:

Acknowledgements

Scarlet:

To my partner, who has to deal with me complaining and stressing and constantly being off in my own fictional world, I adore you. To my son, I love you so much and I hope to God you never read my books.

To Nadine, for listening to my long, excited voice messages about church sex and how in love with Sebastian I am. For trusting me to write with you and creating these characters with me. Love you loads.

Nadine:

To my partner, for listening to my chaotic rants and encouraging me every step of the way. I love you.

To my Mam, for everything. Thank you for being you, I love you.

To Scarlet, for helping me bring these characters to life. I genuinely couldn't have done it without you. Thank you for reminding me to keep going, keep writing and for fighting my imposter syndrome with me. I love you.

To all my non-bookish friends who supported me on my journey and listened to me speak about writing for hours on end despite it not being your thing, I love and appreciate you.

To our beta readers for helping us out on such a tight schedule, we appreciate you so much!

To our ARC readers for reading and helping us get Nessa and Siobhán's story out there. We're so grateful for you taking a chance on this book!

To Sam for the stunning cover - we adore you.

To all our author and reader friends and everyone who has supported us. We would be nowhere without you.

About the Author

Scarlet King is a twenty something year old who lives in Scotland with her partner and child. She loves coffee, book stores, and ignoring her responsibilities in favour of writing. She has a bad habit of falling in love with fictional characters and hopes that someone out there will fall for the ones she writes, too.

Nadine O'Keeffe is a queer dark romance author from Ireland, where she lives with her partner. She loves book, music, coffee, and her cat (even though she swears she's a demon in disguise). She can often be found ignoring the real world in favour of fictional ones, because, let's be honest, they're far better.

If you want to keep up with what the authors are writing and what chaos they plan on causing next, you can find them at the links below:

Instagram: @scarletkingauthor @authornadineokeeffe
TikTok: @scarletkingauthor @NadineOKeeffeauthor
Facebook Reader Groups: Scarlet King-Dom and Nadine's Hunters
Websites (for signed copies and swag!): www.scarletkingauthor.com and www.authornadineokeeffe.com

If you liked this book, please consider leaving a review! A star rating and a few lines helps authors out massively. If you post about this book on social media, please feel free to tag Scarlet and Nadine so they can thank you!

Also by Scarlet King and Nadine O'Keeffe

Also by Scarlet King:

The Revenge Duet - a paranormal why choose dark romance duet (MMFM)

Thieves and Thorns
Revenge and Roses
Ribbon and Rope (a holiday novella, out December 2022)

The Surrender Duet - a paranormal why choose dark romance duet (MMMFF)

Honey and Hellfire
Sugar and Surrender (out February 10th 2023)

Blessed Hearts - a connected series of dark romance mafia standalones:

Broken Vows
Fractured Faith (out May 22nd 2023)

Also by Nadine O'Keeffe:

The Twisted Duet - a college why choose dark romance duet (FFMMM)

Twisted Legacy (out Feb 16th 2023)

Blessed Hearts - a connected series of dark romance mafia standalones:

- Broken Vows
- Fractured Faith (out May 22nd 2023)

Printed in Great Britain
by Amazon

38360683R00179